Doherty '96

3 WEEKS

Family Album

A Mellingham Mystery

SUSAN OLEKSIW

SCRIBNER

NEW YORK   LONDON   TORONTO   SYDNEY   TOKYO   SINGAPORE

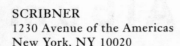

SCRIBNER
1230 Avenue of the Americas
New York, NY 10020

This book is a work of fiction. Names, characters, places and
incidents are either products of the author's imagination or are
used fictitiously. Any resemblance to actual events or locales or
persons, living or dead, is entirely coincidental.

Copyright © 1995 by Susan Prince Oleksiw

SCRIBNER and colophon are registered trademarks of
Simon & Schuster, Inc.

Manufactured in the United States of America

10 9 8 7 6 5 4 3 2 1

Library of Congress Cataloging-in-Publication Data
Oleksiw, Susan.
Family album: a Mellingham mystery / Susan Oleksiw.
p. cm.
1. Police—New England—Fiction. I. Title.
PS3565.L42F36 1995
813'.54—dc20
94-19679

ISBN 0-684-19731-6

To
Eleanor Z. Lodge

ACKNOWLEDGMENTS

Paula Raposa introduced me to the beauty and intricacy of Portuguese lace. Katherine Pinkham, curator of the Beverly Historical Society, trained me in the business of cataloging. There is no Arbella Society, but the architecture and history of the Arbella House are adapted from that of the Cabot House, headquarters of the Beverly Historical Society, in Beverly, Massachusetts.

LIST OF CHARACTERS

Board Members and Volunteers of the Arbella Society

MRS. WILLIAM ROCKLYND (NEE CATHERINE HAMDEN)—
widow and major donor
EDWIN BENNETT—*her nephew, retired clerk, and avid gardener*
GWEN MCDUFFY—*single working mother, with two children*
MARIAN DAVIS—*secretary*
KELLY KUHN—*art dealer and collector*
GEORGE FROME—*volunteer curator*
ANNALEE WINDOLOW—*art collector*
WALTER MARSH—*president of the Society and businessman*
BILL HUNTLEY—*Society treasurer and businessman*
MRS. ALESANDER—*Chief Silva's condo neighbor*

CHIEF JOE SILVA—*chief of police in Mellingham*
SERGEANT KEN DUPOULIS—*a member of the police force*

and other residents of the town of Mellingham

FAMILY
ALBUM

1

A Thursday in July

Gwen McDuffy didn't hear the door shut behind her. It fell to with a sweep and a rasp as the bottom scraped against the sand tracked in since the weekend. It always took her a month into the fall to tease out all the grains wedged into corners and sunk into rugs, resting in sneakers and comic books. In the beginning it had bothered her. Four hours at Mellingham's perfect and beautiful beach usually meant another two hours at home getting rid of the sand and seaweed. She remembered how angry it had made her mother, when she noticed, and Gwen wondered if her compulsion as a parent to gather every grain of sand had more to do with her own childhood than her children's. No one else in the picturesque village on the coast north of Boston seemed to mind the sand that was ever present; as time passed, Gwen hoped she could prod herself to care less and less. But today was another matter. The cocoon that was Mellingham, in its splendid, comforting isolation, was permeable, and seeping in were all the fears she thought she'd escaped, left behind in other places, other times, other lives. But it wasn't so. Even Eden had a gate, it seemed, opening onto the larger world. Today those places long denied, almost forgotten, seemed more real than Mellingham.

She pushed past jackets and towels hanging in the narrow back hall leading to the kitchen. Her eyes glanced from side to side, checking that the ordinary things of her life were still where they were supposed to be. A loud laugh and giggles from the next room gave a focus to her thoughts and feelings; she turned and hurried into the living room.

"Hi, Mom." A young boy looked up from the floor where he was sitting on a worn braided rug holding a typed sheet in one hand and a pencil in the other.

"Hi, Philip," Gwen said, struggling to sound calm. "Hi, Jennifer." She turned to her daughter, who was sitting at a small worktable.

"What are you doing here?" Barely a year older than her brother, Jennifer stared up at Gwen with a look of surprise and almost indignation, as though her mother's appearance had disrupted a secret and important transaction.

The two children waited for a reply, some comment to explain why their mother was suddenly and unexpectedly at home on a sunny Thursday afternoon in the summer. It was Mrs. Alesander, however, who spoke up. Comfortably settled in an old stuffed chair, Mrs. Alesander was an elderly woman who took her baby-sitting duties literally—she sat and babied her charges, thereby tempting them to accommodate themselves to her age and failing capacities, which were strictly physical.

"I was just thinking of having some iced tea and now I have company. How nice," Mrs. Alesander said. She started the series of efforts that would raise her from the chair and carry her to the kitchen. "We just finished lunch and I thought it might be too soon for iced tea, but I'm so glad to have an excuse to have some myself." She turned her black-laced shoes sideways, just missing the half-filled teacup where only moments earlier a single wisp of steam rose to tickle Mrs. Alesander's fingers resting on the arm of her chair. But Gwen was too preoccupied to take in all the details of her own living room; she had to force herself to attend to Mrs. Alesander, who was saying, "And a perfect time for a chat."

"No, don't get up, Mrs. Alesander. I'll get it." Gwen gave a short nervous laugh, moved a hand across her waist, and slowly backed out of the room, her eyes still on her two children. Alone in the kitchen, she leaned against the counter and took a deep breath. Seeing her children at play in the living room made her feel how foolish she had been the last few moments; so relieved was she that she laughed to herself. Then she made her way to the refrigerator, drew out the blue pitcher of iced tea, and set it on the counter. Her knees were still shaking and she had to go to the bathroom. Fear always hit her like that. She moved across the dining room, turning and looking back to the living room at each step as though to reassure herself that the bantering voices of her children were real.

When she returned to the kitchen, Mrs. Alesander had two glasses of iced tea and two of lemonade on a tray. She was adding a plate of oatmeal cookies.

"We're having just a little bit of trouble deciding what to take for the second summer session down at the park. It starts next week. Now, Jennie, she wants to work on her swimming. Very single-minded, that girl. But Philip, well, he wants to try something new, he says. It's got to be something new." She added four paper napkins to the tray. "Actually, do you want to know what I think? Well, I think he's trying to figure out which program the assistant coach is teaching. You must have met him? Nice fellow. Bill, his name is. He's treasurer over at the Arbella Society. Well, anyway, Philip's taken a liking to that man and he is at that age when he's looking for someone to look up to. Philip, I mean. What they call today a role model." She smiled and went on to explain the qualities of the assistant coach so important to nine-year-old boys like Philip, but Gwen wasn't hearing her. Mrs. Alesander's soft, barely inflected voice was like the susurrus of wind in the trees, draining her mind of its anxiety, drawing the tension from her limbs. This was one of the reasons

Gwen had originally hired the older woman, for her irenic personality, even though she hardly seemed capable of keeping up with a nine- and a ten-year-old. But she didn't have to keep up with them, as Gwen soon learned. Jennie and Philip grew delicate in their behavior toward Mrs. Alesander, and with everyone else they grew calmer, kinder, happier. And so did Gwen.

Gwen turned away from the other thoughts, the tiny voices arising unbidden behind her that accused her of cowardice, deceit, and worse. Her answer was always the same. Perhaps it was weak, self-serving, but that was all. She refused to think it could be anything worse. Was it so wrong to want to live in a world that was as loving and as placid as Mrs. Alesander's voice? Gwen followed the older woman back to the living room; she sat uneasily on the sofa and held a cold glass in her hand, but did not drink, her throat closed and dry, the little tick of repeated swallowing gone as though the cloak of a new life could fall away and yet return at the instigation of some other will. The stark fear that had come upon her earlier, while she was doing errands after work on her way to the Arbella Society for an afternoon of volunteer duty, wasn't the usual flash of terror that visited her only in the early morning, before she was awake enough to discipline her thoughts but not sleepy enough to have them masked by dreams. She forced herself to pass through these moments quickly because she knew the cost if she didn't—a fear so deep and pervasive that it would cut through her very being, leaving her hollow, then ripping her apart. Only a will strengthened by practice day after day, year after year, got her through those early moments, into a day padded with the hundreds of ordinary devices of escape—the casual greetings that ensured a rhythm and safety to chance encounters, the job that gave her a paycheck but also a myriad of tasks to fill her thoughts, and the rituals of caring for her children, which, in the way the universe had of surprising her, gave her brief moments of joy so intense that any lengthening of them might cripple her.

With a brightness she did not feel, Gwen jauntily raised her glass and drank, calm enough now to let her mind hear Mrs. Alesander's description of the shrubs Joe Silva, chief of police of Mellingham, was planting alongside the house where he lived, he in the downstairs condo, she in the upstairs one. The older woman interrupted herself every now and then to help Philip read a description in the youth activities brochure, and then resumed her narrative. This was, to Gwen's mind, the only drawback to having Mrs. Alesander as a baby-sitter—she got to hear an awful lot about Joe Silva, and nice as he seemed to be, Gwen just didn't want to be reminded of the police. It was irrational of her, and she knew it, or at least she told herself it was irrational, but she could never quite make herself believe it. She had made her choice, and she knew the costs.

"So, Mom, if you're here, can you take me up to the mall for a new suit?" Jennie asked.

"I'm here, honey, but just for a minute. I thought I left something I wanted to take over to the Arbella Society with me. I didn't realize you'd all be inside. I thought you'd be out playing." Gwen avoided looking at Mrs. Alesander, who peered at her over the rim of her glass; the children had a strict summer schedule, which Gwen knew as well as they did. "Maybe we'll go up later. Right now I have to get to the Society. I promised to catalog a new collection of lace someone donated."

"Can I come with you?" Jennie asked. "Why can't you spend your afternoon off with us?"

"Well, now," Gwen said, turning her entire upper body to look directly at her daughter. Her struggle to conceal her earlier panic made her rigid, remote from the boisterous, boundaryless love of her children, and she once again grew angry at the instigator of her fear. She had thwarted her feelings to keep her children from sensing danger and, iron-ically, had only succeeded in nudging them away. Jennie's plaintive smile drew her back.

She and Jennie had the same chestnut brown hair, which surprised Gwen. She hadn't expected it. When Jennie tossed her curls out of her face just as Gwen had done at the same age, it seemed a sublime act of divine grace. Jennie had been blond, like Philip, until she was three or so, and then had turned darker. Philip had remained a towhead, and probably would be one all his life.

"I didn't know you were so interested in my company this afternoon. We'll do it for sure another time. We're pret-ty busy down there today, getting ready for the board meet-ing tonight. I promised I'd help. I suppose I should get going." Jennie made a face and turned to a bottle of nail pol-ish on the floor in front of her. She had entered the period preceding adolescence with the subtlety of a hurricane. Gwen didn't know if it was the lack of a father, her own fail-ings as a parent, or just all those hormones kicking in. She had given in on the nail polish, recognizing a losing battle when she saw one, and was trying to hold the line on make-up, stockings, fancy jewelry, and everything else Jennie insisted she had to have or she would die. For this moment only, Gwen was glad of the enticement of bright red finger-nail polish. "See you later, guys." She stood up stiffly, a lit-tle too bright for the occasion, then turned back to Mrs. Alesander. "Thank you."

"You're welcome, dear." Mrs. Alesander watched Gwen leave, down the back stairs, the way she had come in. All the way down to her car, Gwen heard the reassurance in Mrs. Alesander's voice that the older woman knew, knew it all, every last horrible moment of truth, all the secrets and fears and shame Gwen had buried, denied, hidden. But she didn't know, she couldn't know, Gwen insisted to herself. What she was really saying in that voice of hers was that

Gwen could talk to her if she wanted, tell whatever was troubling her, and Mrs. Alesander would understand, sympathize, console, soothe. But that was an offer made without knowing how bad the secret might be. Gwen couldn't tell her everything; that was the one thing she couldn't do. And yet, unless she could do something, someone else was going to tell Mrs. Alesander—and everyone else.

■ ■ ■

"You were quite right, Edwin. They've come back beautifully." Mrs. Rocklynd swung her cane at the masses of balloon flowers lining the stone wall that separated her property from the rising and lowering road that led into the town of Mellingham. Some time ago, in her late seventies, she had decided that canes, inlaid with mother of pearl and gold-tipped, or carved from mahogany, or painted like a Ukrainian Easter egg, were an elegant addition to her wardrobe and had begun collecting them. She had canes to match her favorite suits, her broken-in hiking boots, and her gardening outfits; each new cane meant an hour's pleasure in learning the feel of the thing as she swung it out and around and above and below. She liked to watch men jump the first time they saw her swing her cane. It gave her a power society unfairly denied her sex. But canes were a nuisance sometimes too, taking up one good hand when she needed a third or even a fourth, but she held onto her cane with zest, enjoying the sense of abandon that came from throwing out her arm and reaching almost into a stranger's life with her stick. She carried a plain one this afternoon, worn down at the tip and bottom four inches where she had pressed it into earth and gravel during her walks. Edwin Bennett had given it to her a few years ago, and she was especially fond of him. "I thought they'd all be dead after you divided them last fall."

"They're hardier than they look, Aunt Catherine. I see you've planted quite a few more monkshood and campanula. They're doing well." Edwin strolled over to the bed of blue flowers, the monochromatic garden bordering the road a guaranteed traffic staller during the summer months. Tourists slowed, stared, took photos, and some even stopped to pick a bloom or two. Every summer Mrs. Rocklynd threatened to put up a chain-link fence but Edwin knew she never would.

"Can't stand the temperamental ones. Can't move 'em, can't separate 'em." She swung her cane and pushed on to another garden, this one entirely of red flowers. Edwin followed her, an amused, affectionate look on his face. He was used to her ragings at her plants, particularly those that had the temerity to die or fail to thrive. She even grew impatient with a plant that failed to multiply rapidly enough to suit her. Mrs. Rocklynd was that exceptional figure, the gardener who refused to comply with nature.

She was not easygoing, but her attitude certainly seemed to have benefited her. At eighty-four, she forced her way through life with the energy and demands of a much younger woman. Edwin tried to imagine himself as dynamic as she was when he finally got to her age, but he was skeptical. Less than twenty years younger than his aunt, Edwin had recently retired but looked every one of his sixty-five years. Years of smoking cigarettes left deep lines in his cheeks, a sniper's bullet from the Korean War left a scar across his temple and up to his hairline, and the agonies of his earlier years left scars on his wrists.

"You can divide some more of those balloon flowers for the Society this fall. Lord knows, Arbella House can use all the help it can get." Mrs. Rocklynd swung her cane as she surveyed the recalcitrant balloon flowers nodding agreeably in the breeze.

"You really are awfully good to us, Aunt Cat." Edwin

followed her as she moved along the flower beds.

"You think so? Well, let's hope you go on thinking that." She grumbled the last few words to herself, her eyes turned away from him. A foreboding came over him then, perhaps because of her roughness, which was never shown to him though he had seen it often turned on others she thought stupid, foolish, or arrogant, or perhaps something else, something inchoate but certain nonetheless. In unconscious mimicry, his blue eyes slewed sideways as he followed her up to the house.

"Come round back for a drink, since you think I'm so generous."

The tray of cold beer was waiting for them on the terrace at the back of the house. Mrs. Rocklynd settled into a straw chair and waited for Edwin to serve her.

"Maybe you're the one who's generous," she said, taking a sip. The sunlight played on her blond-white hair and on the froth in her glass.

"Me? Generous?" Edwin stared at her. He had never in his life been more than barely comfortable, and that was only possible because he had returned to live with his parents after his tour of military duty and settled into a steady if uninspiring clerical position at a large insurance company in Boston. He had inherited his parents' home but nothing else, and that was fine with him. His wants were few and his aunt was spontaneously if erratically generous. What little charity he had been able to afford had been modest though heartfelt. He settled his long limbs into a straw chair on the other side of the table and looked out onto the back lawn that fell away to the harbor beyond the train tracks. "I think I gave all of a hundred dollars last year." He took a long pull on his beer.

"What about that collection of china?" she asked.

"But that was yours," he said, shocked.

"Only because you wanted it to go to Arbella House. I

gave you your choice. It was really yours and you passed it on to the Arbella Society."

"Ah, yes, I suppose." Edwin hardly knew how to respond to this. The china wasn't his in quite the way his aunt seemed to be implying. Everyone at the Arbella House knew the china was Aunt Catherine's and came to them only because she was ready to donate it. He tried to guess what she must be hinting at and felt increasingly uneasy. "However it got to us, we're very happy to have it. A few of the other members and I were talking, informally of course, about raising some money for new cases for all of the china collections."

Aunt Catherine nodded and waved her hand at him, as if to say she didn't want to hear about the drive for much-needed money to renovate the interior and buy materials for preservation. She had donated generously to that too. He sometimes wondered what the Society meant to her. She gave large sums of money when she felt like it, valuable items from her own collections, and her time as a member of the board. But she was just as dutifully supportive of other organizations.

That wasn't the case with Edwin. He tried to tell himself he gave just as much in time and energy to the Society as Aunt Catherine gave in donations, but he finally let the illusion go. He was there because the Society had become his life, filling the spaces in his heart that he had once thought had been reserved for a loving companion. But there was no one, so the Society became his family (along with Aunt Catherine), a place of warmth and goodwill and fun, and in return he moved from job to job, taking on whatever task needed doing. Right now he was planning a campaign to raise funds for the restoration of the period rooms of the Arbella House.

"I suppose over the years I've donated more than anyone else," Mrs. Rocklynd said in a toneless voice so unlike her usual mode of speech that Edwin sat up and looked at her.

"Are you feeling all right?" he asked.

"Of course I'm all right," she snapped. "I'm just stating a fact."

Edwin waited for her to continue, but when he found the silence intolerable, he said, "Then I would certainly have to agree. Without you, we would be a poor excuse for a historical society. All we would have in Arbella House would be a few broken-down pieces of Victorian furniture and some old crockery." He leaned back in his chair, still leery of her temper and vacillating mood. Though a hard woman, Mrs. Rocklynd was never moody or cranky the way some older people are as they confront the growing reality that their life has moved past the one they want to enjoy. Mrs. Rocklynd's genes had so far saved her from the painful disillusionment facing most of her peers.

"Gave some of my best stuff, too. Good stuff. My mother's silver. My grandmother's wedding gown. The best."

Edwin had never heard her like this, almost petulant, her eyes fixed on her shoes, her fingers rubbing the cold glass of beer.

"The best stuff." She went on, mumbling, "Through you, of course. Through you. You never had to give the Society anything that wasn't top stuff. The best. Right? Right?" She leaned toward him as she said the last part.

He blenched but nodded in agreement. "Absolutely the best, Aunt Catherine, absolutely."

"You're a sensitive man, Edwin. I've always known that. You'd hate having to deal with anything shoddy. Junk. Peasant stuff." She went back to staring at her shoes. "I don't want to have anything like that around either." She threw her shoulders back and looked up. "Want to get it off my hands."

"Get what off your hands?" Edwin asked.

"Thought I'd get someone else to deal with it. What's his name? George Frome. Let him deal with it."

Her words filled the space around and between them, demanding a response from him, insisting he say the obvious, but he knew that once he did there was no going back. He and she had existed for so long in symbiotic charity that he was unskilled in handling discord, unprepared for this new undercurrent of tension. He had no idea what she was talking about, but he was sure it was tied to what he had earlier sensed. His presentiment of danger was justified and now he had to face what the danger itself might be.

"Let him deal with what, Aunt?"

"The house." She spat it out and then took a long pull on her beer. "The house."

"Do you mean—"

"I mean the house," she said, nodding to the distance. "That log house. It's such a ramshackle pile of wood, doesn't belong here, don't know where it belongs. Probably a fake, too."

Edwin pushed himself up straight in his chair. "Well, now, Aunt Catherine." He hardly knew what to say, except the obvious. "I do think we settled all that a few years ago. It is a genuine log house, the oldest surviving house in town, probably built before 1635. That's what our best records say."

"Yes, well, if it were on its original site, it might be worth something," Mrs. Rocklynd grumbled as she looked away from Edwin; she was loath to face him now.

"Who told you that? You know that simply isn't true." Edwin was shocked at his aunt's words. Anyone who researched homes in Mellingham learned right away that houses moved here, there, everywhere, whenever a family felt like moving a house. Years of work might have enabled a family to buy a better piece of land in a different part of town, but not to buy wood to build another house; they solved the problem by moving the old house to the new lot. As a child, Edwin had envisioned the dirt paths of

Mellingham in the 1700s and 1800s full of houses being pulled from one end of town to the other as some families grew, others split apart, and still others moved away. Only the coming of electricity and rows of utility poles put an end to the practice.

"Oh what difference does it make? I'm tired of it. Tired of thinking about it, tired of worrying about it. I want to be done with it." She spoke with effort, weary from the weight of the words in her heart. She put down her glass and stood up. "I told him he could have it. For a reasonable price, of course. Don't go trying to talk me out of it." She raised her hand when she saw Edwin open his mouth to protest. "It's done. That's all there is to it. Have to get the papers ready." She crossed the terrace in a few quick steps and disappeared through a pair of french doors, leaving Edwin and her cane behind on the terrace.

■ ■ ■

"And this one," Annalee Windolow said as she nodded to a large painting on the wall, "came from my mother-in-law." She crossed her arms over her chest, cocked her head to the side, and said, "Ugly, isn't it." With a gentle snort, she turned away and strolled to the far end of her living room, her shoulder-length silky black hair swinging out behind her. Always dressed hopefully for a sudden invitation to lunch at the Ritz, Annalee was wearing a yellow linen dress, white pumps, and a gold and diamond bracelet and earring set.

Annalee Windolow had money, or rather her husband's family had money, and relatives were forever showering her with family pieces—old paintings, some valuable, some not, small sets of crystal, silver candlesticks, worn-out oriental rugs, knickknacks, old tools—and these took their places, if valuable, on the first floor of her home. The remainders were discreetly piled into boxes that Annalee periodically donated to the Arbella Society. Since marrying her husband, Winston, at the ripe age of twenty-eight, just five years ago, she had learned to develop a taste for family pieces and the monthly family dinners that produced them. In-laws, cousins, and siblings invited to dinner often brought an item or two (or a dozen); the older the relative, the greater the likelihood of a treasure (or trinket) arriving in a grocery bag with the dinner guest. As the youngest and newest married couple in the Windolow family, Winston and Annalee could expect the practice to continue until another relative married (probable) or the family ran out of treasures (unlikely), when Winston and Annalee too would be expected to recycle their early gains.

Annalee adjusted to the custom as soon as she learned she was not required to display everything she was given; indeed, she gave every sign of being a docile participant in the family tradition. Winston accepted the object in question without comment until he had rolled it around in his hands, stuck it under a lamp, or peered at it through a borrowed pair of eyeglasses. Once it had registered in his memory, he proffered whatever tidbits of gossip or legend he remembered about it, and the item was duly recorded as a family artifact. Annalee then offered her warm thanks, and the evening progressed. Years of this had taken its toll, however, forcing her to fight back the only way a Windolow could.

"This is the one I wanted you to see. A friend saw it in one of those little New York shops and he knew it was just right, just what I wanted. You know how when you see something, well, it's just what I was looking for. So I flew down. It was very expensive, though. Well, not as much as I thought it might be. It could have been worse, I suppose. What do you think?"

The question was mainly rhetorical, and Kelly Kuhn

knew it. He leaned forward on his toes in order to show the expected interest, his usually cheerful mouth struggling to lift its corners and his mood out of an inexplicable sadness.

"It's very nice, really. Actually, it's, this is what you wanted, isn't it? A nice colonial picture, I mean, a picture of a colonial scene, the table with the fruit and fowl kind of thing. I mean, it is nice." He tried to show enthusiasm as he peered at the darkened signature at the bottom left-hand corner, his sandy blond curls almost brushing the gilt frame. "The artist certainly understood what should be in it for a colonial kitchen. Not a lot of the later ones did, you know."

"You don't think it's really colonial?" Annalee asked with some suspicion.

Kelly twisted his shoulders as though he were trying to say yes and no at the same time, uncomfortable at being put on the spot. In his early forties, Kelly knew when he was expected to flatter, and when it came to his best clients, the ones who responded to his private viewing cards by showing up at the small antiques shop attached to his home and buying whatever he suggested for them on that day, he always managed to tell them what they wanted to hear, partly because he believed if he flattered them when they purchased an object from someone else, they would buy a complementary piece from him. But today he found it hard to tell Annalee that her small painting was a huge find captured at a criminally low price.

"Winston doesn't like it either," she said after watching him struggle to give her an adequate reply. "I knew he wouldn't. He can't relate it to anything his family has given us. Here, I got this one too." She turned to another painting leaning on a chest. "I mean, he has such particular tastes, if you know what I mean."

Kelly did know what she meant, and understanding Winston Windolow's particular tastes had meant the difference between success and failure in Kelly's early years, long before Winston had married Annalee. Winston was a reader, especially of travel books, and when he went on a Continental Kick, as his family called it, he had to have a room redecorated to reflect the works he was reading. Kelly Kuhn had once created a white hunter's African lodge in a Cambridge apartment when Winston was attending the Harvard Business School; later the young businessman had discovered Australia and set Kelly the task of re-creating an authentic home from the Outback. Authentic or not, the room satisfied Winston, and that was all that mattered, for he paid well, and, even more importantly, he was now reading about China in a room on the third floor of a 1920 stone mansion large enough for an emperor's carved bed, which Kelly was currently searching for.

Annalee made a wry comment about being buried alive under family heirlooms, and Kelly laughed, his padded middle carrying on slightly longer than the rest of him. At first he was stunned with Winston's exotic and extravagant demands, not believing that anyone could squander so much money on what were obviously whims, but after a few months Kelly was converted, and his business grew accordingly. His original plans to keep his business stock within modest bounds, primarily American furniture and crafts, had dissolved like banks of snow, and he moved quickly into European and Asian arts and crafts, American paintings, silver, crystal, and whatever else his customers wanted. He knew far less than he admitted, but also far more than he had ever expected to when he had started out.

After working for Winston and then Annalee, he got the bug himself. Until then it had been enough to handle the objects, learn about them, get a good price, then let them go. But one day he felt differently when he was cataloging an impressionist painting he had purchased in New York on a client's instructions. He felt himself falling into the picture, brushed by the pastel flowers and cushioned by masses of green stalks. It cooled him and warmed him at the same time; the room he sat in seemed brighter for the luminous blue sky, and his heart tingled with the lambent light upon the fields. The fragrance of wet grass overwhelmed the smell of a half-eaten sandwich forgotten on his desk, and the crinkling sound of silence, like thousands of cicadas singing miles away, that filled his ears turned into the murmuring of wind rippling through the cypress trees and across the fields. When the picture left him, he was transformed.

After that experience, Kelly sought out every impressionist picture he could afford, and some he couldn't, by known or unknown artists, historical or recent, that might again evoke that moment. Whatever objects he had to sell in his shop dwindled to the few required to satisfy the IRS and the state Department of Revenue. He bought for clients, still conducted invitation-only sales, but increasingly he worked for himself. After a while he even refused to aid clients interested in impressionist art, for fear of losing a treasure to a competing customer. Fortunately, Annalee and Winston, two of his best clients, had never had any interest in any form of art to which they could not link their own families in either historical records or their own imaginations, and in the nineteenth century (as well as every other century) the Windolows were not at all advanced. Even now the senior Mrs. Windolow wasn't all that convinced about European art, although she knew enough to attend MFA exhibits and compliment friends on their acquisitions; overall, she preferred dogs. She wasn't at all sure how she had produced such an intellectual as her son Winston. Kelly followed along behind Annalee, stopping long enough to inspect an antique gilt-framed mirror and admire himself in the glass.

"Does your friend keep an eye out for things for you in

New York?" Kelly asked, wondering where the conversation had gone in the last few minutes.

"Hmm? What? What're you talking about?" Annalee turned back to an early version of the modern painting on velvet, an insipid picture of a stretch of the Hudson River valley on a piece of linen and framed in an extravagant gilt frame decorated with grapes and vines, unable to pull her mind away from her current obsession—the most recent product of the family dinners. Kelly realized too late that he had missed a long narration about newly acquired objects and tried to recall what Annalee had pointed to or touched in her journey around the room. "I really think it should go in the attic."

"Absolutely," Kelly agreed. He wondered if he should pretend he remembered whatever else she had talked about and offer a general comment. He might say, But the rest's okay. No, he might be indicating approval of a hideous 1930s water pitcher that had recently come to be parked in a corner cabinet. It might be wiser just to keep his mouth shut.

"You can see why I wanted the still life. Everything this month has been so horrible," Annalee said.

Kelly was glad he had held his tongue. If Annalee thought that it (whatever that was) was horrible, then it surely must be. He grunted his agreement. It was all he could manage. He had liked Annalee when they had first met, and she'd been an easy client to please—she only wanted quality at a decent price—but now she was throwing him curves with her independent collecting and competitive instincts activated against her in-laws. He was afraid of what was coming, of the reason for her invitation this afternoon. Preparing an official appraisal of some of her family pieces could ruin his business if word got out to the wrong families.

"I figure Winnie and I have to put up with all this stuff as long as we have nothing better, and since he's not going to get anything to replace this—you know what he's like—I figure it's up to me." She turned to him with her hands on her hips. "How 'bout some coffee." It wasn't really a question. She walked over to a tray sitting on a small table between two Federal settees; he followed and sat opposite her.

"I enjoyed buying that picture on my own. I can see why you're in this business. At first I figured maybe you couldn't get a real job, but it's fun. I don't blame you for getting into this. Anyway, I need to learn what you know so I figured I could join the Arbella Society and go to their regular meetings and pick up what I need to know. Get George Frome to teach me. He's already agreed to a few sessions. After all, I do give them all sorts of stuff all the time. They'll be glad to have a donor like me as a full member. So what do you think?"

Kelly didn't dare say what he thought. He didn't even dare think most of it for fear it would show in his face. Instead, he leaned over the coffee tray, raised an inquiring eyebrow, and tried to look as if he were on the verge of bursting into a huge smile. Instead, he looked the way he felt, a hysterical man sliding into madness. Annalee filled his cup with coffee.

■ ■ ■

Perched only three feet from the sidewalk on a granite block foundation, Arbella House rose up in the center of Mellingham as testimony to the town's long-past grandeur as a trading port. The first brick mansion in the town, the house was built in 1781 for a wealthy merchant family, who sold it to the first bank to open in the town, in 1802. Later a family purchased the building, moving in even while the bank continued to operate on the ground floor. Renovations changed the west side of the building periodically, until it finally ended up without door or window. In 1891, the then-current owner, who had received the house as a wedding gift from his father, left it in his will to the town for a historical society, and the Arbella Society was born, taking its name from the ship that brought Anne Bradstreet and the Massachusetts Bay Colony charter to the New World in 1630. Less important to historians but not to Mellites was the journey of the *Arbella* along the coast of what was to be later known as Cape Ann.

Serving as both museum and work site, Arbella House had come to reflect the interests of its many members. The front parlor and dining room on the right side of the center hallway were maintained as period rooms for tourists. The center hallway contained a small gift shop beside the grand staircase to the second floor, the landing two thirds of the way up opening to the landing for the back staircase. To the left of the center hallway on the first floor was the large, comfortable library, opposite the parlor, and behind the library an office, opposite the dining room. In the office, staff (of which there was only one) and volunteers worked side by side on whatever needed doing.

To her surprise, Gwen McDuffy found herself welcomed with genuine warmth and interest when she wandered into Arbella House one Saturday morning with her children and asked about volunteering. Since she only worked a half-day on Thursday, she chose that afternoon for her regular visit. The isolation from all present time afforded by cataloging artifacts from another era soothed her and she worked in silent companionship with the other men and women who appeared less frequently on the same day. This afternoon she had the worktable in the back room to herself.

Over the years, Gwen had grown fond of Marian Davis, the Society secretary and wife of the town clerk, and looked forward to their Thursday afternoons together. Marian saw to it that bills were paid, papers filed, doors locked, telephones answered, and unappreciated volunteers and donors appreciated. Nearly as tall as her husband, Gordon, Marian sprawled behind her army surplus desk, typing letters in her three-fingered method. Her mother had assured her that girls who learned to type were doomed to dead-end jobs, and Marian had taken her at her word. She typed twenty-three words per minute, and as fast backward as forward on her IBM Selectric. No matter, she liked her job, especially on Thursdays when she and Gwen could talk over town affairs without being overheard. Aside from the occasional interruption, such as the UPS man, who had just come and gone, and Kelly Kuhn, who rushed in and out on Thursdays to leave articles for his art student intern (and had also just left), Thursday was a relatively quiet time at Arbella House. George Frome, one of the most active members of the Board of Trustees, would not be in until three o'clock and other volunteers would give tours if a visitor wanted one. It was the best time to be at the Society, in Gwen's opinion.

Gwen pushed a folder of accession worksheets to the side and opened a large cardboard box. Her breath grew still as she unfolded the tissue paper, recalling absentmindedly that the Society had just run out of acid-free paper and acid-free storage cartons; she might have to use an ordinary cardboard box lined with aluminum foil to protect the materials she was now unwrapping until the Society could afford to buy more storage materials. She started to estimate the costs, but her concerns scattered as she lifted from the box a stack of lace-trimmed handkerchiefs, stained and discolored with age, tied with a frayed and discolored silk ribbon. She knew immediately that the linen was machine made, but the lace was not; it must have been saved from earlier silk handkerchiefs and resewn on new cloth, she surmised.

She lifted out each item in turn, making several piles until the box was empty and stored under the table. At the bottom of the box she had found a number of slips of paper with names and dates, and these she attached tentatively to different items in the piles. So intent was she that she didn't hear George Frome talking in the library, only a few feet from her. The white cotton gloves sitting on top of a box of sewing notions and ink-fast ballpoint pens remained there, unused, as she plucked a piece of lace from one pile and laid it flat on the table in front of her. She knew she should have a clean white sheet over the work surface, but she was too eager to stop now. Gently, she moved her finger from leaf to leaf and along a vine to a cluster of berries, the crocheted fruit rising from the ground. Fixing an eyeglass to her right eye, she leaned close to the lace, almost touching it with her nose. Marian went into the library and disappeared among the stacks; the telephone rang but Gwen didn't notice it, nor did she look up as George Frome crossed the room to answer it. Behind her, also unnoticed, came Chief of Police Joe Silva.

"Just let me tell the secretary to take this," George said to Silva, and stepped from the room.

Silva nodded and turned aside to let George pass into the library. In the last two hours he had been befuddled with historical information about the town by a man who could not keep his mind on his task. For weeks now George Frome had worked on getting Chief Silva to personally inspect Arbella House for security flaws, a task Silva considered as much a matter of public relations as safety. But now that the chief was here, he could not get the volunteer curator to answer the chief's more probing questions about security matters with anything more than a grunt and casual affirmation or negation. Frome's love was art history, especially portraits and American primitives as historical documents, and Silva was now numb with what he regarded as useless information.

The sight of the lace restored him. Paying no attention to Gwen McDuffy inspecting her piece, Joe moved to a pile at the far end of the table, the last pieces removed from the box, letting his hand run over the delicate needlework. He fingered the slip of paper, and then the others attached to items in the same pile. Like a priest who sees a magazine lying carelessly on a Bible in a parishioner's home, Joe found his hands straightening the corners of three pieces of lace, laying each one evenly on top of the one below. His eyes were on the lace, appreciating the workmanship, so he didn't notice Gwen McDuffy look up, attracted by the movement nearby.

"Sorry to keep you waiting," George Frome said as he returned from dealing with the telephone caller. "It gets to be a zoo around here. People call up and expect us to know all sorts of things, stuff they wouldn't think of asking a librarian or a history teacher. I tell you. Well, you must know how it is." Frome didn't wait for an answer. "Have you met Gwen here? She's our textile person." George motioned to Gwen, and Silva turned to her. "She knows all our secrets. And someday we'll know hers, eh, Gwen?" He leaned forward and grinned at her.

Both Gwen and Silva winced at Frome's tactless attempt at humor, and Gwen managed a stiff nod to the chief. When he had first entered the room, Silva felt that his coming upon her was a stroke of luck, but Frome had thwarted anything that might have come of this chance meeting. He wanted to say that he had noticed her in the town, made aware of her by his neighbor's, Mrs. Alesander's, fond interest in her, but he knew from experience that that made the innocent paranoid and the guilty circumspect. There were drawbacks to his job, and when he recognized the almost imperceptible wariness come into Gwen's eyes, he held his tongue. She was beautiful in a way few women achieve, with a firm but kind look that hinted at the difficulties he knew she must have faced as a single parent. She mumbled hello.

"New donation. Really good stuff, I hear. Right, Gwen?" George jerked his head around as the doorbell rang. "Damn door sticks. Probably just the mail. Be right back." He rushed off.

"Do you have to identify each piece?" Joe asked.

"I don't, no. We know what most of it is anyway. The donor left us a list. Some of it's Irish. Which I'd recognize anyway." The last was delivered with effort, as though she had to struggle against a barrier to speak.

"This isn't Irish." Joe motioned to the pile he had straightened. "It's Portuguese. You have several different kinds of Portuguese work here." He almost blushed when he realized how eager he must have sounded.

"You know what this is?" Gwen asked, pointing to a particularly fine piece.

"My mother and my sisters do this sort of work." He tried to sound disinterested, but he had never learned to look with detachment on the delicate work that in earlier times might leave a woman blind, her hands and fingers crippled, after only a few years of producing the most intricate and minute designs. He knew exactly how long it took for an expert to make one complete circle, and how long it took a young girl learning to manipulate her fingers like a tool. Each of his four sisters had been put to learning the dying art of Portuguese lace making before they grew old enough to rebel and refuse, and each had learned and then put it aside, except for the youngest. She alone of all the sisters and cousins had taken to the craft, making pieces as gifts and to sell in shops near her home. Her early samples had the evenness and originality of design of the work of a mature woman, and Joe felt a hot pride whenever he looked at the pieces she had made for him. "Do you want the names?"

"Yes, please!"

"This kind of work," Silva began, pointing to a white linen pillow case embroidered in white thread, "is called *bordado a cheio.*"

"Let me write that down," she said, pulling out an accession worksheet from a manila folder. "How do you spell that?" He spelled it for her and she made a show of writing the word slowly, then studying it, but she couldn't conceal from Joe the trembling in her fingers as she began to write. By the time she reached the bottom of the first accession sheet, she was calm, writing out her description in a mature, intelligent hand.

Joe relaxed along with Gwen, but he recalled that nuns and priests were said to have the same experience, that sensation of being discovered by the people around you, that sensation of knowing you were considered different in indefinable ways. It had never bothered him before today.

"And this one," he said, picking up a piece of drawn work, "is called *fios tirados.*" She wrote and he grew less self-conscious. "And this one is *crivo,*" he said, pulling from the pile a piece of linen with leaves in cutwork with different intricate patterns for the body of the leaves, all tied together with embroidered stems and edging. "This part is the *crivo,*" he said, leaning close and pointing to the pattern of the leaf. Gwen drew the cloth to her; for a moment both were lost in the beauty of the work, then she wrote, describing the design in detail and adding a sketch in pencil.

"Thank you," she said, setting the last sheet aside. "That'll be very helpful. For once we'll really know what we have." The slow motions of her hands as she rearranged the pieces filled the time while they listened to George coming back.

"Hi, Joe," Marian said when she returned from the library.

"Now, where was I?" George said, giving Silva barely enough time to nod to Marian Davis. "Oh yes. I'm telling you, Chief, I think if you or one of your men were to really, I mean, really carefully go over this place, top to bottom, you'd find it. There's got to be a way in that we haven't noticed. The cellar is an open invitation, let me tell you." George led the chief across the back hall, into the dining room, and to the cellar stairs.

"Watch your head," George called out as he patted a beam painted gray and posted with a red warning sign.

"If you think anything's been stolen, Mr. Frome, you should make a list. Detailed. So we know what we're dealing with. Then we can circulate the list to dealers and pawnshops. It's the best way." Silva found himself standing under the dining room in a low-ceilinged room given over to railroad history.

"That's just it, Chief. I can't quite put my finger on what's missing. That's where I thought this inspection tour would help—you looking at the house and showing me where someone might be getting in."

"If someone is breaking in, Mr. Frome, there would probably be some sign of it. If no one's breaking in, then your problem could well be internal." Silva shifted into dangerous territory, wondering how sensitive Frome and the rest of the Society might be. Some people refused to believe that one of their own—own employees, own relatives, own friends—could be stealing from them, and were grossly insulted when the police suggested such a thing. Others changed in front of the chief's eyes, letting a character of trust and goodwill fall away to reveal an implacable and abiding suspiciousness. Frome, however, seemed impervious to naive denial and sudden paranoia, almost as though he had another possibility in mind that he hadn't shared with Silva.

Retired from a career in state government though he was

barely fifty-seven, George Frome was a careful man, an early convert to vegetarianism, celibacy, and frugality. A stickler in all things relating to the Arbella Society, he seemed to have no desires to gratify, no needs to fill, no joys to share; yet he didn't seem to Silva particularly small or mean as self-denying people often become after a lifetime of rejecting pleasure. Whatever it was he really wanted from the chief this afternoon after weeks of persuading him to come to the Arbella House, he wasn't telling, and Silva couldn't divine if he was getting it or not.

■ ■ ■

"Now this belonged to my husband's great-aunt Abigail Emogene Eustace—isn't that a wonderful name?—anyway, she got it from her mother or grandmother, who managed to take it all the way to Missouri when she got married and moved out there. Something like that." The last three words punctuated the deposit of the blue-on-white china milk pitcher on the dining table in the Arbella House. Annalee Windolow, resting her hands on her hips and pointing one toe, surveyed the table where a number of family treasures were now spread for the convenience of Marian Davis, secretary of the Arbella Society and long used to the stories and legends that came with Annalee's donations. Marian had known the family all her life, and knew most of the stories already.

The only person in the family Marian did not know well or in the same way—by observing him or her from afar for fifty-plus years—was Annalee, but Marian still had her opinion of the woman. Childless, with a husband who made too much money for her to spend, in Marian's view, Annalee filled her days with the busy work of visiting friends, selecting items for her home, and planning social occasions. The hours of the day were divided by her own series of rituals, several of which revolved around meals, carefully prepared foods she rarely ate herself. She tasted, tested, commented, and left the table hungry for more than food could satisfy; the ritual of meals laced throughout the day helped her pass the time, but nothing seemed to get any better for her. She was bored, though she wouldn't have known it even if someone told her; she thought most people lived listless days. Her looks were a curse, however, an unkind announcement that fate expected much more from her than she expected of herself.

Today was typical, a long afternoon stretching into a blur that threatened to annihilate her, dissolving her personality into the fog that rolled in from the sea, forcing her to inflate small tasks to form a barricade against the world. The hours had threatened to overwhelm her with vacancy until she remembered what day it was: the second Thursday of the month, the day for a donation. Her meeting with Kelly Kuhn earlier in the day to show off her new painting had been satisfying only for an hour or so; after he left she was confronted with the rest of the afternoon, and then she remembered. Once a month she delivered a few choice items to Arbella House, and most of the time Marian Davis was the receiver. To Marian these visits were less exciting, for Annalee seemed to have an inexhaustible supply of odd-ities—knickknacks, stray pieces of furniture, inexplicable nineteenth-century kitchen gadgets, old books whose pages were never cut, old clothes from someone's grandmother. Seeing a sample collection from Annalee spread out one evening for the board to look over had made Marian won-der if Annalee was buying the stuff in order to maintain her role as donor to the Society.

"Now I know you don't have anything like these," Annalee said, pointing to a set of bowls. "I made a point of asking Edwin Bennett before I brought them in and I also looked around myself just to be sure. I certainly don't want to be duplicating what you already have." Annalee offered Marian a knowing look, and Marian's face crumpled into a pasty smile. Annalee's visits took longer and longer; it was almost as though Marian, standing in for the Society as a whole, was expected to earn the gifts Annalee brought. Marian knew her duty, however, and essayed a question about ownership, which sent the other woman off on one of her beloved forays into the past. Marian shifted her weight from one leg to the other, her hands resting in front of her.

Annalee glanced at her digital watch; it was 4:47. She said, "I've still got some time. I can tell you about the rest of it." So saying, she unfolded a napkin to reveal a small china bowl. Marian wondered why Annalee never asked if someone would take notes, or if Marian could remember everything after only one hearing, probably because she knew the answer. When Marian had once suggested that Gwen take notes, Annalee's body turned into a network of strings wound taut but she was saved by Gwen's insistence that she really couldn't stay. And ever since then, Gwen packed up and skipped out the back door as soon as she heard Annalee arriving at the front. It had become a ritual, and Marian wistfully watched her friend leave early once a month.

"Now these are really something," Annalee said, pulling a series of packets from the bowl. "I'll bet you don't know what these are. You don't, do you?" She never paused long enough to allow Marian to answer, nor did she look in the other woman's direction to see if she wanted to reply. (Marian had learned long ago that any attempt to engage in a dialogue with Annalee was futile; the woman wanted an audience, not an interlocutor.) Marian peered at the collection of five seed packets fanned out in the other woman's outstretched hand. She was right in one sense this time: Marian had never seen any of these before.

"Vegetable seeds from the original Shaker community in Mount Lebanon, New York. That's a very un-Shaker-like decoration," she said, referring to the decorative frame surrounding the label. Marian reached out her hand to lift one of the packets, but Annalee drew her hand back and extended her arm over the table, out of Marian's reach.

"Lovely, aren't they? I seriously thought about passing them on to the garden club. That does seem the obvious choice, don't you think?" She frowned at the packets still sitting in her hand. "But then I thought no, that's probably not such a great idea. It may make sense, but it's not really such a good idea. I'm sure you can understand why."

"It's almost five o'clock," Marian said. Annalee picked up one of the packets and started to read the directions in quaint nineteenth-century English. Marian struggled to maintain her smile while Annalee rambled on and on. It was bad enough that it was past the time when Marian usually left work, that Annalee had twice snatched the packets away from her hand, and that Annalee's conversations were designed to elicit agreement where none was felt, but that she should be the owner of something that was actually interesting to Marian was more than the Society secretary could bear. She wanted no more of this. As fast as the tongue of a serpent her hand snapped out and grabbed the packets, so startling Annalee that she broke off in midsentence.

"I didn't know you were so interested in gardening," Annalee said after recovering her poise. "If I'd known—"

"Very interesting," Marian said, interrupting her to hand back the packets. "We close at five." She started to turn away.

"That's what Mrs. Rocklynd said when I stopped by to show her these on my way down here. She was out gardening, you know, that lovely blue garden. She doesn't really like to be disturbed when she's working, dividing and replanting and that sort of thing. I can understand that."

"It's after five," Marian said, trying to move the visitor

toward the door. The idea that Annalee would be sympathetic to the needs of others, even those of a person as important socially as Mrs. Rocklynd, almost pushed Marian to the edge, but she held her tongue. "We close at five."

"Well, yes, that's what Mrs. Rocklynd said. That you like to close at five, but I reminded her that today's the second Thursday of the month and so you don't really close at five. So I came on down."

"I leave at five o'clock, and it's after five now. I like to have my supper before the meeting. And since there's no one else here, the Society's going to be closed until the board members come, but that won't be for a while. And even then we're not open to the public. So," Marian said, walking over to the door and kicking aside the door stop. Marian made no pretense now of her desire to be away, and Annalee, like a child suddenly aware of being hurt, could see no reason for being singled out for such rejection.

"Well, I didn't mean to hold you up, I'm sure." Pretending to be unhurt by Marian's attempts to push her out, Annalee stopped to slide back her sleeve and study her watch. "Now, according to my watch, it's just—"

"We're closed," Marian said.

"And what about—" Annalee turned around to the array of items spread out on the dining table.

"I'll leave a note for Edwin Bennett or George Frome. George went out to get something cold to drink. He'll be right back. He or Edwin will see to your things; now I must insist. We really are closed."

"There's only one of you that I can see," Annalee said as she stepped past Marian, her chin out and her nose up, and only the lightest smirk of superiority playing on her lips. "By the way," she said, turning back from the front door, "Mrs. Rocklynd seemed to think they might be better off in a different sort of place. She has such sound judgment."

"What might?"

"The seed packets. I thought they might make a nice conversation piece, the beginning for a gardening collection—we have lots of old tools, you know—but I'm beginning to think that the garden club might be more suitable. I mean, they'd know how to identify everything and they could explain how all those doodads worked. They wouldn't get confused about the value of the items, either. Have a nice night." Annalee pulled the door shut behind her, leaving Marian with a smile etched on her face. It was 5:23.

2

Thursday Evening

Marian Davis wobbled on one leg and swung the door shut with the sole of her shoe as she leaned into the narrow kitchen extension that also served as the back entrance for the Arbella House. Raising a plate covered with aluminum foil over her head, she made her way past four women making coffee and arranging snacks on plates.

"It's fine as it is," she said in answer to an offer to take the plate. "I'll just put it on the table." She passed into the back of the main hall. The half-dozen others milling around there and in the office greeted her with a smile, a nod, or a quick wave as they completed their preparations for the meeting. The most pragmatic and organized among them, Marian moved on into the library, where a dozen chairs were arranged in a circle around a low table. She deposited the plate on the table and removed the aluminum foil, revealing two dozen oatmeal cookies. Then she opened a large envelope and pulled out a bundle of sheets, placing one on each chair. She was not the first to pass out reports in this manner. When she was finished, she surveyed the confusion in the office from the quiet in the library, her hands on her hips in an attitude of impatience. Shaking her head, she gathered the sheets from the seat behind her and sat down.

Every member of the Arbella Society Board of Trustees

was expected to bring snacks to a certain number of monthly meetings each year. The men stopped at the corner store on the way if they forgot to ask their wives to provide something for them to take, and the women spent the day of the meeting preparing a variety of small sandwiches and sweets for a group of people who had eaten dinner an hour before. Marian fell somewhere between the two extremes. On rainy weekends throughout the year, when she couldn't garden or work outside, she cooked for sunny days ahead; she was just now reaching the bottom of the freezer she kept in the cellar, well stocked during a wet spring.

"Your turn tonight?" a rough voice asked Marian. Mrs. Rocklynd stood beside the table studying the plate of cookies.

"I think there are some other things coming along, if you're really hungry." Marian went back to reading, not because the agenda, notices, and reports were so interesting, but because the older woman irritated her.

"Well, I'm sure we all do our best." Mrs. Rocklynd turned and went back into the office.

When Marian had agreed to serve as the volunteer head of the grounds committee (of which she was the only member) in addition to her regular (and paid) job as secretary, she did so on the condition that no one, particularly Mrs. Rocklynd, would interfere in any way with her decisions. The president at the time was willing to accept her condition but then he was desperate for someone to take an interest in the grounds of Arbella House and relieve him of the chore of bringing his own lawn mower down every Saturday to cut the grass. He was ecstatic when Marian agreed to take on the committee.

"I'm not late?" Kelly Kuhn rushed in through the front door, panting and flapping the lapels on his jacket. "I thought I'd be late. I even thought about not coming, then I thought I should. I seem to spend so much time here. I don't know what good I am. Oh, oatmeal raisin." He grabbed two cookies and pushed one into his mouth while he gathered up sheets in a chair and sat down. "I don't know why I always sit over here," he said as he settled himself near the front door. "We get a place when we first start and then we think of it as ours. People do that same thing in aerobics classes." He blushed as he glanced down at his soft stomach and then at Marian. "I dated a woman who told me that. She taught aerobics and she said after the first class people felt they had their place and no one could take it from them." He laughed again. "Great cookies."

"Thanks."

Kelly busied himself with the notices and reports. He didn't want to be here, sitting thigh to thigh with a man who wanted them all to go to each business in the town for a modest donation to fix the roof, which this past winter had leaked so badly that a carton of old gilt frames had been damaged, or elbow to elbow with a woman who wanted to offer free membership to anyone who brought in a new member. When he had joined the board, he had agreed to identify and evaluate some of the undisplayed paintings, and he had done so, with the help of a college intern and two volunteers, but he was ready to move on. His business had declined so much recently that he now faced the prospect of being broke—for the first time in his life—if he didn't find good pieces he could sell with a big markup to his regular clients. What was he going to do? He glanced at the plate of cookies, then up at Marian, as he stretched out his hand, and found her staring at him. He stopped where he was and realized he'd been opening and closing his right hand in a recurring spasm of panic.

"Anxious to get started, you know. Great cookies." He grabbed another two and gobbled them down.

"I hope you're going to leave some for us. Hello, Marian." Edwin Bennett stepped between two chairs into the center of the circle and moved to the front of the room. "We're going to have a full house tonight."

"And a full night if we don't get started soon," she added. "What's the holdup?"

"The usual. The president wants a full treasurer's report but he didn't come up with all the figures until just an hour ago so he rushed over here and now poor Bill's out there trying to get a week's job done in twenty minutes."

"Oh, gee, too bad," Kelly said. "Well, if it's really going to be late before we get started, maybe I won't stay. It's not as though I have anything to tell you tonight. I mean I don't have a report or anything. My work's about done and I've told everybody all about it a hundred times." He began to bounce in his chair as though he were posting in an English saddle, the rolls of his flesh jiggling as he became more and more convinced that he should leave. "I won't wait. Yeah. I think that's the best thing."

"What's the best thing?" Mrs. Rocklynd stood in the library doorway, where she had been listening to Kelly Kuhn's agitated reasoning. She pulled out a chair near the door and dropped her pocketbook onto it. "We're going to start in a few minutes so there's no need to get impatient. There now, this'll keep you occupied," she said as she stepped aside to let another board member pass with a tray of celery and carrot sticks. "Chew on that for a while." She turned back into the staff room.

"Calm down, Kelly. No one's going to make you give a speech," Marian said. Kelly went pale.

"That would be awful."

"Have you got something you have to bring before the board?" Edwin asked.

"No, no, I'm fine. I'm just thinking that these meetings take a lot of time." A few more board members drifted in to claim their seats as Kelly finished, and they offered their hearty agreement.

"You might be interested in this, Kelly," Edwin said after other conversations sprang up around them. "Annalee Windolow brought in her usual collection of oddities for the month but for once she had something really quite interesting—some early seed packets from a Shaker village up in New York, I think. Never been opened, I don't think."

"Any Shaker furniture?" Kelly asked.

"I don't think so. I just looked at the list Marian left in the box with all the stuff. But the box is out there in the dining room if you're interested."

"I'll look at it before I go," Kelly said.

"Why're we so late tonight?" another trustee asked.

"The usual. George is staying tonight," a woman answered. "He doesn't care if we start on time or not if he means to stay late."

"How do you know he's planning on staying?" Kelly asked.

"He brings his supper in the afternoon and leaves it in the refrigerator. It's always in the way when we're working out there, you know."

"No, I didn't know," he said; the other two women went on discussing George's plans for the rest of the week.

"Just a few more minutes." George leaned in through the doorway, repeated his promise in a cheery voice, and waved to the other board members. Only three seats were still unoccupied: George's, Bill's, and Mrs. Rocklynd's. Kelly Kuhn dived at the cookies.

■ ■ ■

"Does anyone want to add anything?" Walter Marsh, the president of the Arbella Society, glanced around the circle warily and once satisfied that no one wanted to speak, he drew a line of red ink through item number three on his agenda.

"I want to know about Joe Silva," Edwin Bennett broke in. "Where's he on this agenda? Which one is Joe?"

"What's he got to do with anything?" another trustee asked, giving him a challenging stare from the other side of the circle. Kelly Kuhn, who had spent the first part of the meeting sneaking more cookies and crackers, shrank back at the suppressed anger in her voice.

"That's what I want to know. He was here most of the afternoon, wasn't he, George?" Edwin turned to George Frome, who was seated near the door to the office and only one seat away from Mrs. Rocklynd. "That's what Marian said, isn't that right, Marian?"

"I don't think he's on the agenda for tonight," the president said. "Our next item is—"

The other trustees pitched in their views and the president covered his eyes with his hand. It was like this at every meeting, right from his first one, when he came to understand why the Society had a habit of never selecting a president from those who had previously served on the board.

"Ladies, gentlemen, please," the president called out.

"Oh, look at that," Mrs. Rocklynd whispered to the woman on her right. "Someone forgot the dip."

The woman looked down at the table. "I wish I'd thought of that; I wouldn't mind getting out of here for a while. It is exasperating, isn't it? All this, I mean," the woman replied, commiserating with her friend's frustration with the arguments escalating around them.

"Indeed it is. Well, I might as well fetch it now. The dip, I mean. At least I can escape from this cacophony." She eased her way out the door directly behind her while the voices grew louder. Her right leg was stiff as she limped into the hall, but it hadn't seemed necessary to use a cane for such a short errand. By the time she returned with the dip, only one trustee was speaking.

"I don't mind giving the membership report next

month," the woman said; it was obvious that she did very much mind. She shuffled her papers with as much rustling as she could manage while seated in a chair, then folded her arms across her lap and leaned back. "I guess the figures won't change too much between now and then." The president thanked her with more relief than gratitude; he was too old-fashioned to let a woman lose an argument in public under any circumstances, so he had no idea how to resolve the disagreements that arose every month. He relied on Marian for that, but more and more she seemed to be looking elsewhere when he most needed her. He wiped his brow.

"Good. Now what about Joe?" Edwin asked.

"I'd be glad to tell you all about his visit," George said, looking from Edwin to the president, who rolled his eyes up to the ceiling, waved his right hand, and resigned himself to another meeting with a disrupted agenda. He liked his agendas, he was proud of his monthly preparations, and some day, he promised himself, he would actually make it through one to the end.

"Personally, I wanted to wait until I could put together something written so you'd all have a report to study later," George said.

"What are you going on about?" the woman on his left said as she reached for a cracker. "You'd think there was something wrong here."

"There'd better not be," another said. "No one authorized any security work, did they, Walter? We haven't got enough money for a new security system anyway, have we, Bill?"

"What?" Bill turned to the president to rescue him from being dragged into the center of the controversy, but Marian saved him.

"What's the point here?" Marian said. "You wanted to hear about the chief, so let's hear about him."

"Do please get on with it," the president said with a tired smile.

"Gladly. I gave Joe Silva a tour of the Arbella House," George began.

"Is he going to become a member?" a woman asked. "It might be just what we need, someone dynamic like that. I do think he's dynamic, don't you?" The question was addressed to the group in general. "Have you asked him yet?"

"No, no, thank you," George answered the speaker, and with exasperation declined the offer of a cookie from the woman on his right. "Let's not get off the track here." He took the plate started on its rounds by Kelly and passed it to the woman on his left. "It seemed to me," George said, trying to regain the group's attention, "that over the years, and even more so recently, a number of us have noticed items missing, or at least we think we owned things that we can't seem to find now."

"Well, we can't really say one way or the other," the president broke in. "We haven't cataloged very much of what we have. I mean—"

"Yes, exactly," George said, breaking in. He knew the president's habit of specifying each failing and its consequences until he produced a string of disasters in the middle of a board meeting; it was one of the reasons George had become unwilling to work with the man over the last year. George refused to associate himself with anyone who couldn't control his committee members. The idea of accommodating people was a fine sentiment if he worked in an office and everyone had to feel part of a team, but it hardly seemed necessary to carry it to an extreme at a nonprofit organization. After all, George grumbled to himself almost every day, a leader should lead, push ahead, no matter what. It drove him wild to think how slowly things moved at the Arbella House. Collections from the 1890s still sat uncataloged in corners all over the place.

"Well, we are getting on with that," Mrs. Rocklynd said. "Cataloging has to be done carefully." She smiled and the woman on her left pointed discreetly to Mrs. Rocklynd's mouth and offered her a napkin. Catherine declined it, and reached between the chairs for her purse sitting on the floor.

"Sometimes, George, I don't think you appreciate the work we do here," another woman said. "Catherine here, for one, has given years to this society." All eyes turned to Mrs. Rocklynd, who smiled modestly as she pulled her hand from between the chairs. Her handkerchief caught on a rough spot on the chair and fell to the floor. A startled look passed over her face as she cradled her right hand in her left.

"Oh, dear," the woman on her right said. "You've hurt your hand." She pushed her chair farther away, butting up against George's.

"Catherine? Are you all right? What's wrong?" Marian jumped from her chair and knelt in front of the old woman when she failed to respond to Marian's solicitude. Behind her came Edwin. Mrs. Rocklynd ignored the cries of concern all around her as she massaged her hand. After a while she smiled.

"I'm all right. Just hurt my hand, I guess." She laughed.

"Let me see," Marian said, trying to pull Catherine's hand toward her. Catherine jerked it away.

"Don't be silly. I'm perfectly all right. Not even a splinter. Go back to your seat, Marian. All I need is a napkin." Marian reached for one on the table behind her and Mrs. Rocklynd grabbed it from her, twisting it in her hands; she folded it and wiped the patches of sweat from her temples. "I'm fine, just a little woozy there."

When Mrs. Rocklynd had reassured everyone, the other trustees settled back in their seats. Marian nudged Edwin, finally taking him by the shoulders and turning him around. Pale and subdued, he sat with a worried eye on his aunt.

"Walter, I'm fine. Get on with the meeting. Please, George, don't make me feel any more foolish than I already do. Go on with what you were saying."

"If you're sure." George turned to the group again. If he had hoped the board members would be more tractable after Mrs. Rocklynd's mishap, he was disappointed. They didn't modify their behavior for anyone; they pounced on George as soon as he took up his narrative.

"Exactly what do you think is missing if you have no record of what we own?" one said.

"Have you been checking things? Going through each collection?" another asked as she leaned forward, accusing George.

"Where exactly do you think these things are going? Things don't just walk out," Marian said.

"That's just my point," George said and sat back. The room erupted with the dissonance of a dozen cries; even the president was moved to protest.

"I really do think, George, that you have gone too far. As president I must insist that you show consideration for the other board members. None of us is convinced that things are missing. You really are going too far now," Walter said.

"What a monstrous accusation," one of the women said.

"I'm not accusing anyone of anything," George said.

"Not yet, anyway," Marian said. "But you sure sound like you mean to get around to it."

"Do you?" Edwin asked.

"Now, now, let's not get upset. I do think you're all over-reacting. I'm talking about taking ordinary sensible precautions, the kind that any museum might take. We have a lot of valuable things here."

"I thought we didn't know what we owned," one woman interjected. George shot her an exasperated look.

"We don't," another added.

"We are a museum," George lumbered on. "We should

take our responsibilities seriously. We used to have four cups in that service in there and now there are only three."

"What are you talking about? We never had four, did we?" The woman turned to Kelly Kuhn, who looked alarmed at the prospect of giving an opinion.

"That's exactly my point. Anyone could walk out of here with a sterling tea service or an oil painting or an oriental rug. We wouldn't even know," George said.

"We'd notice if a rug was missing. What do you take us for?" one woman said. "You know, right from the start you acted like we were just a bunch of hicks. Well, I think you should know that this place was a going concern, that's right, George, a going concern before you joined. We are very careful with our collections. And we don't let things just disappear."

"Yes, but no one's taken anything, so why should we get all upset?" another added, perhaps feeling that the meeting was getting out of hand.

"Because George has all but accused us of stealing our own collections!"

"Who nominated him for this board anyway?"

The president listened to the comments flying back and forth, watched George growing more and more frustrated, and enjoyed every moment of it. Walter Marsh knew as president he should interrupt the senseless arguing and veiled insults, and redirect the discussion to the central issue—whatever that was—but he so rarely had the chance to see George put out of countenance that he hated to interfere. George's usual sleek smile was gone; the women members who normally fell all over themselves to agree with him were outraged at his sly remarks and weren't going to let him get away with any of it. They would defend themselves and the state of the Arbella House until the building was left without so much as a dishrag, assuming George was right after all. At moments like this, rare though they were, the president had hope. As a trustee defended her scrupulous vacuuming of the oriental rugs in the upstairs rooms, he thought about his agenda. For the first time he could see compensations in not reaching his monthly goal. Maybe next month he'd get to the end. Tonight he was in such a good mood that it seemed like a distinct possibility.

■ ■ ■

By eight-thirty Joe Silva had finished washing the supper dishes and cleaning up the kitchen. He had eaten much later than usual because Mrs. Alesander was waiting for him in his sitting room when he got home at five-thirty.

Mrs. Alesander lived on the second floor of the dark-shingled colonial, which she had converted to two condos when living in the whole house got to be too much for her. With her husband dead, her children grown, and her grand-children almost on their own, she wanted to hear another voice in the house; she was willing to sell half her home to get it. It was the first home Joe had ever owned, and it felt right from the moment he walked through the door. The front of the first-floor condo had two rooms, a living room and a bedroom. Behind, at the back, the large keeping room had been cut into a small bedroom on one end, which Joe used as a study, and a kitchen and bath on the other end. Between them was a large sitting room that looked onto a small lawn that opened into a marsh with the harbor beyond. Joe found Mrs. Alesander settled in the sitting room, the back door open to the smell of the mud flats at low tide, a smell coastal people like the way farmers like the smell of manure; it was a fragrance of time in motion, of a small ball of rock and dirt in a great ocean of darkness reeking of its own energy, a smell of reassurance, of the concinnity of life. It gave Joe such a feeling of peacefulness that he didn't mind finding Mrs. Alesander eating ice cream on his sofa, but then he didn't mind finding her there in the winter either.

After Joe had moved in years ago, he awoke one morning to find Mrs. Alesander in the kitchen and the shocking realization that he, the chief of police, a man raised in a rough city and trained to do a hard job in dangerous circumstances, had forgotten the simplest precaution of all. He had forgotten to change the locks on his doors. After that morning it was too late. To confront Mrs. Alesander with new locks would insult and hurt her, and Joe could not bring himself to do that, so over the years he got used to finding the old woman in his home at odd hours until he came to look forward to her unannounced appearances. He also came to respect her, for she never came without a reason, a problem to talk out, a tip about a teenager unhappy at home and on the verge of trouble, or advice on how to deal with a difficult man or woman. Joe hung his hat on the Shaker peg rack in his bedroom and put away his gun and holster.

"I left some for you in the freezer," Mrs. Alesander said when Joe came back into the sitting room.

"I'll have it after supper." He joined her on the sofa with a bottle of beer. In the silence he nurtured to encourage her to speak her mind he followed the waving black tail of a dog moving through the tall grass of the marsh. When he first moved in he'd been worried a dog would sink into the mud and drown unless he figured out a way to get the animal out. He knew the willingness of the fire department to rescue a stranded animal but also the danger. A home could turn into a glade of blackened sticks in the time it took to recall one engine from an unnecessary run. Now he watched the black Labrador bark in frustration at a duck awkwardly climbing, startled, into the sky. The more Joe settled in, the more he looked back on his original worries with undisguised amusement.

"Did I see you over at the Arbella House this afternoon?"

Mrs. Alesander asked when she'd finished her ice cream.

"I guess you did. How'd you manage that? Out for a drive today?"

"Not quite. Think I could get past your department if I were at the wheel?" She laughed, then fell serious again. "Gwen McDuffy drove me home this afternoon after baby-sitting. Nice woman. Know her?"

The training Joe got in his early years had turned out to be useful in more than police work. He was, for instance, a good poker player because he could slip away from any feelings while he held a hand, but more and more he wondered what else he was slipping away from. Mrs. Alesander's question made him put aside any personal response and think of Gwen as a problem for the department; that he was able to do this smoothly troubled him.

"I'm worried about her," she continued.

"All right. Tell me what it is. Maybe I can help." It was probably just as well that he hadn't got to know Gwen McDuffy, not if she were the kind of woman who brought in the police. Joe knew officers who fell for women on the other side—and women officers who fell for men—and he was not broad-minded enough to gloss over the risks. Maybe all his years as a policeman had changed him, maybe he was prejudiced after all, in a way that was set in his genes, a way he could hide, compensate for, but never eliminate.

"I'm not sure I know what it is. You know she works at the Arbella House on Thursday afternoons. I told her she should try that when it seemed like she wasn't meeting anyone or getting away from the kids. A woman has to get away from her kids once in a while. Anyway, I don't know that she's met many folks over there but I think she likes it. She's got a real sprightly look Thursday afternoons. At least she did, until last week."

Joe thought back over his afternoon at the Arbella House.

It was one of the quietest buildings in the town, no office chat seeping into the silence like Easter egg dye in a bowl of water; it was almost like entering a church.

"What happened?" he asked.

"I'm not sure. Last week she came home after working there all Thursday afternoon looking kind of thoughtful, like she had something on her mind. I asked her if something was bothering her but she said no. Seemed all right when I saw her next. But today— Well, today round lunchtime she came running up the stairs—I heard her coming—and flying into the living room. The kids were just between projects, settling down after lunch and all, just fooling around but I don't think they noticed how panicky she was." Mrs. Alesander pondered the scene in her mind. "I calmed her down pretty much." She patted one hand with the other in her lap. "You know I almost had the feeling that she half-expected some kind of trouble, if you know what I mean."

Joe did know what she meant, though he wished he didn't. It had been obvious, at Arbella House, now that he was forced to see it, that something was troubling Gwen. He had assumed she was reacting to him and his uniform; he hadn't stepped back emotionally to check her reaction to George Frome. Joe tried to recall exactly how Gwen had seemed at George's appearance, but he had been so little interested in George and so much interested in Gwen and her piles of lace and linen that all he could see were her slender fingers touching the roses and vines on the trimming of the handkerchiefs.

"She has two children, is that right?" he asked.

"Jennie and Philip. She's ten and he's nine. Good kids."

For the next half hour she told Joe all she knew about the family and all she could remember about Gwen's early years growing up in Mellingham before she married a boy from another town and moved away. Mrs. Alesander couldn't remember his name, and she didn't like to ask the kids what their other last name was; she didn't suppose it mattered anymore what names children had as long as they had parents (at least one) who loved them. Gwen's parents moved to Florida soon after Gwen married and she had no other family in the area. She was moody as a child, not especially popular or attractive, in Mrs. Alesander's view, but she was nice and warm as an adult and mother. Still, the older woman was worried. No matter how long Mrs. Alesander talked, no matter how she analyzed what she knew about the younger woman, she was pulled back to her original uneasiness. Gwen McDuffy was in some kind of trouble.

It was not what Joe wanted to hear, and he sat with another beer for an hour after Mrs. Alesander left. He had wanted to classify Gwen's standoffishness, her wariness, as modesty, shyness, anything but fear of the police, because that might bring something he didn't want to know about her. When he finished his beer, he felt his fingers tightening around the bottle as though he could crush it as easily as a can. It shocked him to feel how angry he was.

He was forty-seven years old, chief of police in a town that was both haven and prison—haven for allowing him the life he wanted to live as the policeman he wanted to be after brushing up against a nightmare he didn't want to name, and prison for giving him exactly what he wanted and nothing more. He had worked for so many years to get where he wanted to be that he had never considered how he would feel when he actually got there. Now he was there, and the choices he had made unthinkingly, perhaps even unconsciously, revolved around him, spinning tighter and tighter like the wind in a tornado.

He had not meant to end up alone in middle age; the years had slipped past him until the ones he wanted were gone without his noticing. If he were incapable of loving another and knew it, he would have accepted it, but the infrequent encounters with Gwen in the town reminded him that he was not. She stirred memories and seemed to promise some of her own just by her presence. It was perverse that he should get what he wanted, to know her better, but on a professional level.

Joe took another beer from the refrigerator and turned on the television. More and more in the evenings he thought about the people who weren't around him—his parents, his brothers and sisters and their families. Once he might have added Christina, the woman he had expected to marry. For a while he thought he might add Gwen to that list. He fell back against the sofa, the mindless laughter flickering in front of him. For the first time in his life Joe Silva wondered if he'd made a mistake in becoming a policeman.

■ ■ ■

At nine o'clock that evening Annalee Windolow made a decision. She didn't normally like to take decisive action, particularly if it meant mental as well as physical exertion, but the actions of others were threatening to overwhelm her. For the last hour she had kept her husband, Winston, company while he unpacked a box of family treasures his mother had left at the house earlier in the evening, about the size of the one Annalee had left at Arbella House earlier in the day, giving her a feeling of circuitous futility. The living room was now littered with crumpled newspapers and German porcelain, none of which Annalee liked. She couldn't tell if Winston liked it or not, probably because he didn't know himself; he merely embraced, figuratively, whatever his family handed over to him.

Winston Windolow, all six feet of him, was now prowling around the downstairs rooms looking for likely resting places for his new acquisitions. So far Annalee had steered him through the two living rooms (one formal, one informal), the library (more often used for television than reading), and the dining room (already packed with oddities from his family). That left him standing in the doorway to the pantry and the kitchen beyond, sucking in his lips as he scanned the unfamiliar space.

"I don't think this will do at all. Let's look at the living room again." He turned around but Annalee blocked his way.

"We haven't looked upstairs yet. It's very light and open up there and we haven't paid nearly enough attention to those rooms. And I think we should."

"Should what?" He was growing irritated with Annalee as he stared at the door to the formal living room at the opposite end of the hall.

"I think we should pay more attention to the second and third floors, especially since we're going to have so many people coming through." That got his attention, as she knew it would.

"What people?" He began to look worried. Annalee had a habit of surprising him when he had his mind on other things.

"The people on the tour. I've decided to open the house as part of the house tour for Christmas. I know it's a long way off but it will take some time to get the place ready."

"You're putting the house on the tour? I thought you hated those things." Winston forgot all about his porcelain figures and gawked at his wife. She was beautiful in a cold, distant way and she always seemed so mysterious, so deep and unknown. Being around her made him feel he had adventurer's blood in his veins instead of that banker's liquid.

"I've changed my mind. I want to do it now. And you have to help. We have to clear everything out of the downstairs. Everything. Every chair, every rug, every knickknack, every light bulb."

"Isn't that going a little far?"

"No. Everything goes. And then we pull out only what is exactly right for the room. Nothing more. All the leftovers we can put in storage if you want. Or give to the Arbella Society. Or we can sell the stuff."

"Sell it?"

"Or put it in storage. I did say that, didn't I?" Annalee wasn't taking any chances in losing the war over a logistical matter. He could store whatever he wanted for as long as he wanted, just as long as she didn't have to look at it anymore. Enough was enough.

"I suppose that sounds all right." He looked at the oriental runner beneath his feet and the engravings on the wall. "Who comes to these things?"

"Just people from around here. It's nothing to worry about. Let's look at how much room we have on the third floor." She led the way up the main staircase.

Even though Annalee assured Winston that the tour would attract only respectable people, she wasn't all that convinced of it herself. The Arbella Society ran a series of historical house tours every year and at least one home had a break-in a few weeks later. That was in fact the reason Annalee had never given in to the numerous invitations she'd received over the years to participate. She had not a single altruistic bone in her body, and hadn't grown one in recent days. If things went as she planned, she would use the threat of a break-in to cancel her participation at the last moment. Right now she just wanted to make sure she got everything up on the third floor. Bringing back down the few pieces she wanted wouldn't be so hard. It would be years before Winston caught on, if he ever did, and by then it wouldn't matter.

"You certainly have changed, Annie. You always said you didn't like house tours or the people who have them, and here you are offering to help the Arbella Society raise money with a tour yourself." He followed her up to the third floor.

"Don't be picky, Winston. And don't call me Annie. It's so ordinary."

"Sorry, dear." He squeezed her buttocks.

"You're not paying attention, Winston." She brushed his hand away. "We can get someone in to pack up all the small things. Most of them will probably fit in here." She walked into a large room with eaves and windows looking out toward the harbor. She could see a strip of blue off toward the horizon, a view that meant nothing to her but a lot to the real estate agent who showed them the house. It had seemed to her then and did so even now that anyone who bought a house just for the view from the third floor was a fool. But, as her mother had always said, there were all kinds of fools. She watched Winston as he poked around the boxes and broken lawn furniture stored since their arrival. Her mother certainly was right about that.

After a few minutes of quiet exploration, Winston said, "If you put everything up here, Annie, won't the rooms be awfully bare?"

"I'm taking care of that. And don't call me Annie. You saw the painting I bought. Well, Kelly Kuhn thought it was okay even though he didn't want to admit it. Every time he sees something he thinks is really valuable, he gets glassy-eyed and he breaks out into a sweat. He thinks no one notices, but it's so obvious."

"Poor man. You should be more sympathetic, Annie."

"Don't call me Annie. Why should I be sympathetic? I pay him enough to be rude to him if I want to."

"A Windolow is never rude, Annie."

"Winston, one more time," she said, turning to him.

"Sorry, dear."

"All right, then." She glared at him. "I have a very sensible plan. I'm going to take Kelly along on trips to a few galleries and watch how he reacts. When he comes all over sweaty and flaky, I'll know I've got a great find. Of course, I'm only going to pick up a few things to fill out the downstairs." She added the last qualification when she saw a puzzled look gloss her husband's face.

"He'll catch on that you're using him."

"No, he won't. But if he does, I'll pay him a small finder's fee. That's fair."

"I suppose so." He turned around to survey the room again. "This will make a nice study. We could put up shelves over there and put out some of Mother's china. What do you think?"

Annalee smiled. She thought it was going to be much easier than she had expected.

■ ■ ■

At 9:31 George Frome closed the back door on the last departing member of the Arbella Society Board of Trustees. The Arbella House was finally, blessedly, quiet after almost two hours of acrimonious debate. It was the first evening he could remember in a long time in which the entire meeting had lurched beyond his control. It was those damn women. They had no sense of what he was trying to accomplish. He pushed the lock and slid the bolt, then stood in the quiet. Finally he had the Arbella House to himself.

It was a good thing, too. He had plans for this evening that would be hard to explain to anyone else, so he had restrained himself until he knew he could be alone. What he had to do required concentration and time, neither of which would come in a house full of volunteers during the day. With the level of curiosity rising in inverse proportion to the financial support given, volunteers were, to George's mind, an encumbrance, one that he had to avoid at all costs if he were to resolve his current doubt. A late evening was the only time that was suitable, George had concluded. When he saw car lights draw a bright yellow sheet across the front hall, he turned from the door to the refrigerator behind him.

Ever since he had joined the Arbella Society, George had finagled the trustees to leave him alone in the building at least one night a week, one night when he could feel himself owner of all around him. It irked him to have skeins of old women wedging their way in beside him at a worktable, or swooping through the galleries, or hatching plans in the office. Because they gave most of the items needed for the collections he was always nice to them, especially Mrs. Rocklynd, but he was convinced in his soul that they didn't really have the capacity to appreciate the artifacts they dragged out of their attics or found in the back drawer of a grandmother's sideboard. They put nineteenth-century Limoges figurines in the same box with a plate of macaroons for an evening meeting. They even used their old china, serving generic-brand crackers on Lenox plates. He didn't know which offended him more—the sweets that were part of every meeting or the proximity of antique and dessert.

George opened the refrigerator and lifted out a plastic food container. Refined sugar never crossed his lips, neither did meat, eggs, nor milk products. Well, almost never. Those who thought they could call themselves vegetarians while still eating eggs or taking dairy products earned only his disdain. The world offered enough in fruits, vegetables, and grains to satisfy any healthy taste, and he said so whenever anyone asked him why he wasn't eating what they were offering. He closed the door to the kitchen, checked the front door, and turned off all the lights downstairs except those in the central hallway.

The streetlights outside illumined the dining room,

reminding him that in all the rush before the meeting he hadn't had time to look at the collection Marian had left on the dining table, the most recent donation from Annalee Windolow. Vaguely he recalled Edwin's comment that one item in particular was worth a look as he poked through the box. The china bowls were interesting if not especially valuable, but in one were five packets of vegetable seeds. A few seeds, tiny, pale shavings of life, had dribbled into the bowl from a frayed corner, but otherwise the original seal of the packets seemed to be intact. George held one up to the light from the window to read the text as the telephone rang. Snorting in irritation, he slid the packet under the oatmeal cookie resting on top of the food container and held both in place with his thumb as he hurried to turn on the answering machine. He'd had enough of the Society for one day. All he wanted now was his dinner and time to reflect.

The second floor of the Arbella House was just as varied as the first floor. Over the library and office was one large room used as a gallery and meeting room. The front room on the opposite side was a late eighteenth-century bedroom and the room behind it contained a permanent exhibit on the history of the town of Mellingham. George had wanted the exhibit placed on the first floor, where it would satisfy the slothful curiosity of the few people who wandered into the Arbella House expecting a typical museum. He was outvoted, however, and the exhibit stayed where it had always been, drawing tourists and a few locals up to the second floor where they would have even greater opportunity to damage irreplaceable materials.

The third floor repeated the second in design, but here the collections were stored. In the large room chairs were stacked on chairs, bureaus backed up to dry sinks, beds leaned against settees. The lack of order dismayed George and he tried not to think about it. The front room held clothing and textiles, and the back room weaponry and old cycles for one or two people. He had suggested selling some of the items but all he got for his efforts to upgrade the collections was a litany of whose father, grandfather, or brother had donated this rifle or that unicycle.

On his way from floor to floor he flicked off every light until he climbed the stairs to the attic (it pleased him that they were wider and finer in craftsmanship than most staircases in modern homes), unlatched the door and pushed. He turned on the light as the door swung open, letting folds of hot air tumble over him. In the winter it was cold, in the summer hot. Uninsulated, unfinished, the attic was all eaves and dark patches, with a flight of stairs in the center leading up to a skylight that opened onto an old widow's walk atop the slate roof. He shut off the light on the third floor. Only the attic light served him now.

Despite the heat and musty smell of wood, he loved it up here, standing alone above the town, the Society, even the coastline. He discovered the attic one day while prowling around the third floor after he first became a trustee. Until then he'd really had no reason to look over the entire building. When he asked about the door at the top, Marian, the secretary, gave him the key and told him to show himself around. He had. That was a stroke of luck, for him at least.

George climbed up to the skylight and opened it. The hot inside air lifted a bit but outside it wasn't much cooler. He left the window open and descended, sitting on the lower steps. Leaning against the brick face of the central chimney on the east side were half a dozen oil paintings in various states of disrepair. A few months ago George had discovered a stash of paintings behind the second chimney on the west side, a stash he thought he must have overlooked the first time he inspected the attic, though he recoiled from admitting that he might have actually missed anything. After looking at them closely, he changed his mind.

The paintings were spread along the brick face so that

George could view each one from where he sat. Half were portraits and half were still lifes, all done in an early primitive style. He was studying them because he was sure he had seen them before, but he couldn't remember when or where. He had only a vague idea when, but that had given him an inkling of how they might have come to be hidden there. He wasn't certain—the details were elusive—but he had become obsessed with teasing out the memory, thus his late night visits to the attic when all others were gone.

George took a last look at the faded packet, reading the archaic English and hoping Annalee's gift of Shaker seeds was a prelude to a more valuable gift of furniture. She was an annoyance, shallow and demanding, but he had agreed to give her informal talks about paintings so she could become an informed buyer. Two months of that should tell him if it was going to be worth the effort.

With a sigh, he put the packet into his shirt pocket and nibbled the cookie before pulling the top off his plastic container, dumping loose seeds into the salad. He didn't approve of sweets, particularly the sort Marian made, but he liked throwing away food even less. The taste was always strange to him, never growing familiar though it was redolent of his early years as a boy. He let his mind drift as he swallowed a large piece of the cookie, wiping his hand on his pants leg. A few seeds fell to the ground. He let them go; they could hardly be worth saving after all this time. The unopened packet was what mattered, a historical record of an important development in American history. It galled him to think he had Annalee to thank for it.

Such concerns melted away in the attic. He dug his fork into his salad. Every night in warm weather he made the same meal—lettuce, tomatoes, sprouts, broccoli, red onions, and carrots—with a variety of more exotic and spicier toppings. His simplified diet allowed him to concentrate on more important matters, like the paintings. He leaned forward. When he knew where he'd seen them before, he would know what his next step was, and he was sure there was a next step. George stuffed a forkload of vegetables into his mouth and chewed and gulped. Just as he swallowed he looked down at his salad and shook his head slowly from side to side. The heat was getting to him. He took another bite. A moment later he stopped chewing, his eyes bulging, then he spit out the food. The plastic container fell from his hands as he groped in his lap for a napkin.

Leaning back to let the nausea pass, George gagged. Then the room seemed to grow dark. He tried to stand but his legs gave way beneath him; he fell forward onto his knees. Beads of sweat fell from his forehead, his chest hurt. A tuft of cool air tumbled down the stairs and brushed across his shirt. All he could think of was the story about the dog and his master in Alaska, or was it Canada? It was a story about cold or friendship or something like that.

George tried to push himself up from the floor but he couldn't make his muscles work. His mind was cluttered with scenes of a dog in snow and ice and a man with a fire that wouldn't burn. But he could see light. There was light everywhere. He blinked. The rough plank flooring was turning yellow. He was so cold.

3
Friday

Most of the time Marian Davis liked Friday mornings; they were quiet times when she could work on whatever she wanted—except once a month, when she had to type up the minutes from a tape recording of the board meeting on the preceding night. Perhaps in honor of the last day of the week, or the day after the board meeting, on Friday Marian wore khaki slacks instead of her usual linen skirt and starched shirt. Today she also wore sneakers and a loose tan jersey, making her look like a faded tulip leaf balanced on her green leather swivel chair. She might have come ready for cleaning out the cellar.

The minutes usually took her all day, not only because she typed a mere twenty-three words per minute but also because she had trouble making out the precise names board members flung at each other as the meeting neared its inevitable end. Some of the trustees had limited imaginations and used the same epithets month after month, like slot machines with only three settings; but others amazed everyone with the variety and majesty of their barbs. And these, in Marian's mind, were worth preserving.

That wasn't what the secretary told the president, however. For him she had a different argument. She wasn't going to rewrite the ending of the meeting just to make a pleasant and inoffensive report. No indeed. After all, historians in later years might want to know what people in the 1990s were willing to fight over, to which the president replied with what had become his standard response. It might make more sense, in his view, and would certainly be more efficient, if these future historians searched for what the members of the Arbella Society didn't argue over. Marian silently agreed, but since she typed the minutes, she made the decision about what to include or exclude, with one exception.

She shut off the tape recorder and typed the last six words she had heard. It was already ten-thirty and she was still on the acceptance of the minutes from last month's meeting with all the necessary changes duly noted. The one time she had omitted the corrections, she had received a carefully typed note from a certain member ordering her to include them. And so she did, with a vengeance.

She turned on the tape recorder to hear George Frome's voice making the corrections, as usual; she turned off the machine. She punched two final letters and looked up at the lines already typed on the sheet resting in her typewriter. The name Frome was misspelled, as it was every month. Again, she punched the on button on the tape recorder, and the president's voice spiraled upward, from a groan into a pleasant thank you.

"Hello, Marian. Why's it so quiet in here? Where is everyone?" Annalee Windolow managed to walk toward Marian's desk while looking over her shoulder into the hall-way and dining room, and then into the library.

"Marian?" Annalee said looking directly at her. Marian raised her head with a quizzical look while she typed the last three letters of a word (two of them incorrectly). "I hope I'm not interrupting you. I'm looking for George. George Frome."

Annalee began her conversations with Marian in precise-ly the same way every time, so Marian had decided on a series of conversational ploys. Although she originally told herself that she was merely trying to teach Annalee some manners, the secretary now openly admitted that she delighted in punishing her for various slights, intended or not. When Marian once realized how far she'd gone down the pleasant path of revenge, she rationalized that it was no more than a mode of defense, a way of keeping Annalee's sharp tentacles from leaving hundreds of tiny cuts as she embraced her officiously. Annalee never seemed to notice; she only thought Marian Davis improperly schooled, if she thought of her at all.

"He's not here," Marian replied. "If I'd known yesterday that you had an appointment this morning with him I would have mentioned it to him last night at the board meeting."

"I forgot to mention it. Anyway, he said he'd meet me here at ten o'clock," Annalee said stubbornly. Marian glanced at the clock, which now said ten-fifty.

"He's still not here."

"He has to be. He said he'd meet me."

Marian leaned back in her chair, wondering just what made people turn out like Annalee; she looked normal enough. From that she progressed to wondering just how far she might push Mrs. Winston Windolow. "I arrived right on the dot of nine o'clock and no one else was here."

Annalee turned away from the library door. "Well, where else would he be? We spent a lot of time working out this arrangement; he knows it's important to me. I guess I'll just have to wait. For a while at least." She turned into the library and browsed among the stacks, once again managing almost an entire conversation without making prolonged eye contact with Marian.

The secretary turned on the tape again, listened to a few more words, then shut it off. Alone in the office she could conjure up the villains on the board who mumbled, slurred their words, or burped in the middle of their main point, but with Annalee only a few feet away Marian was shy about her secretarial skills. She rested her fingers on the keys, depressed the space bar, and listened to the comforting sound of the platen moving behind the ball. She typed a word, erased it, tried again, then stopped and pushed herself away from the typewriter. With Annalee in the next room, she couldn't work She was not independent enough to ignore the gossip she feared Annalee would start around town if she heard the older woman thumping one key at a time like a minuet. To conceal her dilemma, Marian turned on the recorder and rapidly wrote down the comments, shutting off the machine far less often than when she was typing the words.

"Doesn't George drive a black car? A new one?" Annalee was leaning against a window, her fingers pressed against the glass, her eyes fixed on something outside. Marian ignored her. "I'm sure that's his car. It has that sticker in the window." She stepped back. "He must have already been here when you came in. I'll have to go up and look myself." She spoke directly to Marian.

"No, you will not." Marian startled herself with her severity, but she didn't try to soften it. "If he's here, he's way up on the third floor and that's closed to the general public." Marian scribbled a few more words while Annalee waited with an imperious look on her face, which collapsed into consternation when she absorbed the idea of being part of the general public.

"Well, if I can't go up to the third floor, you'll have to. I can't wait all day."

"Are you asking me to go up to the third floor to look for George?" Marian asked in a meager attempt to return to her more common politeness.

"Would you mind?"

Marian thought it unnecessary to answer literally and left

the room. It was just like George to arrange some kind of meeting here, something with no connection to the Arbella Society, just so he could seem more important to someone like Annalee Windolow, a woman who never gave a donation that was ever anything they needed, like cold cash. Marian swung up the stairs to the third floor with new plans to ask the board for an intercom system, but this thought was interrupted by the speculation that no one used them anymore, people being much more interested in beepers and cellular phones, which meant that no one would have to go to the trouble and expense of installing an entire system as a permanent part of the building. Maybe she'd ask for a set of beepers that the Society officers could wear when they went to the upper floors.

On the third-floor landing she turned right, toward the back workroom with military artifacts. An acrid smell fell on her face like a wet cloth as she came to the stairs to the attic. The attic door was open and the light on. "George?" She called out loud enough to be heard on the third floor but not below. "Wouldn't you know it," she muttered to herself. "Up here all the time without letting any of us know so we'd have to flit around looking for him. What is that smell?"

Marian turned up the stairs to the attic, her hand on the railing. It started to bother her that she had been saying awful things about him to her husband, Gordon, at breakfast and to herself in the office all morning, and yesterday she hadn't been particularly kind either. Whenever she sniped about someone, whenever she let loose all the stored-up hostility, she finished only to find the object of her ire making up for it in some way. If she said nothing, of course, George would go on being outlandish, underhanded, and troublesome; if she said exactly what she thought of him, he'd show up an hour later with a considerate gesture and a donation large enough to fix the roof. It never failed.

And now, considering what she'd been saying and thinking about him for the last couple of days, he'd probably come back after lunch and offer to have the Arbella House painted. Well, it could do with some fixing up.

Marian climbed to the fourth step and called again, her voice carrying easily through the open attic door. She could even hear a few cars on the street below, so she knew the skylight was open. "George, are you in there?" Why did he have to pick the worst spot in the building to do his work?

She climbed two more steps and stopped. Directly level with her eyes were George's leather moccasins, and beyond she could see a hand, a swatch of his shirt. She climbed one more step and saw George sprawled across the attic floor. Uncertain for three seconds what to do, Marian ran up the remaining steps and knelt down beside him. She laid a hand on his shoulder, touched his hand, called out his name; she had her answer in the skin that felt like putty against her palm and the smell that her mind was now recognizing. Holding her hand across her mouth, she backed out of the room, and slid against the wall as she made her way down the stairs.

■ ■ ■

The attic was clean now. The police had not only removed the body of George Frome but a young member of the state police, unable to help the EMT crew maneuvering a swelling and decomposing body into a blue plastic bag, had sidled away from his partners and busied himself with collecting the far-flung remnants of George Frome's last meal. He had scoured the floor well beyond the chimney after inspecting behind the paintings resting against the brickwork, and declared the area clean just moments after the chief heard the zipper gaining speed. The smell lingered.

"Looks like a heart attack, or something," one man said to

Chief Silva after the others had disappeared down the stair-well. "They're taking him over to the Sara Meya Funeral Parlor."

"I don't mind telling you, I sure was relieved when I got a look at the front of him." Sergeant Dupoulis wiped his neck with his handkerchief. "Ah, if you know what I mean, sir." Silva did and said so. It was a relief to him too to find George Frome dead apparently from natural causes, even though he knew he'd have to wait for the official report.

In his mid-thirties, pudgy and unmarried, Sergeant Ken Dupoulis was doing just what he had always wanted to do—serve on his hometown police force. When Joe Silva arrived in Mellingham in 1985, Dupoulis was one of the few who thought the new man might open up other career paths for the hometown officers, though George Frome had not been specifically what he'd had in mind. "But we got all the usual info, anyway," Dupoulis added.

Silva nodded again. He had been alone in his office try-ing to come up with a solution to the summer parking prob-lem (a necessary but futile task) when the call had come in, and he'd walked over from the station after hearing Sergeant Dupoulis radioing that he was just pulling up in front of the Arbella House.

"Oh, we found this in his pocket," Dupoulis said, hand-ing over a small plastic bag with a seed packet inside. "It looks like it's never been opened but there's a tiny hole at the top corner. It might belong to the Society, but we weren't sure."

"I'll ask in the office before I go," Silva said, taking the bag. "Anything else?"

"For all his healthy dinner, he still had a sweet tooth. They picked up what looked like an oatmeal cookie along with the other scraps. Anyway, I'll get back on patrol now," Dupoulis said, his mind already composing the sentences he would use to open his report. The sergeant had the long slender fingers of a painter, but he showed no interest now or in earlier years in anything artistic; he was serious, almost to an extreme. His single burst of creative expression was in the Day-Glo sweatshirts he wore on his days off, which brought out genial ribbing among his friends and fellow officers.

The sergeant lumbered down the stairs, his excess pounds reminding the chief that he meant to warn the department as a whole to avoid weight gain or face mandatory weight limits imposed by the board of selectmen. He reminded himself to remember to make the speech he'd been preparing for Monday morning, but he knew he'd forget anyway. It was getting harder and harder to remember his mental lists, and he felt oddly weakened by this, as though his memory had become wanton and willful, teasing him by drawing away just outside his grasp, frustrating him and making him feel foolish. He was starting to feel vulnerable to youth. Even until this year he'd thought the vulnerability of the old was physical, and he'd defended himself against that encroaching weakness by staying in good physical shape. And he had; he was as strong and as quick as a thirty-year-old. And even though he was willing to acknowledge that it was really a matter of genes, he allowed himself to feel just a little bit vain about his condition.

That was a mistake. Fate got him another way—in his mind. Now he began to understand the threat that was youth—not strength, health, money, but merely a fewer number of years and so fewer worries. Joe was convinced that even thoughts were programmed into human beings, ensuring that no matter how we might struggle, we would harbor certain fears and worries on schedule; he believed this for he had no rational basis for feeling less able today than he had a year ago. The worst of it was that he needed his memory now more than ever.

George Frome had made a point of showing Chief Silva

the attic on Thursday afternoon, walking him up the stairs
to the door with frosted glass windows, around the staircase
up to the roof, then around both chimneys and the eaves,
waiting for Joe to notice the paintings stacked against the
central chimney. There were five of them, but they were
jumbled together, so Joe saw parts of some, the back of one,
and the brown wood of the old frames. Now they were
spread along the brickwork, each painting facing outward
in full view, just the way the police had found them when
they'd arrived.

Silva sat on the stairs, where George Frome had probably
been sitting before he collapsed on the floor, and studied the
paintings. George had wanted him to notice them, and he
had, but Joe couldn't see anything special in them. They
were just paintings—two portraits and three still lifes—and
old, or so Joe guessed. The clothing and faces of the portraits told him that, and the rabbit hanging on a peg next to
a pheasant suggested the same for at least one of the other
pictures.

But why were they up here? The attic was otherwise
empty in every corner and under every eave. Hot in the
summer, cold in the winter, this was no place to store valuable artwork, or anything else. In all the time Frome spent
showing Silva around the Arbella House, they spent a dis-
proportionate amount of time here in the attic. And then
Frome came back to it last night, after everyone else had
gone home, with his dinner, as though he meant to spend
considerable time here. Doing what? There was nothing to
do here but stare at the paintings, and from the way Frome
was lying when he was found, that must have been exactly
what he was doing.

The chief leaned closer to the paintings, his arms resting
on his legs. It didn't help; he still couldn't see anything special in them. He dropped his head into his hands. George
Frome had wanted something from the chief of police bare-

ly twenty-four hours ago and now he was dead. Joe shook his head. The smell was getting to him, that and the heat; he felt woozy, almost sick to his stomach, tired of the smell of death and the uneasy feeling that George Frome had left something undone.

Joe pulled the attic door shut behind him; at the bottom of the stairs he stretched a piece of yellow plastic ribbon across the bottom step, from the banister to the wall. Whatever George Frome had been up to, it didn't matter now. What he had left undone would remain undone. Perhaps that was true of everyone. Perhaps no one ever died when they had finished their life, perhaps there was no such thing as a finished life, no matter how old you were when you went. Every life was an interrupted one, for there was no right time to end life, only an untimely break.

Joe descended to the second floor and heard voices below; they came upon him as a foreign sound, remote and strange until he made himself listen to them. Gradually, they brought him back into his ordinary world, and he was grateful. He was finding it too easy these days to dwell on his mortality and to take a view of life so remote that he was no longer part of it. That was dangerous. A man was meant to live day by day, reading the signs of his neighbor's deepening friendship and thinking no farther than his child's next smile. Maybe that, Joe thought ruefully, was really the problem with his life. He had nothing to keep him attached to it.

The talking stopped abruptly as the chief turned into the office. Marian Davis and Edwin Bennett watched the chief come into the room and waited for him to speak.

"I've put a seal on the attic, just in case there's anything unusual about Mr. Frome's death." They nodded.

"Poor man," Marian said. "I didn't even know he was sick."

"Do you know what happened?" Edwin asked.

"It might have been his heart, but I can't say," Silva replied. "Not yet." He shrugged his shoulders. Edwin's face was pale, strained, and Silva realized that Edwin must be eight or ten years older than Frome. When the other man turned his face away, for a second Joe saw his uncle, a man who had gone unchanged through war, hurricanes, near financial ruin, remaining the same cheerful man until the best friend of his childhood died suddenly of a stroke. It changed his uncle more deeply than the death of his own parents. Edwin looked as moved now as his uncle had then. Our mortality is announced by the death of a friend.

"By the way, there are some paintings up there," Joe began.

"There are?" Marian asked. "There shouldn't be anything up there. Nothing at all." She stopped, her indignation dissolving. "I never even noticed them. Good lord." For a moment she saw again the prone figure and the swollen fingers, felt again the shoulder beneath her hand.

"What sort of paintings?" Edwin asked, trying to cover Marian's sudden change and his own shock.

"I can't say. They look like two portraits and three still lifes. They look old," Silva said, embarrassed at giving such a poor description.

"What on earth are they doing up there?" Marian said to Edwin. "Come to think of it, what was George doing up there? Wasn't there food around?"

"Yes," Silva said. "We picked it up and took it away. The whole place is clean now. I've left the skylight open—for the air. It might do some good." It was the right thing to say, but that attic was going to be unpleasant for some time to come.

"You know, Chief," Marian began, catching his attention with her new formality, "he always ate his supper here if he could manage it but I never knew he ate up there in the attic." George Frome's death had disassembled one of her strongest fantasies about him. "I always thought he ate in the dining room. On the dining table. I thought he got a kick out of sitting in there and enjoying it as though it were his own." She was ashamed of how unkind her thoughts appeared, but more fascinated by the gap between fantasy and reality.

"You knew he was going to be here after all of you left last night?" Silva asked, surprised at the freedom that Frome had enjoyed in the house.

"Oh, sure," both Marian and Edwin said together. To Silva that only made it sadder, that George Frome, admired and respected, even envied in a twisted way, should prefer to eat alone rather than with one of his colleagues in town of an evening. Silva put the thought from him.

"What do you know about this?" Silva asked, showing them the plastic bag. Edwin took it first, examining it closely.

"Marian, take a look. Isn't that one of the seed packets Annalee gave us yesterday?" Edwin said, handing it to her. "Let me check."

"It looks like it," Marian agreed. Edwin returned with the other four seed packets and showed them to Chief Silva.

"You got them yesterday?" Silva asked.

Marian groaned. "I really shouldn't say anything, but once a month Annalee Windolow comes over here and unloads some of the stuff her relatives unload on her. That's too strong," Marian said, lowering her head and taking a breath. "I don't know what's wrong with me today." She closed her eyes for a few seconds and began again. "Some of the stuff is okay but nothing for a museum, no matter how small, but once in a while she comes in with something interesting. Yesterday she showed up with that box of stuff in the dining room and she had five seed packets from the Shakers in New York. They're probably about a hundred years old. The seeds probably aren't any good as seeds, but it's nice to have the original packaging. We might be able to use it in an exhibit about commerce in the nineteenth century, if anyone wants to do it."

"These things were here when George Frome went upstairs to eat and do whatever else he meant to do up there?" Silva asked.

"Oh yes. Annalee was here yesterday for about an hour; she left at around five-thirty. I really had a job getting rid of her."

"What time do you close?" the chief asked.

"Five o'clock. I wanted to get home so I could have supper before the board meeting. I just left the stuff on the dining table." She turned to Edwin. "Did you put it all in the box?" Edwin nodded.

"They're just seeds, Chief," Edwin said when he realized how carefully Silva was examining the packets.

"I expect so." He smiled and handed back the other four.

"Can we bring the pictures down?" Edwin asked.

"Not yet," Silva said. "We may want to have another look around." He promised to let them know as soon as they could reclaim the artwork.

The chief left the Arbella House dissatisfied at what should have been considered good fortune in a tragedy—a sudden death that was no more than a heart giving out. Instead of feeling relieved, however, he felt saddened and weary. There was something awful about the way George Frome had died, or was it more than that? Frome lived alone, ate alone, died alone. He was like a few hundred other people in Mellingham and thousands of others in the area, not to speak of the millions in the rest of the country. Still his death was unsettling, stirring up a corner of Joe's memory allowed to sit in shadow. He remembered the woman officer who had rescued an old man from a lingering death in a rat trap that had been his lifelong home, his gratitude to her for finding him a place in a nursing home, her regular visits until he was happy and no longer needed her, she said. It didn't fit with the life Joe knew was hers and one day he asked her and didn't get the answer he expected; instead her words were irradiant. She was a striver for independence, privacy, autonomy, her only articulable goal for years, and then she achieved it. Now she was trapped in a personality she had created and couldn't reach far enough to leave it behind. She didn't have to look anything like George Frome for his death to remind Joe of her—or of himself.

In that painful moment that fate kindly gives us only once or twice in a lifetime, Joe saw exactly where his life was going, and he didn't like it.

■ ■ ■

Kelly Kuhn stepped on the brake, looked in both directions before stepping on the gas, and turned left onto Main Street. An hour earlier he had left a client in Boston who was examining a pair of Sheraton side chairs and planning a trip to Charles Street during the remainder of his lunch hour. Kelly said nary a word. Lunchtime has come to be a time for everything but lunch, he thought sourly, for shopping for groceries, picking up shoes at the cobbler, getting a haircut, dropping in at a bookstore. White-collar workers understandably enjoy the opportunity to get away from the steel-gray frame that encloses them and rush about town while eating a sandwich. It was the same in Mellingham. There weren't many of these employees in the small town, but Kelly Kuhn was one of them only reluctantly. The lunch hour in his view was sacred; it was time meant for food. He resented the fate that had so distorted his life that he couldn't enjoy a large bowl of cheese-filled pasta shells at the Family Café or a hot pastrami sandwich at the Harbor Light.

Kelly massaged his stomach, whose pain grew in intensity the more he dwelt on his predicament. When he had agreed to evaluate and identify, during his free time, the collection of paintings and drawings at the Arbella House, modest though they were, he expected to make a few extra dollars to add to his own buying fund. He was wrong, a turn in his life's events becoming far too frequent for his peace of mind.

Unwary and uninterested, he had agreed to sit on the board if it would facilitate his work with the pictures. George Frome said it would. Kelly signed on and showed up for his first meeting only to learn that no professional who served on the board could be paid for services rendered to the Society. Kelly barely made it through the evening, his eyes bulging in his head as he tried to focus on the paintings, most of them next to worthless, but not all. He was going to spend hours over the next several months frittering away time that might be more lucratively spent elsewhere, and he only vaguely understood how it had happened.

Life was getting away from him; there was no doubt about it. First he got tricked into evaluating pictures for free, then he had to spend all that time at Arbella House sitting through all those meetings. And now that intern. It was enough to make him irritable, and Kelly tried never to be irritable; he might alienate a prospective client.

Kelly parked his car behind the Victorian town hall and lumbered across the village green. When George Frome had promised him an assistant, he hadn't explained that Kelly would be expected to train the young student in the intricacies of art conservation. Nor had he explained to Kelly how peculiar young people could be today. Unmarried, childless, Kelly didn't even own a cat. No other breathing, coughing, warming life impinged on his moods, his needs, his own desires at any time, day or night. But the student intern had changed all that, calling up the Society to change her work hours, workdays, even her work duties whenever she felt like it. More often than not, she ruined Kelly's schedule. Today she was ruining his lunch, and he was chewing his lower lip in frustration.

He heaved himself into the traffic without looking, fell back a few steps when a driver honked frantically at him, and tried again. He rapped at the door three times before Marian pulled it open and said, "What do you want? You, of all people. I would have thought that at least you wouldn't fall to such depths. Oh hell, come on in if you must."

Stunned at this reception, Kelly looked around to see if the culprit intended in Marian's speech were hiding behind him, but apparently the fellow had skipped away. "Well?" she said.

"Thank you," he said when she closed the door behind him.

"I suppose now you do want to go upstairs," she said.

"Why would I want to do that?" Kelly gave her a fretful glance and headed for the dining room. "Where is she?" he said when Marian followed him to the doorway.

"Who?" Her irritation was growing.

"My intern. She changed our time to lunch this week so here I am," Kelly said.

"Oh, Kelly, I completely forgot." Marian became conciliatory. "It went right out of my head. She called this morning to say she can't make it until next week. I forgot to call you. I'm so sorry." Marian clasped her hands close to her face and shook her head. The shock of discovering George's body had severed her attention from the ordinary events of the day. Appointments were forgotten, friends talked to enemies, the future was a blank. "Kelly, you should know—"

"She can't come?" Delight and anger struggled for possession of Kelly, and delight won. He pulled at his wristwatch. "I just have time for lunch at the Harbor Light."

"Don't you want to know what happened?" Marian said in surprise as Kelly rushed past her. "I thought that was why you were here. You know, just coming to find out what happened. I'm so sorry." She trotted after him. "It's about George. He's—"

"She'll tell me, don't you worry." Kelly fled through the front door, cutting off Marian before she could add any more to the misery that was his volunteer job at Arbella House. Getting all sorts of gory news from his intern was bad enough, but to have to put up with it in the form of messages from Marian was more than he could bear. For almost eight weeks, since she began as a student intern at the Society for her summer project, Kelly had heard every detail of the girl's life, the unsuspected throbbing in her boyfriend's temple when he was getting an erection during an argument, the way her mother sneered at her artistic ambitions, her father's sympathy, the cost of her new sandals. Kelly turned it all into white noise, having given up on getting her to listen to him. She was in fact oblivious to his every word, except a direct order delivered in a stern, almost angry voice.

He supposed he put up with her because she at least took a direct order when he gave one. She would run up to the third floor, never making a sound on the stairs, dig out the next set of paintings for him to work on (for the most part her judgment was tolerable; only two or three times had he sent her back to replace her choice for something else), and carry them downstairs. She would dust them off, sand down a tiny corner for the new catalog number, and check references in the library, talking all the while. Kelly simply got used to her. He hoped never to meet any of her family; he felt he knew them better than he knew his own relatives.

Today he was free. Whatever else he might have to do today, he didn't have to put up with that girl. He could have a nice long lunch, call a few clients, perhaps visit a few auction houses to see what new objects they had. This was much better, he said to himself as he crossed the street.

Much better. He might recommend it to the rest of the people at Arbella House. Now that he thought about it, Marian was looking a little peaked this afternoon.

■ ■ ■

Marian Davis closed the heavy front door of Arbella House and made it all the way past the small table selling Arbella House notecards, local history books, and postcards before the front doorbell rang again. She halted for a moment, then went on into her office.

"One of you has to take another tour. Six people are waiting in the library," she whispered, "and someone else is at the door." She ran back down the hall before either of the two women could reply, and opened the door to two women in their thirties.

"We just thought we'd drop by," one of them began, but Marian didn't bother listening to the rest of what she had to say. In the last two hours, since the news had spread through Mellingham that someone had died in a surprising manner at 33 Main Street, young and old had suddenly taken an interest in Arbella House; in the last two hours Marian had sent off more small tours than she had in the last year, pressing into service the three retired women who came several times a week to do the unnoticed but necessary work of the society—the cataloging, envelope stuffing, and hostessing that kept any museum going. Now they were taking tours around the first and second floors, entertaining visitors with random bits of history, local legends and recollected scandals, and a few bits of fiction to entertain themselves. It was a certainty that no two tours were getting the same information.

Marian trotted once again to the main door, opened it, and tacked to its center a sign announcing tours every hour on the half hour. It was just two-thirty; only two more tours to go. She slammed the door shut just as three teenage girls straggled up to the wrought-iron railing. Back in her office, she closed the door to the library and sat exhausted at her desk.

"The ghouls," she said. "Whoever would have expected it?"

"If I'd known before I drove up, I wouldn't have come today," the other woman said; her companion had volunteered to take the next tour.

"I should have closed the house. Just closed it," Marian said. "That's what Walter suggested. Of course, no one else on the board agreed with him. Wouldn't you know it? The one time he gets to make a unilateral decision, to assert himself as president, with no danger to himself or anyone else, he takes a poll of the board. That man is hopeless."

"Well, at least we'll make some money." She glanced over at Marian for confirmation. She was glad to be free of the decision too; no one wanted to appear callous at such a time, but it seemed a shame to pass up an opportunity to get people actually inside the house. And they did so need the recognition.

"Oh dear. I've completely forgotten about collecting the entrance fee. Oh, how could I?" It was a rhetorical question; Marian did not want to be told that she was too upset to view the death of George Frome in anything but a personal light.

"Well, maybe they'll all remember us in the fall, when we do our usual collection." Forty years as wife, mother, teacher, volunteer, had trained her to think of the future, of the next time that would always come; because there was nothing that could not wait, there was nothing that did not have a second chance. If the Society missed one opportunity, it would catch another. Opportunities were sometimes like mosquitoes.

"They only want to see the death site—scene?—whatever they call it. Everyone wants to go up to the attic; that's all they talk about," Marian said in disgust. George's death was threatening to push her into a narcissistic funk.

"Good thing they weren't here last night," the other woman said.

"Why?" Only the confusion generated by an apparent non sequitur could break through to Marian at such a time; it was one of the reasons she was so fond of her Friday morning volunteers. They were such original thinkers.

"I hear George practically accused everyone of letting the place be robbed blind."

Marian shifted in her seat, and grew thoughtful. It was something of a relief to view George in the old way again. She thought fondly of their last argument. "George did seem to hint things were disappearing and we were remiss for not doing something about it. I liked George but he was a tough one. I think he liked to shock people."

"You're probably right. You found him in the attic, didn't you? He was having his supper up there with a bunch of paintings? Can you imagine?" the woman said. "I had no idea he was so lonely. Of course, if he was odd like that, he probably would be lonely."

"I can't imagine George being lonely," Marian said. "It's such a common emotion. And he always seemed so, I don't know, so far above such feelings. He always seemed to be on the verge of something better, more exciting than whatever it was the rest of us were doing. We were so pedestrian compared to him. And this week. Well, this week he was so chipper, so upbeat, especially this week."

"Probably pep pills or something. People take anything these days."

"Not George," Marian said. "He was a real fanatic about what he ate. Wouldn't touch anything that came in a package. He did all his own cooking, from scratch."

Both women pondered this, imagining a man not far

from them in years spending hours each day preparing meals in his kitchen, but one was more skeptical than the other.

"He was odd. I said that, didn't I, Marian?"

"Yes, you did. Men get strange if they don't marry," Marian said. She was calm now, the excitement generated by the unusual number of visitors had been worked through, leaving her much as she always was, hardworking, serene, but with some of her older prejudices surfacing. "I don't know why I said that."

She didn't want to admit that she did believe that marriage was meant to be a kind of rounding out of the personality, and she was in her core uneasy with unmarried men or women. She couldn't imagine their lives, what they thought about, how they made decisions, what the future looked like to them. Whenever she found herself chatting with a single person, she felt as if she had to explain her own way of life as a married woman. Marriage impinged on her thinking and rearranged her time, even her personality. Once George demanded to know why she couldn't finish a grant proposal a day early and she could only lamely recite her husband's name. It had seemed enough until then but thereafter she was more circumspect when she worked with unmarried people. Now she tried to remind herself that it wasn't George's fault that he was different. She reached for a pile of letters. "I've been saying horrible things all day about someone who just died. I feel terrible."

"Yes, we have, haven't we. Funny, that. We all got along with him, counted on him," the volunteer said. She was not one for false feeling; it didn't bother her at all that a man might die unmourned. "Of course, it is awful for the society."

"He didn't have any family, did he?" Marian asked. The other woman shook her head. Marian cast around in her mind for something compassionate to say. It was troubling to discover how callous she was about him since his death;

she had thought of him as a friend. Granted, she didn't like him very much, but he was good for the Society. He raised more money than anyone else, came in with all sorts of artifacts donated by the people he cultivated, and gave everyone a sense of mission. He was good at his work, but he knew it, and that was the problem. He was conceited. Yes, that was it. "He was conceited."

"What did you say?"

"Oh, I didn't mean to say that out loud," Marian said.

"Well, you're right. He was conceited. And lately he'd been even worse. He was starting to sound like an arrogant old priest—out to save us from ourselves." She showed no signs of being one who might capitulate.

Marian sliced open an envelope with a dinner knife and pulled out a letter announcing a meeting for directors of small museums. She set it aside for the president, the only one who might qualify as the director of the Arbella Society, now that George was gone. She opened the next envelope and unfolded a letter; from the folds fell a business card.

"Oh," she said, turning over the discarded envelope. "Oh dear, well, I guess there's no harm done." The other woman looked over expectantly. "It's a letter for George from an architect who specializes in recovering old homes after bad renovations." Marian read the letter; then she read it again.

"Advertising?" the other woman asked.

"No. George wanted to hire him," Marian answered, puzzled.

"Whatever for? He lives in that apartment building downtown. It's not old enough to need renovation, is it? When was that built anyway?"

"Sometime in the sixties, I think." Marian went on reading. "Maybe he was going to move," she said as she set the letter aside. She was ashamed of her less than noble sentiments about the dead man. She was old enough to have grown up with, and to have accepted without question, a tradition of never speaking ill of the dead, but she learned as an adult to acknowledge her feelings. Today the two ways conflicted, leaving her ashamed and embarrassed. George Frome was dead but his death was releasing the ill will she had stored up for years, and Marian resented him for even that. George Frome, demanding and aggressive and charming in life, was turning out to be just as unsettling in death.

■ ■ ■

Chief Silva pulled at the starched collar of his summer uniform, and felt a drop of sweat break loose and slide down the center of his back until it finally broke, then spread into a rib of his undershirt. It was hot and getting hotter though it was almost five o'clock. Unlike most of the men in his department, he considered shutting down the air conditioning a legitimate cost-cutting measure, whereas his men argued that they were entitled to one modern accommodation while working in a nineteenth-century police station authentic right down to the plumbing. Silva sympathized but no more; they all sweated together. Today Joe didn't mind the heat at all; he even savored it. Here it was, five o'clock on a Friday afternoon and it looked as if he was going to have a quiet, uncomplicated weekend. The last thing he had to do was clear up his desk. He pulled open a drawer as he reached for the ringing telephone.

The lawyer was friendly, relaxed, in the same way Joe was, as he said, "I thought I'd help you clear up one last loose end. I have George Frome's will and other papers, and the closest relative he has is a cousin in Ohio. I think that's where he is." The man rustled through some papers, then read a name and address to Joe. "I'll get on to him about George. See what he wants to do."

It was indeed a last loose end and Joe was glad to have it

taken care of. He let the lawyer ramble while he watched the minute hand on the clock skip languorously toward five-fifteen; his mind strayed to other matters before he suddenly felt he'd missed something in the conversation.

"Would you mind repeating that?" he asked the lawyer.

"Well," the man paused, and Joe feared he must be asking him to repeat something simple or obvious like Frome's eye color. "I just meant that it's too bad it happened now, right when he was on the verge of getting something he said he always wanted."

"He told you this?" Silva asked.

"Yes. He had me draw up the papers just last week," the lawyer said, sounding puzzled.

Silva took a deep breath, resigned to giving away his earlier daydreaming. "What, exactly, was he about to come into possession of?"

"I thought you'd never ask," the lawyer said, sounding pleased. "The log house. Mellingham's one and only log cabin. It's not far from you, either. You know that little tiny shed that looks like it's used for storing boats or garden equipment? The clapboards are falling off, the foundation is just a pile of rocks about to roll away? Well, beneath all that mess is a log cabin, the oldest surviving house in town, the only true log cabin left in this area, and all owned by Mrs. Rocklynd. She agreed to sell it to George. Finally." He paused. "Too bad how things happen, isn't it?"

Silva agreed, trying to recall the rundown building he occasionally glimpsed in the winter on his drive home. He might live in a condo cut from a colonial house, work in a Victorian police station, and preside over a town that looked as if it stopped growing in the nineteenth century, but there was enough of the poor boy in him to wonder why anyone would want a rundown shack even if it did contain the remnants of a historical treasure.

"How definite was this sale?" Silva asked.

"George seemed to think it was as certain as his will. He asked me to add a codicil."

"Can you tell me who gets what?"

The lawyer hesitated, weighing his duty as an attorney with his position in the small town of Mellingham and in Chief Silva's circle of reliable sources. He chose. "He left a few things to some longtime friends in Boston, and the rest to two cousins out West."

"Nothing to anyone here in town?" Silva asked. The lawyer repeated his information, perhaps not finding anything surprising in the disposition of George Frome's wealth, whereas Silva pondered the dead man's disregard for all the friends in a town that had been his home for virtually his entire life. Then again, maybe he, Joe, was the odd one. He didn't even have a will, and he assumed, if he thought about it at all, that his brothers and sisters and their children would just arrive and take care of his home, divvying up his possessions as they saw fit. That made sense to him. But George Frome's way, for a man of no close relations, made no sense at all.

"Anyway, I'll take care of the arrangements. George was a man who looked ahead, always ready for the unexpected. Too bad he didn't get to enjoy his retirement after all that planning."

The lawyer was glad to help Joe in any way he could, but after repeating his basic information, finally ended the call. It was almost five-thirty and Joe recognized that uneasy feeling in his stomach, the feeling that said reality will not be what you're thinking it is. He tried to push it away, but that only made him think instead about his last meeting with George at Arbella House, and the elaborate and lengthy tour the other man gave him, the details about architecture, furniture, art that George dropped at every step, while not saying one word about the log cabin he was acquiring, an acquisition so definite and significant that he had his lawyer making preparations, and perhaps so secret that no one but his lawyer should know. The thought teased Joe as he cleared his desk of the work of the day.

"Chief, the ME's on the line. Insists on talking to you." Officer Daley leaned into Silva's tiny office as he delivered the message, then withdrew. The eruption of noise that was the changing of the shifts was over, and the evening shift was settling into its routine.

"I'm going to ruin your weekend," the voice on the line said. "I'm over here at the funeral parlor. Nice place. Ever been here?"

Silva listened as the man went on, then interrupted him. "Get to it. Give me the bad news."

"Aconitine."

"What about it?" Silva asked.

"Well, in simple terms, we found aconitine in a food that was part of the salad."

"The salad? What're you guys doing over there?"

"That got you, didn't it." The man chuckled. "Well, don't get fired up, Joe. It's real simple. One of my people laid out the food scraps, just to check, you know, and then went off to do something else. I'll have to talk to him about that. Anyway, one of the morticians came in, thought someone had left some garbage out, from lunch, maybe—makes you wonder what goes on here—so he started to clean it up. Then, what do you know, but the guy looks like he's going into shock. So we get him a chair and I pick up the stuff he's dropped and pretty soon I'm feeling pretty queer myself. So we grab the food back and my assistant went to work on that." He chuckled, then shouted like a circus barker. "Forget George! Get that salad!"

"And? What happened?" Joe asked.

"I told you, aconitine. Something in his food had aconitine in it."

"You mean George Frome's salad?"

"Right. Or his cookies. Well, probably not the cookie. I just thought I'd let you know."

"What about George?" Silva asked.

"What about him?"

In a steely voice, Silva said, "Did George eat the whatever it was, and if he did, what effect did it have on him?"

"I got you. We ran the test. He ate it, all right. And it killed him. That's the effect it had on him. It killed him. Pretty fast too."

"What does that mean? Is that normal? Abnormal? What?"

"Hmmm, well, yeah, hmm." The medical examiner didn't want to commit himself and treated Silva to a variety of sounds.

"Can you tell me how it works?" Silva asked, trying to keep the sarcasm out of his voice.

"Oh sure. Well, first contact gives a feeling of tingling, burning, numbing, inside the mouth or outside, on the skin. Limited contact probably won't kill you. The real danger is from ingesting it. Some people vomit, get blurred vision, have trouble breathing. Let's see. The blood pressure slows down, some people sweat, get giddy, some even have convulsions. The body gets cold, the limbs are paralyzed; death usually comes from respiratory arrest. Some go into a coma, some stay conscious."

"Would he have had time to get help?" Silva asked.

"Maybe, maybe not. In some people weakening of the limbs comes on fast. If that's what happened to the deceased, then no, he wouldn't have been able to do much. He would have been in too much pain. The way he eats probably made things worse."

"You mean up in all that heat?" Silva asked, trying to follow a conversation that sounded as much internal as directed at him.

"No. From the looks of his stomach, he swallowed a good

mouthful without even noticing. He must have gulped his food. That's very bad for the digestion, very bad. What's the matter with people they don't know that? You wouldn't believe what we find in people's stomachs these days—"

"What's the likelihood that George got this aconitine into his salad by accident?" Silva asked abruptly. He didn't want to know what the medical examiner was finding anywhere.

"By accident? Pretty queer accident, if you ask me." Silence, then laughter. "You are asking me, aren't you. Well, like I said, pretty queer accident. I mean it doesn't come in anything that's edible. And if he'd put it in his salad, he'd know it, unless he cooks with gloves on." He stopped again, whether to contemplate cooking with gloves on, or his dinner awaiting him, or something entirely different, he didn't say.

"Could you spell it out?" Silva asked. "What difference does it make if he wore gloves or not?"

"Aconitine is absorbed cutaneously. Through the skin in plain English. If he came across it and by accident dropped it into the bowl, he'd feel it too—tingling, burning, lots of signs. That's how we got on to it. The mortician just touched some scraps. Doesn't take much. I think the official dose is something like two to four milligrams. That's not much."

"So it couldn't have gotten into his salad by accident," Silva repeated.

"Not very likely," the man said.

"Frome had an old packet of seeds in his pocket when we found him; my sergeant pulled it out and bagged it. I've got it here. I'll send it over. Let me know what's in it, okay?"

"Aha, the murder weapon!" The man sounded pleased as he acted out his role in his own private melodrama. "But it probably isn't, not unless they're pretty strange-looking seeds. The aconitine was in some slivers, look like tiny potato scraps. That kind of thing. We're still testing. No identification yet. But send that stuff over, anyway. Can't hurt to look."

"What about the cookie?" Silva asked.

"Could have been in it. Could have. Could have. The cookie's all crumbs. He must have fallen on it, Frome. Got crumbs mashed all over his shirt. Like a kid." He was still chuckling when Silva replaced the telephone receiver.

Somehow Silva just couldn't see this last tragedy in the same way as the medical examiner.

4

Friday Evening

Six o'clock on a Friday evening in July still feels like the middle of the day, especially in Mellingham, which had that warm, soft, small-town sound of summer evenings. It was not the time to announce a murder but that's what Chief Silva had on his hands. Off duty and making plans for a vacation, Sergeant Dupoulis nevertheless wanted to be in Silva's office just after five o'clock despite the heat, the awkwardness, the extra work.

"We've lost some time," Silva said after reporting the medical examiner's telephone call. He was pleased that Dupoulis spent less than thirty seconds on regretting his error in not recognizing the death as a suspicious one at once and moved into what needed to be done. "I'm going over to Frome's apartment to see if there's anything there to help us, but I'm not expecting too much. It seems to me we have to concentrate on Thursday afternoon and evening at the Arbella Society."

"That's a lot of people and a lot of time," Dupoulis said. He was calculating the full range of work ahead of him, blocking out the time necessary for interviews without any thought for what had already filled those spaces in his weekend. His girlfriend might have commented that this was typical of him, of his perversity that turned the ordinary balance of a life upside down. Sergeant Dupoulis liked to work whenever the chance arose; he also liked to fish. In a picturesque coastal town with a history of fishing, Ken Dupoulis longed to cast for trout—the freshwater variety. His idea of a vacation was heading to the hills and a good stream where he could smell pine trees instead of salt marshes, watch for ospreys instead of egrets, and drink the cold river water when he was thirsty instead of opening a flip-top can. He was anathema to his family, who could not understand his wayward tastes. An undercurrent of life in Mellingham was the oft-spoken belief that the town had everything, meant as an allusion to its beauty, coastal pleasures, and safe life, but understood more metaphorically by others to include the dissatisfied, the secrets and sadnesses of the unnoticed, and the disloyal native son who, at least in one case, enjoyed inland more than coastal pleasures.

"With luck this won't cut into too much of your vacation," Silva said, knowing he cared more about this than his subordinate, who was still young enough to believe in work above all else. Silva was willing to let it go, at least openly, because he made sure his men got vacations whether they wanted them or not. He refused to add to his own burdens by encouraging a policeman to narrow his focus to work alone. Such men proved a liability, dangerous in the end, their dedication to duty becoming an obsession, then a handicap, and finally a blinder until they made a mistake and couldn't see it. Dupoulis was never going to have the chance to fall so far.

"I've drawn up a list of everyone we should talk to, at least the ones I know about," Silva said, handing the sergeant a sheet of paper. "That's the entire Board of Trustees of the Arbella Society—they were having their monthly meeting on Thursday night—and anyone else who was there on Thursday. We may have to branch out but the medical examiner says the poison was part of George Frome's meal, which he brought to the Arbella

Society when he came over in the afternoon." He looked at his notes. "Take the names checked off and see what they recall about Thursday."

"What're we looking for exactly, or don't we know?" Dupoulis was an eager policeman, determined to do as much as possible in the best way; all he wanted was a pointer, a sign telling him where to apply his prodigious energy. Silva understood this and was willing to give him less and less direction, forcing him to make his own choices. Dupoulis belonged to that new school, begun with the first baby-boom generation and blossoming with today's youth, that thought failure on the way to success a waste of time, the result of nothing less than a superior refusing to offer guidance or applying unreasonably strict standards. Silva had softened much of this attitude but Dupoulis still had a way to go before he expected to run down a few dead ends as a matter of course.

"We're looking for someone who could have poisoned Frome's supper, which he seems to have brought with him to the Arbella House to eat in the attic," Silva said. It rankled that so much time had gone by; board members were liable to blur this past Thursday into all the preceding ones. "I want to know why he was up there with all those paintings."

"How much of a secret was it that he was up there?" Dupoulis asked.

"Hard to say," Silva replied, recalling his earlier talk with Marian Davis. "Marian said he often brought his supper with him, especially on Thursdays. He liked to eat alone after everyone else had left, after the board meeting. She thought he was just using the dining room; she didn't seem to know he was eating in the attic. The shock of finding him blocked that out at first." Silva paused. "At least that's what she wants me to think. We'll have to check all that."

"Why couldn't he look at those paintings downstairs,

where it was cooler? Sort of, anyway." Dupoulis grew increasingly sensitive to the heat as his weight went up, a correlation he hadn't yet noticed. As far as he was concerned, George Frome was a bit strange.

"That's one of the things we have to find out," Silva said. "But this is where we begin." He nodded to the list of board members. "Now." Dupoulis looked up at the clock. "We've lost too much time already." The sergeant nodded. He too felt the change that comes within after the discovery of a new purpose.

■ ■ ■

Chief Silva turned right onto Main Street, opposite the direction he would have taken if he were going directly home; the only cars parked along the curb belonged to the early guests at the small restaurant across from the village green. The town was quiet now, though he knew that would change when children rushed out to hoard with play the long hours of sunlight. Silva followed the road as Main Street turned right at ninety degrees and sank down to sea level, then left. In seconds he pulled over to the side of the road and parked across from an apartment building.

Built in the 1960s on the site of the old gray stucco Horticultural Hall, the small brick building of nine small apartments on three floors had been Mellingham's one and only flirtation with modern life of the sort assumed to be found in big cities. Thereafter, buildings remained more in tune with nineteenth-century New England design, and over the years residents forgave the architect, builder, and owner, and came to look on the building as their own brush with "the real world." The landlord kept the grounds neat in the summer and the parking lot plowed in the winter, and the building well lighted all year round. People who moved in expecting to stay only a year or so were still there when it came time to retire or go to God. George Frome was one of them.

Chief Silva unlocked the apartment door with the super's keys, and felt the heat slide over him, down his back and arms, inside his shirt. He snapped his head back for a moment. No one had pulled the shades in the two-bedroom apartment on the second floor, and the sliding glass doors, which opened onto a small balcony, concentrated the heat of a full July day.

Chief Silva had already learned, from Sergeant Dupoulis, that Frome had been living in the building since it opened, but the chief did not stop the super when he launched into a history of Frome's life as a tenant. Indeed, so deep were Frome's roots in the ground below the Larkin Building, as it was known, that Silva was more than a little disconcerted when he stepped through Frome's front door. From what Silva had just learned about Frome's long years there and from what he already knew of the man's interest in history, especially local, nineteenth-century life, the chief expected to find a comfortable living room cluttered with pictures, decorative objects, sofas, rugs, and all the other things collected over a lifetime. After his first look, Silva checked the number on the door, but he was in the right apartment.

Silva closed the door and crossed the bare wood floor to the windows at the far side. Frome had a corner apartment, with the front windows and balcony facing south, but the man apparently cared nothing for fresh air. No wonder he could eat dinner in an attic in July and not feel suffocated, Joe thought as he slid open the window. It wasn't much cooler outside, but at least the air was moving. He walked around the living room, the sharp noise of his shoes on the wooden floor echoing around the bare walls. The living room contained an old wooden sofa with pillows, in beige, against the outer wall, and two old canvas director's chairs. Nothing softened the space—no rug, no pictures on the walls. A single floor lamp stood by the sofa. A low counter with stools separated the living room from the kitchen, and it too was spare. A few spices stood in a small cardboard box, worn and floppy from years of service, against the wall.

Growing more curious as a man than as a police officer, Joe began opening the cupboards, moving from right to left, from those by the outer wall toward the inner corner and the refrigerator. The first two, over the stove, were empty; the next one held baking soda, cornstarch, flour (stone-ground wheat), honey, and seasalt. The two over the sink were empty. The next two held a few unmatched dishes, glasses, cups and saucers, and serving bowls of various sizes. The two over the refrigerator were empty. The lower cupboards held an assortment of cooking pans, casseroles, and other equipment. One drawer held cooking utensils and another held cutlery, not more than two of each. George Frome was a man determined to be alone. Even if a more gregarious impulse had arisen in his heart, he had ensured it would be thwarted by his stock of food, dinner service, and dining facilities.

Joe's first apartment had seemed bare, but it was nothing like this. He had moved into a studio after he got his first job and before he joined the force. His mother had taken one look at its dirty sterile walls, which he promised to wash and paint, and the dingy kitchenette, and mobilized the family. In one weekend everything was scraped, patched, painted. The tiny refrigerator was stocked, and the room was furnished with a foldout sofa, a café table and chairs, and a comfortable reading chair. The sofa looked suspiciously like one his uncle hoarded in his rec room in the basement, but no one would tell Joe where it came from. The only new items were a crucifix and a picture of St. Anthony his mother hung on the walls while Joe was carrying boxes. Later that Sunday evening, when they had all gone home, he found his favorite soup, *caldo verde*, in the refrigerator, along with bags of *linguiça*, *chauriço*, and other meats, and a six-pack of cold beer. Frome's apartment didn't look as if anyone had ever left anything for him to enjoy.

Silva pulled open the refrigerator door and wasn't surprised by what he saw. On the bottom shelf were three kinds of lettuce; just above were loose tomatoes, half a red onion in a plastic bag, a box of mushrooms, and another bunch of frilly green leaves, but this one Joe didn't recognize. He picked it up; beneath it lay two brown roots, like dirty carrots, one whole and the other scraped into a point at one end. Neither one looked familiar to Joe and he bagged them both. On the top shelf was mineral water, a half-empty container of apple juice, and a bottle of lemonade. "I'd starve to death in this place," he mumbled as he made his way to the hall.

The bathroom had bright red towels, so far the only admission of any passion in the dead man, but the medicine cabinet belonged to the man who had stocked the kitchen. The cabinet contained an aloe deodorant, baking soda toothpaste, and a few other items. Only a bottle of aspirin suggested that George Frome had the feelings of other mortals.

The first and larger bedroom held a twin bed, which fit the small space well, and a floor lamp. A low pile of books, historical novels, lay on the floor by the lamp. The closet held a limited wardrobe of summer and winter clothing. Underclothes, sweaters, and socks were piled neatly on the top shelf; there was no bureau. In this room alone Frome had put shades on the two windows. The second bedroom held a straw reading chair with a floor lamp, again no rug, and two low bookcases filled with an assortment of school texts, histories, and reference books. None of them looked new, or even faintly interesting to Joe. A large map of Mellingham hung on the wall over an old wooden desk, the single attempt at decoration—or was it merely another reference?—in the whole apartment. On one corner of the desk sat a notebook with drawings, notes about antiques, meetings attended, and drawings of art objects. Joe idly flipped to the end and a drawing of a couple of birds hanging from a peg; Frome had reworked it several times, apparently not satisfied with the design. Scattered across the surface of the desk were a number of photographs from the 1950s and even earlier. As best as Joe could tell, the more recent ones were of a carnival in the park near the harbor, the older ones of a child. The names and dates of all of them had faded from the back or never been recorded, but they ranged from the 1930s to the 1970s, judging by the hair and clothing styles. The faces looked vaguely familiar, and he assumed they must be of residents of Mellingham he didn't quite recognize.

The sight of them bothered Joe, for they were an odd assortment to leave lying around, as though Frome brought pictures home from the Arbella Society to identify, instead of working on them there, as other volunteers did. If he did do that, he hadn't got very far. There were no notes on the backs and no notes on scrap paper on the desk.

Joe checked the desk drawers, but these held leftover paper, apparently gathered to use as recycled notepaper, a few old pens (dried out), and a telephone book. Disappointed, he slid open the closet door; he found what he was looking for on the top shelf. He pulled down a box with several manila folders, marked "Important Papers," "Family Papers," and the like. In one he found Frome's last statement from his checking account, which showed a balance of over three thousand dollars. The figure was approximately the same in earlier statements; George Frome liked a large supply of ready cash. His bank books and other financial statements also showed a relatively high balance, providing Frome with a more than comfortable income, enough so that he could go on saving even after retirement.

Certainly, in light of the other rooms, Frome had no use for the money he did have.

The chief put the papers back on the shelf and returned to the living room, self-conscious at the sound of his steps. It was a wonder the other tenants had never complained about the noise, unless George always wore rubber-soled shoes. Out of curiosity, Joe checked the bedroom closet again; he was right.

The apartment depressed Chief Silva. It wasn't just the thin film of dust over everything, except where George had walked or worked, though that disgusted Joe too, who saw no reason why a man couldn't do his own cleaning at least until he married. It was the deprivation of it all that bothered him most, a deprivation self-inflicted. Never before had Joe been in a place that so threw him back on himself, that made his feelings pulsate in him, made his views stand out with such contrast, like a black silhouette portrait cut swiftly but accurately. Life was to be enjoyed, the passions pursued, beauty embraced, not shunned. With the exception of his red bath towels, George Frome was a man who rejected life and all its sensuous pleasures. There was no fine cloth to feel beneath the palm of the hand as he sat reading in a comfortable chair, no fragrance of spices as he cooked, no smell of freshly cut grass drifting in through the window in the early morning, nothing soft or cool under the feet. George Frome was a man without senses.

Frome had made a meager life without cause, for no matter what his problems might have been, he had had a decent job with the state and had made decent money for years. But he certainly never spent any of it, as far as Joe could see. George Frome had lived a life from which all pleasure had been excised, focusing his attention on his work and then, after his retirement, on the Arbella Society. He had no close friends as far as the police knew, and no enemies, and yet he was dead.

The achingly spare living room was no fresher after the window had been open for almost an hour, but it still chilled Silva to be in it. A man who lived here, so dulled in his appetites, hardly seemed a likely candidate for murder, but Joe had long ago come to believe that those who circled around the core of their intended life, poking at it, thinking about it, never embracing it, were the true candidates for a tragic end. They sat on the periphery and drew or bent others to their ways, and one of those ways always included violence. George Frome died because he wouldn't live.

■ ■ ■

Silva wound his way up the steep hill, glad to leave Frome's apartment behind (he couldn't bring himself to think of it as a home, anyone's home); at the top he took a sharp left, then at the end, where four roads met, he turned right, driving past a vacant lot that had once been a high school, on to the next intersection, and another vacant lot above a playing field, where another high school, once an elementary school, had stood. Lingering near a pair of benches, half a dozen teenage boys jostled and boxed and razzed each other, calming down as three girls approached. The cluster of young people, moving together and apart, lengthened into the single bulging, curving line of an amoeba until a single couple split off and moved away to start over again the tension that holds them together and pushes them apart in undulating rhythms of energy. None of them signaled the fate that might leave him—or her—living the life of George Frome, but Joe knew it was there in one of them, fated like the color of one's eyes unless a sudden rush drove one to falsify fate, trick it, slip away while no one noticed. Their lives were shaped for them, just as the lives of their elders had been.

The twelve members of the board of the Arbella Society,

all of whom attended the meeting on Thursday night, revolved in his head, along with the few others who had had opportunity to tamper with Frome's dinner, such as it was, thought Silva, who was a meat-and-potatoes man.

Silva drove past the mound that was all that remained of the old school, the grassy dirt falling away to a playing field, with a dozen benches dotting the gentle rise; he parked when he saw whom he expected to see. Bill, the treasurer of the Arbella Society, who was explaining to a young player why the last call was a strike instead of a ball, answered the chief's wave. Silva walked over to the group of parents, talking to each one; Gwen McDuffy sat off to the side on a bench watching the game, an informal affair begun by families who ate early and then rushed off to the playground. The rest of the players and their families would come later, closer to seven o'clock.

"Yours?" he said to Gwen McDuffy, nodding to the kids at play.

"Not all of them," she said. "Just two." She pointed to a girl playing left field and a boy sitting on the bench for the other team.

"Nice-looking kids," he said.

"Thanks." She smiled and went back to watching. "How come you know so much about lace?"

"My sisters had to learn it," he said, "but only the youngest one has taken to it. All Portuguese girls learn it. She made a set of *amostras* for me, when she was learning." He stopped, at a loss to explain what he meant. "*Amostra* is a pattern, a square. Sort of like a small sampler." He was suddenly very aware of his accent, which emerged now only when he was speaking Portuguese or was with friends and family at home. It bothered him that it had appeared without any warning.

"Where are you from?" she asked, as though she could divine his thoughts and identify his most vulnerable spot.

"The Azores. São Miquel." He had worked for years to eliminate the sibilancy and the fullness of vowels that were obvious in Portuguese, qualities that gave density and weight to his English, a language that had always seemed thin to him. Even so, he wanted his English to sound American, but his words betrayed him.

"That's a beautiful word, *amostra*," she said. "And that was a lovely idea of your sister's. Do you still have it?"

"Oh yes. I keep it in my office. It's beautiful. She has excellent hands. She still has the graceful, delicate fingers of a child, though she's far from being a child now." He thought about the young woman who was the most beautiful of his four sisters.

"It's so unusual to meet a man who knows anything about needlework," Gwen said. "I never would have guessed what those pieces were yesterday if you hadn't said something. All I could tell was whether or not they were crocheted or lace; I wasn't even sure about whether they were machine made or handmade."

"How long do you do that sort of thing over there?" Silva said. "That close work can make for a long afternoon."

"I usually get there after lunch. Yesterday was a long day because there were a bunch of people coming through for tours and George, of course, wanting to show you around." She nodded to Silva as she said this. "Are there problems I don't know about?" she asked.

"Some. I should tell you," Silva said, realizing he was stuck now, "that we're looking into George Frome's death. It wasn't accidental, as we first thought."

"I see." Gwen looked down at the ground. The thought seemed to weigh on her rather than cause her pain. "I talked to Marian; she said he was just lying there. I guess we assumed he'd had a heart attack. The danger of assumptions." One side of the field erupted in squeals and yells, and both turned to the game.

"Which side is winning?" he asked. Gwen told him, and he said, "Your family wins either way." She laughed and nodded. They watched the ball game in silence for a few minutes, and then she looked over at him, her face a mixture of musing and watchfulness.

■ ■ ■

The news that George Frome had died of poisoning while carrying on secret and highly questionable dealings (as the grapevine reported) in the attic of Arbella House had captured the imagination of the people of Mellingham to the exclusion of everything else but the time of high tide (for beachgoers) and humidity (for tennis players), and a few other concerns too unimportant to list. Gossip centered around the dealings in the attic rather than the manner of death or the murderer, and Arbella House loomed ominously over the town, its board members and volunteers exuding an aura of mystery the closer they seemed to be to the center of the crime.

The average Mellite was wrong in almost every speculation except one—the eerie glint at the center of the crime. Marian Davis saw it, too, but she never considered for a moment that the townspeople saw her in its penumbra. George Frome's death was like a bizarre tale told for the benefit of visitors from out of state eager to imbibe a little of the eccentricity of New England. But it wasn't a story, and it wouldn't go away. This observation had been pushed on her repeatedly by her husband, Gordon, who urged her to set the murder aside until she had recovered her equilibrium and could look at it objectively; he recommended a vigorous hike at the Audubon Society. She declined, insisting she was too upset. In fact, so upset was Marian Davis that she refused even to ride over to the Audubon Society and merely sit in the car and listen to the birds while her husband hiked a nearby trail, forcing him to go alone. Marian sat pensively on the back terrace of their colonial home, blind to the bird feeders swinging under the weight of marauding squirrels. When she heard a car door slam, footsteps on the sidewalk leading to the driveway, Marian rose.

"I knew you'd be coming," she said to Chief Silva as soon as he drew close; she motioned him to another chair. A glass sat by a pitcher of iced tea, and Joe accepted her invitation to help himself. Watching the chief of police mix in sugar and crush a slice of lemon over his glass made him seem ordinary, unthreatening. Every action spoke of normality, of an evening with nothing more serious to discuss than the next local elections. It might have been the heat, the informality of his sitting back and complimenting her on the tea, or her own wish to be free of the tension within her—whatever her motive, she said, "I've been thinking about it all evening, ever since my neighbor called me during supper. I can't believe it. I mean, I believe it happened—you know what I mean. Gordon's gone for a walk. He thinks I'm taking it too hard. How should I take it? Right under my nose," she said more to herself than to him. "I was there all afternoon and all evening. And I never saw a thing." She stopped. "Chief, it must have been an accident."

"It wasn't. I think I can assure you of that." He listened to the litany of expressions used every day to aid the comprehension of the incomprehensible; her recitation had an automatic quality that put Silva on his guard. "I'm glad you were there all afternoon. Tell me about George Frome"

"George? Poor George. That poor, poor man. I can't believe it," she muttered to herself. Her reactions had a subdued, almost impersonal quality.

"Tell me when George came in. Do you remember?"

"Remember? How will I ever forget? He was there most of the morning. Then gone for lunch, then back at three with his supper. There until I left. Always the same. Poor George."

"I'm sorry if this is hard for you, Marian, but I do have to know." He spoke with the easy familiarity that was the first sign that he was studying her like a stranger, looking at facets of her personality he had neglected in the years he had known her. "What do you remember about yesterday? Tell me about the meeting."

"That meeting." She shook her head. "As bad as it was, it wasn't our worst; it was pretty much our usual meeting. Lots of arguments, the agenda out the window, no one in control, except maybe George." She stopped to think about this. "No, I think even George lost control this time." The exercise of thinking about the past as a visual experience seemed to calm her, freeing her to see it unemotionally, as though she were watching a movie rather than reliving a moment.

"What were the arguments about?"

"You, mostly." She smiled when she saw his reaction. He twisted around in his chair.

"Could you explain that?"

"George invited you to come to Arbella House and inspect our security, didn't he?" Silva nodded. "Well, he said at the meeting that our security was terrible. I don't know what you told him, but he hinted that our collections were just walking out the door." It was obvious she hadn't agreed with him. "Well, that got everyone upset, well, maybe not everyone, but a lot of us. Most of us, I'd say. George bossed us around over a lot of things but this was really the worst. It was tantamount to saying that we didn't know how to take care of things. And you know that's not going to go over well at the Arbella Society." Her mouth set in a disapproving line.

"People took it personally, did they?"

"I'll say. It completely derailed the meeting. We argued

about it until after nine o'clock or so, at least until our usual ending time, and then we quit." She took another sip of her drink, and leaned back, stretching out her legs, her ankles almost as white as the canvas sun hat on her head. "I suppose that's a sign that it wasn't the absolute worst thing he could have done. We didn't come to blows. We noticed the time and stopped. Don't make too much of it. It happens every month. We never finish an agenda."

"So you think there was nothing unusual about your acrimonious evening," Silva said as much to himself as to her.

"We always argue in circles and then we quit and go home. That's not unusual. What was unusual, I suppose, were a few other things."

"Such as?" A part of him wanted to hurry the investigation along, to recapture the time that had slipped away since Frome had died, while he and everyone else thought the death a natural one. It was early in the investigation, perhaps, but late in the timing; if he'd had any idea earlier in the day that George Frome had been murdered, he probably wouldn't feel so pressed now.

"What else, what else? Let me see. Kelly Kuhn was talking about resigning; he was very jumpy, he always is, but this time he was really antsy. Catherine Rocklynd hurt her hand. We have to get new chairs and meet upstairs where there's more room. Edwin Bennett was distracted for the first part of the evening but he warmed up when the big fight broke out. I think that's about it. At least that's all I noticed." She crossed her legs, relaxed now that she was helping the chief find his way through the confusion that was the Arbella Society.

"What happened to Mrs. Rocklynd?" Silva asked.

"I don't know; she apparently hurt her hand, from the way she was massaging it. But she said it was okay. It didn't stop her from saying what she had to say during the rest of the meeting."

"What did people eat? Did you happen to notice?" Silva asked, changing directions.

"Food. Let me think. We all bring food at different times. I brought"—she stopped and stared at the chief—"I brought oatmeal cookies. But Kelly ate almost a whole plate himself. Everyone saw him." Marian grew defensive.

"I'm just collecting information at the moment. We're tracing the poison right now," Silva said, afraid her wild swings from meditative calm to rampant fear would thwart a useful review of the afternoon and evening. "My sergeant mentioned that your cookies had been found," Silva said.

"Don't waste your time on my cookies." She laughed. "George wouldn't have anything to do with them."

"Why not?" Silva decided not to tell her what had been found.

"George? He was a strict—I mean strict—vegetarian. He didn't approve of any processed foods either, especially something sweet like cookies made from bleached flour, refined sugar, and factory-dried raisins, among other things. He always made me feel so unhealthy, as though I ate french fries and greasy burgers all day." Marian wrinkled her nose as she recrossed her legs and sat up straight.

"Sounds like you knew him pretty well. Did you know he was about to come into possession of something he had wanted for a long time?"

"George? No. He didn't say anything about it last night. Are you sure about that? I'm sure he would have told me, or one of us." She looked worried. "Maybe he just didn't have time. It was a wild evening. What was it he was getting?"

"The log house Mrs. Rocklynd owns." Silva spoke calmly, but Marian gaped at him. "You doubt it?"

"I don't believe it for a minute. Catherine would never let that house go. Never. And even if she did, she wouldn't give it to him." Marian was adamant.

"I'm afraid it's true. He was all ready to buy it."

"But she loves that house. I know it's a mess, a falling-down, grungy mess, but it's the oldest house in town, and the only log house in the entire area. It's part of her family heritage. She'd never sell it. And if she did, she wouldn't sell it to George. If she were going to sell it to anyone, she'd give it to Edwin Bennett."

"So she might be willing to let it go," Silva said. "To Edwin Bennett. Do you mean she would actually give it to him, or sell it to him for a nominal price?"

"Well, moot point." Years of command behind the Arbella Society desk had left Marian unprepared to be contradicted or corrected; she struggled to accept Silva's challenge gracefully. "If she were going to sell it, I suppose she'd sell it to Edwin for a dollar. It's easier than a gift."

"You seem pretty sure of that," Silva said. "After all, if it's as old and as important as you suggest, she could get a lot more for it by putting it on the open market."

"Be serious, Joe." Marian smiled and shrugged, throwing off the formality of the Society secretary. "This is Catherine Rocklynd we're talking about. That house has been all over town. Every time her family bought more land and built a bigger house, they took that little cabin along with them. At first it was just a house, cheaper to move than building a new one, but then it got to be important to them. In the last century, when they bought that nice old house, they put the cabin out in the back. Now you're not going to tell me that anyone whose family goes to all that trouble to preserve that cabin is going to turn around and sell it just for a few dollars."

"If it's so important, then why is it in such disrepair?"

Marian had enough sense to see the flaw in her argument, but she didn't like it. "True, true." She shook her head and smiled at him piteously. "It's this way, Joe. Catherine is more Yankee than she wants to admit. Fixing it up would mean spending some of her own money on it, and that's something Catherine rarely does if she can avoid it. The talk is that she'll leave it to Edwin Bennett. He'll move into her house, sell his, and use the money to fix up the place, including the log house."

"So why did George tell his lawyer that he was getting the log cabin?" Silva asked. He still had trouble separating this colonial house of split logs and plaster from the cabins made of round logs he saw advertised for people who wanted to build inexpensive housing on their own land.

"He was making it up," Marian concluded confidently, then paused.

"Yes?" It was obvious she had remembered something.

"It's so far-fetched, Catherine selling the log house. I mean—maybe you're right." She drew away from him. "There was a letter. It came in today, for George; I opened it by mistake. It was from an architect who specializes in restoring colonial buildings. He was agreeing to work for George on something." Her own experience of the morning undermined her convictions. "I never would have believed it. If you'd told me Catherine was going to give George that house, for any amount of money, I wouldn't have believed it. Not for a minute."

■ ■ ■

Edwin Bennett had not made a will. It didn't occur to him because he had so little to call his own and no wife or children to leave it to. The death of his parents many years earlier had seemed almost anticlimactic, the physical end to an emotional and geographical distancing that had begun years ago, almost since he reached adulthood. They were good people, he reminded himself through the years; he had no grudge against them. People couldn't really help their feelings; we just have them and we have to accept them. His parents had theirs, and at least did him the courtesy of not hiding or denying them. They were never false to him. And so their death was a sadness but not the revelation of mortality, and the instigator of questioning, that the death of parents so often is. But the death of George Frome in the last twenty-four hours was—a revelation, a shock, an instigator. He was younger than Edwin, living the same kind of life.

The small, white clapboard house with a bow window in front and a mansard roof at the second floor had always seemed large to Edwin, at least when he was a child. From the side kitchen window he could look across the driveway into the neighbor's living room and watch the family in the evening, or he could run out back and find someone else at play nearby. But that wasn't really what made it seem large and open and greater than it was.

From his earliest years Edwin knew his aunt Catherine's home as his own. Since his parents had moved to Mellingham when he was barely two years old, he had always had a place at Aunt Catherine's. His parents went there for Sunday afternoons, an evening of games, or just a chat when they were driving by. He dropped in at his aunt's home as readily as he waved at his neighbors. He had not one home but two. Aunt Catherine's brief marriage to William Rocklynd during World War II, when she was in her thirties and Edwin was barely into his teens, hadn't changed anything between them. William went off to war and never came back, and he took on that romantic cast reserved for experiences agreeably set aside. Aunt Catherine kept a few pictures of him around but after a few years he was regularly mistaken for a cousin, later an uncle or someone's brother. Who he was faded; he became just one more face among the many encircled in brass or silver or polished pewter. Edwin came to think Aunt Catherine had married him not from any passion set loose by the war but from a simple desire not to go unwed all her life. After William's death, she went about her days freer, more confident, as though a difficult chapter in her life had been closed.

Now Edwin had the same feeling in his own life. George Frome had changed his perspective dramatically in the last twenty-four hours just by dying. Frome's death spoke of mortality, but not only Edwin's. It spoke of Aunt Catherine's; it spoke of the death of a person who had been impervious to the buffeting, weighing, pulling of time. George had been like her and now he was gone. Someday Catherine Rocklynd would also die, and that would change him even more.

For all of his sixty-five years, even during his aunt's brief marriage, Edwin had considered himself her heir without ever having actually formulated it in those terms: it wasn't that he was covetous or greedy; he wasn't. He lived a life of modest tastes and though he longed sometimes for the freedom and wealth to travel, to be stretched by discovering other peoples living in other ways, he accepted graciously what life had given him. It had been Aunt Catherine, on the contrary, who had made it known to him that all her property would some day be his. At first she said no more than a mild order to take care of this telescope when it was his, or to oil the table when it was his. Eventually, he understood what she meant, and took especial interest in learning how certain pieces of furniture were cared for, how the old cameras worked, when rugs were cleaned and by whom. He had gained a lifetime of knowledge about his aunt's possessions, learning and filing and practicing as though the Federal home far out on Main Street were a museum whose curator's job he was to accede to.

But he had been wrong, apparently, though how wrong he didn't know. At least part of Aunt Catherine's estate had been destined—however briefly—for George Frome, a rearrangement of life as he knew it that had the effect of revealing to him that he was not who he thought he was; he was not Edwin Bennett, he was merely some fellow who had imposed on a nice old lady who was too kind to admonish him openly. The drawing back was swift and liberating, as well as unjustified. Nevertheless, it prompted him to write his own will, if for no other purpose than to discover where else he had ties. The experience was enlightening, for he had few friends who seemed natural recipients of his accumulated wealth, such as it was. He liked many of the people he knew well enough to give them something, but he wondered how they might feel about receiving a major gift from him. Would they recognize at once the paltry emotional life he had lived, reaching into old age with no one to care for, no one for whom he might understandably want to share his life's gain? Or would he look ridiculous?

That last fear was the kicker. He wasn't sure where it had come from but for all his adult years it had confronted him at corners, outlined in black even seemingly simple choices, and sometimes made him hate himself. He relied on sheer, blind willpower to get himself past it at crucial moments. This might be one too. Nothing could be more ridiculous than an aging man desperate for friendship, except any man who thinks he can live on the edge of community, friendless, without consequences. The choice was easy for Edwin, though its execution might not be.

Edwin walked through the kitchen to the screened-in back porch and leaned against the inside railing. It was half an hour past first dark, the voices were beginning to sound secretive, private, as voices do at night. The wind had shifted not long ago, bringing cooler air from the ocean, along with the smell of salt spray. Too much of his life had been focused on another part of Mellingham, and not enough on his own part, for his parents' closeness to Aunt Catherine had taken him away from circles he might have been part of. They were still out there, revolving through the streets and lanes of the town, like interlocking gears, separate but meshing. Some he knew from the Arbella Society, some he saw at other local events. Many he could meet without any noticeable change in the pattern of his days, which was important to him. More than anything else, he wanted the security and stability of his life to remain the same while he inched his way into another world. He saw no contradiction in his desires. The only question that remained was, Was it too late?

5

Saturday Morning

Edwin Bennett rang the bell by Mrs. Rocklynd's front door, then turned to walk around the garden. The doorbell told his aunt Catherine that he had arrived. It was a signal that announced only; it made no demands. Mrs. Rocklynd heard it and went on with what she was doing, waiting for Edwin to come in through an open back door when he was ready, or until she felt like joining him outside for a walk around the grounds. This morning she looked down from a second-floor window, saw him approaching the front garden, and rapped. Edwin turned and waved; when she saw him turn up to the house she gingerly grabbed a teak cane, from the Philippines, and made her way downstairs.

The knock on the window was a relief for Edwin; he stood on the grass looking back at the house as the last of the morning fog lifted, burned off by the July sun, like his anxiety melting from the sheer pleasure of such a day. The sight of his aunt's face at the board meeting Thursday evening as she cradled her sore hand had shocked him so much that merely seeing her invigoratingly bang on a window unleashed feelings damped down in him since then. He hadn't realized how crucial she had become to his life, though surely a man of his years, sixty-five, should have accepted mortality by now. And he had. It was his aunt's mortality that had eluded him until Thursday night. He took a deep breath and one last look at the blue front garden, eager for a splash of yellow or red to reflect his new mood.

Edwin found his aunt in the library, a dark room with floor-to-ceiling bookcases filled with leather-bound volumes originally purchased by her father, grandfather, and so on. The books were the foundation of her education, achieved largely at home at a time when few women went beyond high school. She motioned Edwin to a chair as he stepped through the french doors leading to the terrace at the back.

"I think I've finally found the answer," Mrs. Rocklynd began without any introductory pleasantries. "I was looking through my great-great-grandmother Hamden's papers last night and found just what I wanted." Edwin was used to being greeted with comments that belonged to earlier conversations, or new ones Aunt Catherine held with herself; with a few minutes to listen, he could usually tell which sort of conversation he had joined. He settled back in a leather reading chair to find out.

"It bothered me," Mrs. Rocklynd went on, "that the cabin was built after" (she emphasized the preposition) "other homes in town were built which we know had clapboards. Those haven't survived, but still—"

Edwin nodded as he picked up his place in the ongoing debate about the log cabin, which stood at the back of his aunt's property, near an inlet of the outer harbor. Even though it was the oldest surviving house in town, it wasn't the first known to have been built in Mellingham; still, the log cabin seemed to want to claim first place by dint of construction if nothing else. No other log homes had survived; few were even known to have been built contemporaneously.

"We do tend to think the so-called simple technique is also the first one to develop. The primitive form of house building is supposed to give way to the more sophisticated," he said.

"Exactly. And in this case, we'd be wrong," Mrs. Rocklynd said with passionate intensity.

"Really? You mean the cabin belonged to Mellingham's first hippies? In the seventeenth century?" Edwin queried mischievously. Mrs. Rocklynd cast him a reproving look. "Or perhaps just our first antisocial element?" Mrs. Rocklynd raised her head skyward. "Our first poor, then?"

"Edwin," she said, turning toward him, "such levity does not become you." He smiled at her. "Edwin? You have a stupid look on your face. You know I don't like stupid people."

"Sorry, Aunt. I guess I'm just feeling a little lightheaded today." He grinned.

"Don't get fey on me, now." She watched him, uncomfortable at such behavior.

"I should be more decorous, I suppose, under the circumstances," he said.

"What does that mean?"

Her sharpness of tone startled him. "I was thinking about George. You do know that—"

"Yes, yes, of course I know. You think I'm a hermit?" She turned back to her desk. "It'd be hard not to know in this town." She shook her head. "When's the funeral?"

"Not for a while yet, obviously."

"What does 'obviously' mean?"

"Oh, you haven't heard—" He sat up and started over. "The police think George was murdered. It was all over town last night."

"That's just malicious gossip. How can you lower yourself to listen to such talk? Really, Edwin, sometimes I worry about you. No one would dream of trying to tell me a story like that." Her eyes roamed to a portrait of a stern-looking woman in a black, high-collared dress hanging over the fireplace.

"It's not a story." He proceeded to name the links in a chain that began at the Sara Meya Funeral Parlor. "The police won't like it when they find out the mortician has been telling everyone what happened at the autopsy, but since one of their own people was involved, an assistant, I think, they should have expected the worst." During Edwin's rambling explanation, Mrs. Rocklynd gave him a perplexed stare, the kind newcomers found beaming down on them when meeting her for the first time at one of her semiannual parties, given not for her own pleasure, as she frequently reminded people, but to fulfill her responsibility to the community. Raised in part by an eccentric grandmother (a euphemism for an unhappy woman who fabricated a world in an otherwise hollow home), Catherine Rocklynd rattled off her duties like Latin paradigms, and gave them as much scrutiny. There was much in her life she never questioned. Edwin missed the intensity of her gaze. She returned to her desk, putting away her papers while he rambled on about how Chief Silva might handle the indiscretions of the funeral parlor, whose owner would not want to lose the goodwill of the police department.

"I can see why it has you rattled," she finally said, unperturbed. "He's a few years younger than you, isn't he?"

Edwin nodded, embarrassed that he had apparently let his feelings get out of control. Her comment was not a perceptive observation but rather a rebuke for having given so much of himself to fruitless speculation. The news of George's death had released a confusion of emotions, each one struggling for supremacy, like snakes in a basket, making him feel completely at the mercy of his feelings in a way he had not experienced since he was a teenager. The subsequent news that George's death was murder only added to his turmoil, injecting into a calm and orderly life an element of chaos and danger. Edwin had never encountered anyone who was later murdered. Nor had he ever known a murderer.

"You know, the building was locked after we left and

Marian said it was locked when she got there in the morning," he said. "You realize what that means?"

"I know what it means for me," she said with spirit. "Nothing. Absolutely nothing. I'm not going to go around suspecting people. I've known everyone on the board for years and almost everyone else who volunteers there just as long. I'm going to go on with my life just as I always have. I refuse to think ill of my friends."

"Yes, yes, I see your point. Still, we are going to be looking at each other differently now." He shifted in his chair.

"No, we're not. We don't have to give in to that sort of thing. Suspicion. We are who we've always been, and absolutely nothing can change that. Nothing." Edwin readied himself for a rendition of one of her more eloquent narratives on the Hamden family and its place in Mellingham, but she merely shrugged. "It's not any good getting worked up for any reason. Here now. You've come over for breakfast and I've kept you in here talking nonsense. Come along. Let's have something to eat," she said.

"Good idea." The intuition that something about George's death was bothering her lasted only a second; he didn't want to think about it either. "I want to tell you about this new nursery on Route 1. It changed hands in the middle of the season." He followed her out onto the terrace. "So now they've got some huge mistakes in orders and all sorts of problems. The upshot is, lots of plants, dirt cheap." Aunt Catherine groaned at the pun. Edwin chuckled. "Thought I'd go over and get a few things. I noticed some balloon flowers out front that aren't doing too well. Shall I look for replacements?"

"That would be wonderful. Don't know what's wrong with that front garden this summer. Awful touchy some of those plants."

"Not to worry, Aunt. We'll get everything fixed up. No one'll ever know there was ever any problem."

■ ■ ■

Gwen McDuffy pushed through the heavy wooden doors of the public library and stood for a moment in the dark vestibule, its walls of dressed New England granite cooling off the sweat already formed on her bare arms and face. She had left Jennie and Philip playing at the park with a group of friends while she went off for her Saturday morning round of errands, but the minute she had driven up the steep hill that was the center of town she pushed aside all thoughts of a regular day and headed for the town parking lot. Having the library open on a Saturday morning was a luxury she had grumbled about along with other residents, preferring to see local tax money spent on projects she thought closer to her life, but now that she needed the resources of the library, she was glad her side had lost. The 1886 granite building, designed originally as a memorial hall, became this morning the most vital building in all of Mellingham. Gwen almost laughed at how her perceptions had changed over the last few days.

She pushed through the main doors and turned right, walking through the old stone hallway that was originally a war memorial and now sheltered the main circulation desk. Straight ahead, on the west side of the building, the hall opened into a two-storied reading room with bookcases lining the walls and tables with chairs dotted around the floor. Once the offices of the Grand Army of the Republic, the room was a pleasant mixture of children's books, magazines, encyclopedias, and other reference books. She passed a freestanding bookcase with depleted shelves sporting a sign announcing Books Available for Beach Reading. The hard covers among them were chewed at the corners, wadded at one end where the pages had been splashed by a wave or iced tea, and broken at the spine. Some of the paperbacks were held together by elastic bands. She had never noticed the sign before, and thought back to the few novels she borrowed that exhibited a white belt around the dust jacket advising patrons Do Not Take This Book to the Beach; she made a mental note to check out this case before she chose anything from the other room.

Gwen made her way to the bookcases beneath the large Palladian window facing the street. There was little call for library services this morning, it seemed, and she had the room all to herself as she moved to the bookcases rising up the wall. Cars drove by on Main Street, and tourists knocked hesitantly at the door to Arbella House, across the street.

Farther along Gwen came to a series of dark green volumes with gold lettering. She ran her hand along the top row, then down to the two rows below. She read the spine, the same on each of the sixty-two volumes—*Massachusetts General Laws Annotated*—and looked around behind her, listening to the voices of the newly arrived patrons in the center hall. To her right, between the reading room and the vestibule, was a small office, but the light was off and the desk clear of all paperwork, its blotter and other appointments neatly arranged. It was different now, not at all as she had remembered it from her childhood, when it served as the children's room, a cozy corner for storytelling late in the evening during the summer months and a Saturday morning reading hour during the school year. Her first week back she had brought Jennie and Philip to the library to show them the children's room, but it was closed, an office filled with professional librarians conducting a meeting on coping with difficult patrons. It wasn't at all what she had expected.

She reached for the first volume in the series, opening it to the title page, which informed her that she held in her hand the first part of the Constitution of the Commonwealth of Massachusetts. She put the book back and glanced along the rows until her eyes rested on four dark green paperbacks at the end, the index for the current year. Each volume was thicker than any other book she could ever remember reading, but she pulled out the first one nonetheless and turned the pages. Her finger ran down the columns of entries, guard dogs, guard rails, and on to aged persons protective service hearings; answer to interrogatories; deeds and conveyances, notice of appointment; and divorce, mentally deficient and mentally ill persons. She read on, the words running together in a confusion of terms and phrases that seemed to rearrange themselves at will, producing as many technical forms as mathematically possible, like a game played for lawyers and judges, a game she had wandered into and was now being told by a four-volume index she couldn't participate in. The index was a gatekeeper, not a facilitator, offering access with one word and taking it away with another.

She had felt this way before, tricked into trusting only to discover the deceit too late. It angered and scared her, prompting her to struggle again with words and requirements she couldn't understand. Only the realization of what she might lose kept her going, searching painfully for an answer that might not exist.

Settling on one entry, Gwen replaced the index, withdrew another volume and began to read. A slight trembling moved its way up to her knees, then her hips; she dropped into a chair and clasped the book between her knees. She chided herself for her weakness, for letting a doubt grow into a fear, for not knowing an answer she should have sought years ago. I have to read this, she urged herself; I have to. So saying, she opened the book again, but her good intentions only led to greater confusion. The text was clear enough to her to let her think it was irrelevant to her search, but the subsequent paragraphs in small print reciting in incomprehensible English one court decision after another mocked her. She put the volume back and tried another one.

For the next hour Gwen, confused and tense, read every entry that seemed relevant, but she got no nearer to solving her problem, as she viewed it. Two more patrons wandered into the reading room, claimed a book, and wandered out before Gwen gave up her search.

Even wearier than when she first arrived, Gwen drifted into the hallway, where two librarians were chatting complacently. Across the hallway was the fiction section, and unlike the larger reading room, it was bustling with patrons. Two men sat in leather chairs reading newspapers before the large stone fireplace, a stack of novels by Dick Francis leaning against one of the chairs; a young mother pulled out a novel by Anita Desai while her baby swatted its toes in a collapsible carriage; a young man was discovering the West of Louis L'Amour; three teenage girls were comparing the merits of The Baby-Sitters Club series by Ann Martin with the Sweet Valley High series by Kate William. Two boys brushed by her carrying books by Christopher Pike and R. L. Stine.

The buoyancy in their movements tugged at her, for she had heard nothing to suggest so many people were here; it tossed her down, back into herself. It seemed like a metaphor for her life—the bright easy world of other people taking its course around her while she struggled, unseen and unacknowledged, with an intractable, almost insoluble problem, one that she had to solve or give up living if she failed. A wave of self-pity rushed over her. She hated herself when she got like this, going over and over the wrongs of her life with no way out, just as there had been no way out as a child, no escape, no reprieve. But she had escaped. Maybe it wasn't a moral judgment on her that she sank so low and sometimes stayed there for days, pretending nothing was wrong.

She turned to gray lead inside when she tried to fight her way out of the dark. It was bad for her and bad for the children. Thinking about how her moods might be affecting them sent her deeper into her own worthlessness. At such times the only recourse was turning to the obvious: a recitation of how much they needed her, which was never as much as she needed them. She couldn't and wouldn't imagine a life without them, but she had to discover a way to save them from her own darkness.

A mother with a stroller smiled at her as she wheeled her way out of the fiction room while Gwen went in. Perhaps what she ought to do is forget about her sorrows, her fears, forget about the threats and danger. If there was no solution she could risk applying, then she might as well let the consequences build while she got on with her life for at least as long as fate allowed. After all, she had her two children to raise, and that was all that mattered.

■ ■ ■

During his many years in uniform, Joe Silva rarely wondered why he did what he did. A thoughtful, meditative man about whatever confronted him, he nevertheless was not inclined to deep introspection or any periods of self-doubt—about anything. At least not until recently. The feelings he had discovered in himself over the last few days had surprised, irritated, then troubled him. Now he was avoiding examining the most recent development—the change wrought by the news that George Frome had been murdered. Frome's death had injected him with energy and purpose, his doubts and regrets an unpleasant memory. That was what bothered him. He had the unsettling suspicion that he was using a murder investigation as a drug, covering up a personal discovery he didn't want to deal with. He tossed the folder onto his desk, rubbed his hand over his forehead, and wondered if every American male was destined to go mad by the year 2000.

Silva pulled out a pad of paper from beneath the pile of folders, setting the Plexiglas cube displaying squares of handmade lace and crochet work on the windowsill, and began his notes. His brief talk with Gwen McDuffy the night before had been followed by a short talk with the treasurer of the Arbella Society; as a result Silva felt he had a good overview of Thursday and Frome's death. George Frome had died from something he ingested late Thursday night. Scraps of his meal contained the poison aconitine; the source of the poison was still unidentified. Frome was apparently alone in the building at the time of death; the Arbella House was locked when the Society secretary, Marian Davis, arrived for work on Friday morning. The first-floor central hallway lights, which were regularly turned on when the house was closed up at night, were on. The only other lights on in the house were those in the attic where Frome was found.

One window of Silva's office looked out on the village green, to the Victorian town hall on one side, sitting back from Main Street, and the granite and sandstone library beyond, where not long ago he had seen Gwen McDuffy going up the walk. The sight had sent him off on his musings, none of them productive, he told himself. Perhaps the problem was the victim. George Frome was an unlikely choice, as far as Silva could see. He had lived in Mellingham for many years, if not his entire life, and had taken on a more active role for himself over the past two years, since retiring from his job with the state government. Generally well thought of and friendly to everyone he encountered, Frome had been a familiar sight to Silva as he arrived at Arbella House, visited Town Hall, or did his errands around town. Well liked, charming, an old unmarried townie, George had no enemies that Silva had heard of.

But there the chief was wrong, and he knew it. Before him, in all probability, somewhere on the list of trustees and visitors to Arbella House on Thursday, was the name of George Frome's murderer, the name of one person who had reason to poison a likable, aging gentleman. Already Silva and Dupoulis had eliminated several of the board members after talking with Marian Davis and some of the women members. Silva rifled through the piles on his desk for the report of Dupoulis's conversation with four of the trustees.

Marian insisted that from her desk she could—and did—see everyone who came into the building by the back door as well as anyone who went out to the kitchen after they walked through it into the main house. (The front door was always locked.) Despite Silva's delicate probing, she would neither alter nor soften her stance. She insisted that Gwen McDuffy entered through the kitchen when she arrived on Thursday, the first person to arrive, after Marian, for the afternoon. A small group of visitors came for a tour, which Marian conducted, thus leaving Gwen alone for a brief period—before, she insisted, George Frome arrived with his supper and left it in the refrigerator at three o'clock. Marian also insisted Gwen left before five o'clock, before Annalee Windolow arrived. Gwen walked straight through the kitchen and out the back door. Then Annalee arrived and Marian was held—against her will, she wanted Silva to know—until almost five-thirty, when she dashed home to get her supper before the meeting. At the time she left, Arbella House was empty, all other volunteers having gone by four o'clock and George having stepped out for a cold drink. Her deference to the chief by not cataloging his visit Thursday afternoon along with all the others was the first reminder of his position. He literally didn't count.

During every investigation he conducted, no matter how large or small the problem, there came a moment when he knew he was an outsider, despite how much the person might try to hide it. It was nothing personal—he understood that—but he was not one of them, not born and raised to the quirkiness, biases, skewed visions of life as lived in Mellingham. If his job hadn't declared him a manifestation of another mode of thinking, his birth and upbringing certainly did. He was a foreigner, literally and figuratively, and time had inured him to the Mellites' inability to speak freely in his presence and to their automatic slide into defensiveness in times of crisis.

Marian Davis was thus only the first to remind him of his place; there would be others. She had defended Gwen to the best of her ability, and had far less enthusiastically vouched for Annalee Windolow.

"You're quite certain you didn't leave her alone for just a minute while you answered the door or the phone?" Silva had asked after listening to Marian's account of the treasures accumulated for the month.

"Don't I wish," had been Marian's reply.

Nevertheless, Annalee Windolow had brought the seed packets into Arbella House, and until Silva knew exactly what was in them and whether or not they had killed Frome, he was not going to cross her off his list. She and Gwen got a note and a question mark, as did Marian, who was alone at almost five-thirty in the building after everyone else had left.

Silva expected obstacles in his initial interviews but the one Sergeant Dupoulis had conducted the night before with four women in their sixties, who seemed to serve on the board as a single bloc, was a severe disappointment. The four members arrived together, voted together, chose volunteer projects together, and disputed every feature of the board meeting together. And that was the problem with their statements—they had done everything together. They prepared the foods together, set them out together, and inspected them together after Mrs. Rocklynd passed a critical aside to the president. Each and all insisted that none of them had a moment alone in the kitchen. To do what precisely? was a question Dupoulis had ducked at least four times; Silva, the sergeant warned, could expect to be asked the same as soon as one of them spied him on the street.

Dupoulis's warning amused Silva, for the chief was accustomed to being queried (even interrogated) by disgruntled residents and found the role of sounding board an easy one. The sergeant, in contrast, took it personally, as a challenge to his worth as a police officer, to his judgment as a man. More than one retired schoolteacher asked for her old elementary school student when she wanted to complain. Sergeant Dupoulis came to resent every call. Silva found himself smiling; there were advantages to being an outsider sometimes.

Dupoulis's last report concerned the treasurer, Bill Huntley. Silva could guess what was in it without even turning the page. Silva had seen Bill at the playground last night, as he expected to and so did everyone else who knew him. Rain or shine, winter or summer, Bill was playing a game, planning a game, getting a team ready for a game, preparing the playing field for a game, or teaching neighborhood kids how to play a game. He worked as an accountant, volunteered for the Fire Department, served on a number of boards for local nonprofit organizations, but his heart was at second base, and so was his body if he didn't absolutely, positively, without question, have to be somewhere else. To the best of his recollection, he had arrived at Arbella House about twenty minutes before the meeting was due to start (he knew the time because his team was in the bottom of the sixth inning when he left the park); while other members were in the kitchen or wandering around the library waiting for the meeting to begin, he set to work on the books at Marian's desk until the meeting started. He was one of the first to leave and went straight home to get a sandwich, since he didn't have time to eat at the park before the meeting. His wife vouched for his presence the rest of the evening; together they were sewing team insignia on their children's uniforms.

Dupoulis had next interviewed Walter Marsh; the president's narration confirmed much of Bill's. The two arrived at Arbella House simultaneously and Walter hovered around Bill, feeding him figures for his calculations; after the meeting, the president accepted a ride home from the treasurer. Walter's wife vouched for him for the rest of the evening; no doubt his teenage daughters would emerge to do the same if needed. Dupoulis's final interview was with a man who got a ride from his office to Arbella House and was picked up by his wife at nine-fifteen. He never went into the kitchen and suggested he might never go into Arbella House again after Thursday night. Silva crossed three more names off his list.

Chief Silva was not happy at the result. The work so far had eliminated more than half of the board members. The remaining trustees and volunteers hardly constituted the usual list of suspects—Marian Davis, Gwen McDuffy, Catherine Rocklynd, Edwin Bennett, Kelly Kuhn, and Annalee Windolow. Some of the best of Mellingham.

■ ■ ■

Kelly Kuhn added up the column of figures, checked the total, and tossed his pencil in the air. He was clenching his fists in ecstasy when the pencil landed on the floor behind him, hitting the worn green rug with a muffled plop. Working in the small office attached to his white clapboard home since six-thirty this morning, he had added column after column, moved figures from one column to another, then another, raised some amounts and lowered others. Now, after more than three hours, he had finally reached the total he wanted. The calculating he had struggled with had at long last produced the figure that was a permission for him to buy again. A small watercolor for sale in a Boston gallery was now within his reach. He clenched his fists and bounced and wiggled in his chair with glee. After a brief period of frozen terror, he was back on track, once again reaching out to the impressionist art that gave his life meaning. He leaned around in his chair, searching for the flying pencil.

The office was almost a perfect square, the result of enclosing a garage and winterizing it several years ago. Soon after it was done, Kelly moved in dozens of pieces—paintings, chairs, boxes, lamps, vases—but the room hadn't been full in months. The period when his business had spread to the first floor of his home, sprawling from the living room into the dining room, was long past. Now only a few pieces, bought on orders from his best clients, met his eyes. He spotted the pencil beneath a Sheraton table with maple veneer. Inflating the value of that object had enabled Kelly to achieve his goal in the end; he had no doubt he could get his client to pay the inflated price. The greatest challenge in keeping to his plan would be Annalee Windolow.

Kelly checked his watch—it was 8:43—and lumbered off to shower and dress. He returned just before nine to arrange a number of colonial paintings around the room, checking for the light as it fell through the windows, and moving a canvas out of shadow, or slanting it in the sunlight to cut down on glare. The gate in the stockade fence swung open just as he settled the last canvas into place; Annalee Windolow breezed into the room.

"Well, at least you're still functioning," she began after Kelly greeted her. "No, thanks, no coffee for me. Why does everything look so different? Did you expand this place?" She looked around. "It looks so much roomier."

Kelly rushed toward her with a chair, which he placed in the middle of the room, arranged so that she could see the paintings he had set out.

"Thanks," she said as she sat down. "I was over at the Arbella Society yesterday morning when they found George. Do you know what that is like?" She half-turned to him. "No, of course you don't. You weren't there. Well, let me tell you. There is nothing, absolutely nothing more gruesome than being in a house with a dead body. I mean, it just oozes distress. Oozes it." She shuddered while Kelly hovered beside her. Her words hammered for his attention but had no greater impact than a child's fist on a pillow. His thoughts were not on murder, but on penetrating Annalee's defenses and pocketbook.

"So these are them," she said when she was no longer interested in talking about George Frome's death.

"Yes, these are the ones I told you about," Kelly said, instantly alert. "After we talked, on Thursday, wasn't it?" She nodded. "I remembered after we spoke that I did have some paintings of the sort you said you were interested in. I was pretty sure I still had them and I did." He beamed at her and the paintings.

"Maybe I will have some coffee," she said. "No, make that tea. Have you got any tea? I'd love some."

"Tea. Right. Just a sec." Kelly rushed into the house wondering if he had any tea. He didn't want to leave Annalee in there alone for too long; that could be a serious mistake. He had learned the hard way about how easily she got bored if she had no one to talk to. As part of his plan to get to know her personal taste when she first became a client, he had invited her to attend an auction with him. Quite to his surprise, she had seemed content to wander around the rooms with him, examining the items on display. Overconfident, as he later realized, he left her side for what he thought was no more than a minute to talk to another dealer, and found her gone when he returned. He spent the rest of the afternoon tracking her down, reconstructing how she had made the acquaintance of a woman who sold only 1950s antiques, including comic books; the dealer had led her off for afternoon coffee. Annalee ended up buying the first Donald Duck comic book ever printed, *Donald Duck Finds Pirate Gold*, Four Color No. 9, published by Dell in 1942. There were at the time only eighteen copies in mint condition, and Annalee bought one of them. Cost: $4,200. Kelly almost broke down and cried.

To his great relief, Annalee was pacing the room when he got back, walking up to a painting, then stepping back, cocking her head from side to side, twisting this way and that, as though the picture might improve if she changed her pose.

"Tea?" Kelly offered.

"You know, that one looks so much like that painting I got in New York. Maybe it's by the same artist. How would I figure that out? Do you have any Sweet 'n Low?"

"Sweet 'n Low. Right. Just a sec." Kelly rushed back to the kitchen.

"I was so disappointed yesterday," Annalee said when Kelly returned with two pink packets. She took them without a word. "George Frome had promised to help me recognize paintings of the colonial era. You know. Primitives. That kind of thing. Now I'm stuck. It's really a pain in the neck." Kelly fussed around in front of her, sliding a canvas into her line of sight while she spoke. If she wrinkled her nose, he pulled it away and tried another.

"He was so interested in helping me," she said.

"He, uh, was very thoughtful like that," Kelly said, sliding another canvas in front of her.

"Gee, that sort of matches the one I got in New York. Let me look at that."

Kelly carried the canvas up to her chair so she could study it. He told her the little he had been able to learn about it, embellished the stories that seemed to be attached to it, and tossed out the names of a few artists known to be working at the time, letting Annalee make the assumption that one of them, if she recognized them at all, was the painter.

"How much?" she asked. Kelly thought of the hours spent earlier at his desk and the near-endless column of figures, and then the one that finally brought him the total he wanted. He quoted a figure. Annalee opened her eyes wide.

"Early American," he said. "In excellent condition. Unquestionable provenance." She pressed her lips and frowned.

"All right. I'll give you a check."

Kelly coughed to conceal a gasp. To make sure she had heard him correctly, he repeated the price. Annalee nodded and drew a checkbook from her purse as she settled herself at Kelly's desk. He watched over her shoulder, seeing that the balance figure in her checkbook easily covered the price he had quoted. He knew she had a budget for buying paintings but he never thought it would be so large. Her balance would cover two paintings like the one she was buying. What a collection he could have if he had the Windolow resources!

"Shall I wrap it?" Kelly asked when he had folded the check and slipped it into his pants pocket.

"A plastic bag will do."

Kelly scurried off to find a bag, his thoughts scattered by the feel of the check pricking him through the thin cotton of his pants pocket. The expectations of haggling, cajoling, negotiating for three quarters of the price he had asked had guided his every move this morning, so he was unprepared for this immediate and huge success. The amount of money he had just received was more stimulation than he could readily absorb. He yanked a bag from a pile in his front closet, and hurried back, fumbling with the handles.

"Why do all these old paintings have all these little stickers with numbers on them?" Annalee asked. She was holding the canvas on her lap with her left hand while she picked at a brown label on the bottom stretcher with her right hand.

"That's nothing. Pay no attention to it. Here." He dropped the bag and inked over the sticker with a black magic marker. "It's just an old cataloging number. Pay no attention to it." He maneuvered the painting into the bag.

"I'm really sorry your lessons won't work out. With George, I mean," Kelly said as he handed her the bag. "Perhaps I could help?"

"Thanks, Kelly, just the same, but I think I'll get someone at the Arbella Society. They do that kind of thing for free. And since we do support it with public funds, I figure I can just go over there and get my money's worth."

"I don't think they get any public money," Kelly said, perplexed.

"Well, whatever. Anyway, what are you going to do with the rest of those pictures?"

"These?" Kelly turned back into the room, unable to believe his good luck. He was on the verge of making two sales in one day, even if the second one took a little longer to reach fruition. "I promised to have some American primitives for a client who visits Mellingham in August. Of course, since you've seen them first, I can show him whatever I have left next month. They'll be here for a while longer, anyway."

"August? Hmmm." Annalee ran her tongue over her teeth behind her lips, creating one of her more grotesque faces as she pondered the remaining pictures and the time between now and August on her way down the path. When Kelly heard her car door slam shut, he clenched his fists and bounced with glee on the balls of his feet. His entire body jiggled and jounced with joy.

■ ■ ■

When Silva was a child, he was always the first at the playground on Saturday mornings, not because he was eager, but because he was used to getting up early, at four or five in the morning at the sound of his father moving around downstairs. At the first sound of the new day, be it his father in the kitchen or a car starting in the driveway next door, he was awake, alert, out of bed, and on his way, soundlessly moving around the room. His actions were swift, graceful, efficient as he filled the space of time opening up. It was a drive in him, like addiction in another sort of person, and the day never failed to satisfy him. His younger siblings didn't have this feeling, but for Joe it had led to a lifetime of early mornings filled with the odd jobs of life while he waited for the rest of the town to wake up.

Because of his early habits, therefore, he was surprised to arrive at a home to find the person he wanted to speak to already gone, just as much an early person as Joe but not at all as constrained by convention to wait until seven or eight or nine o'clock before getting on with the business of the day. Discovering that Edwin was an early riser too made up for not finding him at home until relatively late in the morning.

"If I'd known, Chief, I would have stayed here, but it was such a gorgeous day and I wanted to get up to New Hampshire early so I could get back before the day was gone." He pointed to the pots and seed packets scattered on the ground in his backyard. "Wildflowers. This is star of Bethlehem, fairly common," he began, his eyes glistening with pleasure. He named three more before he stopped himself. "I'm sorry. I got carried away." He couldn't seem to think of what to say next. "Have you come about George? Inside?" He led the way in, explaining his early trip up north. He spoke quickly as he went about closing the windows and turning on the air conditioner to low. It was one of the few Silva had seen in use on the first floor. Like other

New England towns, Mellingham was dotted with old clapboard houses and these were dotted with tiny air conditioners hanging out of second-floor windows or, less often, first-floor bedroom windows. Few people had gone so far as to expect such comfort in the home during the day. It seemed immoral, somehow, at least to the older members of the town, except for Edwin, apparently, who adjusted the vents and sat down across from Silva in the living room.

"Marian called me last night after you were there. I stay up pretty late reading, and she knew I'd want to hear about it. Awful thing to happen. Poor George. Just awful. We weren't close but I never would have thought something like this would happen to him." The blankness of disbelief suffused his body, making lax the muscles that broke ground and turned soil without his needing to take a deep breath. His knees bowed out and his hands rested on the cushion as he stared back at Silva. "How did he die?"

"He was poisoned," Silva said. "Aconitine."

"Aco—" Edwin broke off in midword. "But that's—"

"That's what?" Silva asked.

"That's a plant poison," he said, as though the word itself might be dangerous.

"You're familiar with it?"

"Yes. Every gardener is, I suppose. It's common in, oh, what's the family name?" He rubbed his forehead. "I can look it up for you." He started to rise but Silva stayed him with an upraised hand. It was enough to know that Edwin recognized it.

"I can't believe it," Edwin repeated, shaking his head. "What can I do to help you?"

"Tell me about Thursday, for a start. I'm trying to get a clear picture of what happened during the day and later at the meeting."

"I only know about the meeting. I brought Aunt Catherine and we must have gotten there, say, at a little after seven, I guess. A lot of other people were already there."

"The talk after the meeting must have been interesting. I hear it was quite an argument," Silva said.

"It was but I didn't stay for the aftershocks, you might call them. I'd had enough. I drove Aunt Catherine home and came straight on here. Those evening meetings can get to be a strain sometimes." He brightened up suddenly. "You know, Chief, we'd love to have you on the board. Maybe you could keep us on the straight and narrow. What do you say?"

"Thanks, but I've got enough to do." The last thing Silva expected was an invitation in Mellingham to serve on the board of such an organization. He wasn't sure what to make of Edwin's offer other than the impulse of a generous man. "Tell me about the meeting itself," Silva said. Edwin assented; he was a willing narrator and began after a few comments to sound like a sportscaster, letting Silva know who was seated where, who said what, what votes were taken, put off, how long each topic took and where it ended (if it did), and how people reacted to each step in the meeting. "That's quite a spiel," Silva said when Edwin had finished; but for all its length, his narration reminded the chief of how selective memories are.

"I heard about the meeting breaking up into one of the usual arguments," Silva said.

"It wasn't one of the usual ones, but the arguing was the same. We always argue," Edwin said, with a smile. "It's in our nature. I told you you could help us with that."

Silva smiled. He knew enough of Mellingham to agree with him, even if Edwin meant it facetiously. "I'll keep it in mind. What I want to know is whether you noticed anything unusual about George Frome or anyone else."

"You mean other than the usual?" Edwin asked.

"What does that mean?"

"George was a bit different from the rest of us. We bicker a lot, and argue over the least little thing, but we do respect each other. We know we're all trying to keep the Society going and enjoy ourselves along the way. But George—" He paused to consider the enigma that was George Frome. "Well, he was different. He was always telling us what was best for us, trying to maneuver us into agreeing with him before we even knew what he was up to, that sort of thing. We're just a small-town organization but we're still capable of making some pretty interesting discoveries. People forget this is where some important records are—in little historical societies all across the country. One might be negligible by itself, but several thousand add up to something. George acted as though we were too stupid to recognize the importance of a Civil War diary or anything else."

"How did people feel about that?" Silva asked, though he didn't need to. It was a wonder George Frome had been kept on.

"Do you really have to ask? He drove us crazy, but he did a lot of work too. A lot of work." Edwin's respect for the other man's dedication was obvious.

"George Frome is a problem for me. He was one person I never got to know at all; he never called the station for anything, never complained about anyone or made his presence known to us for any reason. Who was he?" Silva tossed out the question, but it was anything but a throwaway to Edwin, who stalled by rearranging pillows behind him. He cleared his throat and said, "He was George Frome, long-time resident and friend of all the right people."

"That's a slogan, Edwin. You can tell me more about him than that," Silva said. "Or don't you want to?" If Silva had wanted to startle Edwin Bennett, he succeeded admirably. The other man sat up straight, his mouth dropped open; he gawked at the chief.

"Here, now, Chief. Don't you think that's a little strong? I didn't mean to be flippant about it. I just meant—well, I don't know what I meant. He was just George, that's all."

"What do you mean, just George?"

Paler in face and stiffer in limb, Edwin looked around the room. "Well, he has no family around here that I know of. He's always been interested in the Arbella Society and after he retired he started spending most of his free time over there, taking stuff in, showing tourists around, leading historic walks through town, that sort of thing. I don't think I ever thought about his having any other life. He never talked about anything else." Edwin looked back at the years of George Frome and the Arbella Society, years when time was taken for granted, squandered on activities people couldn't even remember weeks or months later. But there were no threads of other colors woven into the fabric of Frome's life. "The only thing George ever did after he retired as far as I know is the Arbella Society, especially donations. That was his main task. It was always George's role to receive everything that came in, no matter what collection it belonged to. I don't know how he got the job, but he relished it. He was sort of our gatekeeper. He had a good eye, so it made sense for him to do it."

"How literally do you mean that? That he was the gatekeeper? Is he the only one who knew what was coming in?" Silva asked. This practice alone could bring Frome into conflict with just about everyone else in the Society. If this was typical of their policies, it was no wonder they were always at each other's throats.

"No, not exactly. He looked at everything, said yes we wanted it or no we didn't. Then he made some kind of note—I'm not sure about his record keeping on this—and then sent it on to the department that should have it."

"That's a lot of control for one person, isn't it? Or am I behind the times when it comes to historical associations?"

Silva asked. He caught himself in mid-thought and rephrased his question. It might distract Edwin to tell him that he had never belonged to a historical society in his life, nor had any of his immediate relatives.

"I guess so," Edwin said. "We never thought much about it, at least not that way. We were just trying to make it easy for people who wanted to donate things." He smiled. "We do have a grand idea of ourselves sometimes. We thought of George as streamlining, taking all the first questions and passing on the best stuff. Hmmm. I don't think we would have let him set up that system if we thought we were giving up control." Silva let that stand.

"So he could turn something down and no one would ever know, except Marian, if she remembered seeing whatever it was arrive."

"I suppose," Edwin admitted.

"He was also the first to discover family secrets if someone donated old letters or journals, for instance."

"Now, Chief, be serious. What kinds of things do you think people give us, anyway? Besides, we all know each other's secrets in Mellingham. That's the point of a small town. Anything serious in this town and, well, you'd be the one to know about it." Edwin laughed, but he couldn't conceal his nervousness.

"I'm glad to hear you have so much faith in my department. For my sake let's try an example." Silva thought about what he had seen on Thursday afternoon. "There was a box of lace that was donated some time ago, and I saw Gwen McDuffy making notes about it. Tell me what the procedure is using the lace as an example."

"Lace. That comes under costumes and textiles. Okay. Someone calls up and says she's cleaning out her mother's attic and has a big pile of old lace. Do we want it? Marian will probably say yes, bring it down—she's like that, never say no to anyone, you never know what they might have—

and then she'd tell George it was coming. Nothing formal, just, Hey George, I got a call today from a woman who's bringing in some lace. I'll let you know when it gets here. Clear so far?"

Silva nodded, suppressing his opinion that the historical society had policies and procedures of the same vintage as its collections. "Go on. Marian just remembers who calls and what they want."

"Right. Good memory, Marian. Anyway, when the stuff arrives, Marian takes it and if it isn't already in a box or bag, she puts it in something. We have an awful lot of people wandering through; it's too easy to step on things, or pick them up and put them away and never see them again. So she puts it in a box, and she would have told George the next time she saw him. Or talked to him."

"And then it became his responsibility," Silva added.

"Well, not exactly. We're not quite that strict. I don't think we ever think of it as anyone's responsibility in that sense. But George would look at the stuff when he came in and say yes it's okay for us to take or no, we didn't want it. That happened sometimes. You know, some things can really cost us a lot of money. We might want to accept some furniture, but it if needs a lot of repair work, it's not worth it for us."

"And you tell the donor that?" Silva asked, curious.

"Well, no, not usually. Some people think we're hinting for money if we tell them that. One woman was furious when George told her her bureau needed too much restoration work. She accused him of trying to hold her up for more money and took the bureau back. We wanted her to, but not quite like that." He sighed at the recollection. "It's never easy. You think it would be, but it isn't. Most of the time we just say we can't use it. Sometimes people give us things that they want us to use in specific ways, like their grandmother's secretary. It can only be used in the front parlor. Or lace has to be framed and hung. That can be a problem, especially if it's not a very good piece. Sometimes people give a nice picture but we don't want another like one we already have and the donor says we can't sell it, so back it goes." Edwin was growing relaxed again as he tried to detail for the chief the intricacies of donations to the Arbella Society. "We're just a small local society; we can only do so much. We have to stick to our mission, which is local history. Some people, with really nice paintings or antiques, get the idea they should give their stuff to a local museum like us, but unless it has some local historical value, it may not be a good gift. We can't always afford the insurance or the security fees to take care of some of the things people have wanted to give us. We're really into preserving local history so people have a better sense of how one town fits into the larger history of the United States."

"What about the box of lace?" Silva asked, trying to get Edwin back on track. He was also beginning to wish he had picked another example.

"Oh yes, the lace. The lace was made by a lot of old families around here and it came to all belong to one woman who is pretty careful about what she collects. There used to be lots of old families making it, mostly for themselves, you understand. So the box of lace arrives. Well, if George— well, the new gatekeeper, whoever it is—says no, it goes back; if he says yes, it goes to the person who should have it. That just means that it sits in the office or the dining room until the right volunteer comes along and takes it away. Now lace, that's costumes and textiles, and that's Gwen McDuffy, so that means Thursday. She comes in one afternoon a week. So she'd come in and look at it and take it up to the third floor until she could get around to it, or she might start working on it right away, identifying it and cataloging it."

"So he was the only one who knew all the things that had

been taken in by the Society over the last few years?" Silva summarized Edwin's description of the acquisitions process, trying to accurately reflect the extensive power and knowledge Frome had acquired.

"Well, if you want to look at it that way, you could take it even further; he was probably the only one who knew everything that was in the Society."

"The only one who knew everything?" Silva repeated to be sure he had heard the other man correctly.

"The only one. There's a storage room on the third floor, right above the gallery, and I've seen him in there more than once, just going through stacks of things, not looking for anything, just looking at them, seeing what was there. I interrupted him once for a phone call, but he didn't seem embarrassed about it. It wasn't a secret. He liked to know what was what, what was where, and all that. I would guess he was the only one who really knew everything that we had."

"Sounds like he's someone to be missed," Silva said.

"I suppose," Edwin said, willing to grant Frome the credit he deserved. "For all his arguing, I guess he did do a lot of work. But those of us who have been there longer have a pretty good idea of the entire collection; we just didn't go about our work in the same way." Silva noted the bluster in Edwin's last comment, and the reservoir of envy beneath it.

"He seemed to think that the Society had some problem. You know I was over there on Thursday afternoon getting a tour of the building and all sorts of questions from George on keeping the building secure. The implication, which he wasn't trying to conceal, was that things were going missing."

"Yes, well, that came up at the board meeting." Edwin frowned.

"What do you think he was getting at Thursday evening?" Silva asked. "Could anything be missing? That seemed to be what he was implying."

"It might be with an ordinary person, but nothing was ever simple with Frome." Edwin shook his head; beneath his resentment at what Frome's death had shown him was a deeper feeling of distress at what Frome's death was doing to the Society. "George was good for the Society, but he could also be a problem. He could complicate things no matter how hard you tried to keep him to a simple yes or no. Now, take that lace that came in a little while ago. Gwen seems to know something about handwork, even does some herself if her own clothes are any sign. But I'll bet that George had a few things to tell her about the donations— regardless of whether he was right or not—that he made her put into her cataloging notes. He'd tell her something— he did this with all the volunteers—then stand over her to make sure she wrote it down. He knew a lot, but he thought he knew a lot more."

Silva recalled the thin slips of paper with misapplied terms pinned to some of the pieces. If those were George Frome's, Edwin was right about what the dead man did and did not know, at least when it came to Portuguese hand-work. "What about the oil paintings he had up there? Have you given them any more thought?"

Edwin bristled, as he had on Friday morning when Silva had first mentioned the pictures. "That's no place for paint-ings. Think of the heat! The dryness! I can't believe George would take them up there. He was always so particular about good things." His indignation at Frome's behavior spoke of a deep competition. "Where are they now?"

"Still there. You can bring them down tomorrow. I may want to take one last look. They're the only things we found up there. Could someone else be responsible for taking them up there?" Silva asked.

"You mean George just found them?" He considered the idea. "I suppose he could have stumbled across them when he went up there to eat on the roof, to catch a breeze, enjoy the view. But it's so unlikely. Who in the Arbella Society would be so stupid as to put good pictures or good anything up there? That's a horrible place. A steam bath in the summer, an igloo in the winter." Edwin grew leaner as he spoke, his anger stretching him to a taut thinness. George Frome's death was sad, but the mistreatment of art was a tragedy.

6

Saturday Afternoon

There comes a time in every life when motives no longer matter, when the reasons why something is done, the reasons that drove the doing in the first place, no longer hold the mind or bind the heart. The thoughts that once guided a step to the right instead of the left, determined a response or a dream, bundle together in clusters to be put away with a personality of the past. Gwen had reached that point, when all her reasons deserted her and left her alone in the present, unsure how she got here but unwilling to alter her circumstances.

The children, Jennie and Philip McDuffy, tumbled out of the second-floor apartment at one o'clock, their lunch half in their mouths and half on the kitchen table, as they raced to the beach to get the best spot with their friends before the crowds overwhelmed the pristine sand. Their promptitude on the weekends always made Gwen wonder at their lassitude on school days, but she was glad they were off on their own now, for she needed more and more time alone to think through the things on her mind.

Spread before her on the living room rug, a braided rug in muted blues and greens and reds she had purchased for twenty dollars at a yard sale, were three shoeboxes of photographs and a brown three-ring binder with plastic display pages. Over the last few days she had grown especially conscious of how precious her children were to her, and was thus inspired to lay out their lives in plastic and oils. She dumped the pictures out onto the rug and started sorting them into piles, only two at first, then three. Philip with plump fists and a cowboy hat, sharply focused but with no background, went into the stack on the left, and Jennie with her arms around her brother and a big smile out of focus went into the one on the right.

The piles grew, and when she was finished sorting, Gwen transferred each one to its own shoebox, except for the third, which she put into a paper bag. The next task seemed more appealing to her, for she smiled as she opened the binder and pulled it close to her. Pushing aside the shoebox on the left and the paper bag, Gwen dumped the pictures from the remaining shoebox back onto the rug and again began sorting. This time the underlying principle was obvious; she arranged the pictures by the age of the child therein until she had several unsteady piles. These she then arranged in the display pages, leaving room to write in dates, names, and places, for which she had purchased a white-colored pencil.

Gwen lingered over the last few photographs, taken by Mrs. Alesander only a few weeks earlier when Jennie and Philip had finished the school year with awards for citizenship and science. Gwen stood between them at the bus stop, stiff paper awards blowing out in one hand while they tried to keep hair out of their eyes with the other as Mrs. Alesander posed and photographed them numerous times before she ran out of film.

By the time Gwen was finished it was well past three o'clock, but she was not ready to stop just yet. When she rose from the floor, she was stiff, and surprised at how much time had passed. In the kitchen, she filled a glass of water, set it aside, then placed the second box of photographs on the counter. Taking the first one in her hand, she lit a match and set the photograph on fire, watching waves of heat slide across the film, the red and yellow lip of the wave rushing over the face of a woman forgotten long ago. She dropped the picture into the sink, watching its last corner bubble and melt. For the next hour Gwen put match to film, twisting the picture in her hand to lure the flame to burn upward, blowing on a lazy wave of heat, dropping the last corner before her fingers were singed.

After an hour the smoke alarm in the front hall went off, sending a high buzzing through the neighborhood. Gwen ran for a chair, climbed up, and pulled the top from the alarm nailed to the ceiling. Scratching and cutting her fingers against wires and metal, she pulled out the battery and the alarm was silent, but the smell remained. Only then did she notice the acrid odor that pervaded the small apartment. She pushed open all the windows, the front door, the door at the bottom of the stairs, and the back door onto the porch. A sheet of smoke drifted toward the kitchen window, then lurched through. Gwen began to worry a neighbor would see the smoke and call the police. She turned on the radio and went back to the sink to burn the last three pictures.

Gwen gathered up the photos left in the paper bag and sorted through them again; there were only a dozen of them, some black and white, and some of a man and a woman other than Gwen, of the man alone, of both with older people in a town not Mellingham, and of another man with Gwen and alone. She stuffed them into an envelope, which she taped shut, going round and round the envelope with masking tape; she slipped the package between two sweaters in her bottom bureau drawer. The smoke was almost cleared from the kitchen, and the smell was leaving the front of the apartment. It was nearing four o'clock and she still didn't want to stop for lunch.

In the hallway outside the bathroom stood a closet for

the washing machine, and beside it a shelf for folding and sorting, where Gwen had earlier that morning left her basket of laundry. She moved it to the floor, and began pulling out the clothes and dropping them into the washing machine; some she put aside on the shelf. When the basket was empty she went to the kitchen for a pair of scissors. Inspecting the clothes on the shelf, she clipped away stray threads and an occasional frayed tag from an unfamiliar department store. Partway through she began to sing to herself.

The water poured into the washing machine while Gwen turned to the children's bedrooms. Philip was tidy, conscientious about putting away his toys and clothes after each use, even arranging them in more harmonious groupings so the dinosaurs wouldn't fall off the edge of his bookcase or his comic books get spoiled by soda cans on his bedside table. He had always been like this and Gwen marveled at it; she had never seen anything like it in her family before. She checked each shelf in his bookcase, pulling out an old book that had once been part of a library before being withdrawn and sold, and flipped through the pages, tearing out a manila pocket with the name of the library, before putting the book back. Then she checked through his clothes, buttoning collars, folding pants on hangers, and snipping away frayed threads and the like. She did the same in Jennie's room after straightening it up, for her daughter was nothing like her younger brother in her personal habits.

By the time she heard Jennie and Philip climbing the steps to the kitchen, their bickering and whining the badge of a successful afternoon at the beach with their friends, one that left them wearied and worn, Gwen was sitting in the living room enjoying a glass of iced tea and a late afternoon snack. The silence after her work was done had been one of her rewards for everything else life demanded of her, and now she was ready to enjoy the sound of two tired-out and sun-burned children who were certain to be difficult all evening.

■ ■ ■

"I have to talk to the chief." The young man brushed away the brown curls flopping over his forehead and jutted out his chin. His lip trembled, undermining his belligerent stance; his fists were clenched in front of him, and except for the notebook in his hand, he could have been any young man in his twenties out for the day in carefully ironed jeans and a plaid shirt. Mickey Concini was not going to let Sergeant Dupoulis send him away. "You don't understand. I have to talk to him."

"He's not here. I just told you that. I'm sorry, but he's not here." Sergeant Dupoulis put his hands in his pockets and studied the younger man. "What's the matter with you, anyway?"

"The matter? What's the matter? You don't know? It's Saturday afternoon. I'm just checking the local stations to make sure I don't miss anything for the Monday edition, just in case something actually happens around here, and what do I find? I mean what do I find? Here? In Mellingham?"

"For God's sakes, Mickey. What did you find? The secret to the conspiracy behind the assassination of JFK? Another Boston Strangler?"

"George Frome was the social columnist for the *Traveler*, for years. He shows up on all the old lists of who was doing what when. My editor probably went to school with him. If I miss this story, he'll kill me."

"So? The chief's still out. If you don't want to talk to me, take off. Come back when the chief is here." Dupoulis allowed himself to slouch as he filled the doorway to his office.

"Aren't you supposed to be polite to me? I mean, I'm a member of the estate."

"The what? What estate? What're you talking about?" Dupoulis grew irritated, and Concini pushed his hand through his thick hair.

"You know. Journalism. My editor is always saying we're part of some estate. You know. Status." He leaned forward on the last word, shoving his chin into Dupoulis's face.

"That doesn't cut any ice with the chief. Or me. You should know that by now. He's out. Come back later." Dupoulis took a step forward in an effort to move Concini closer to the door.

"Hey, listen, have a heart. I can't leave until I find out what's going on. If I miss this story, my boss'll kill me. He thinks I can't handle it as it is. We sort of missed out on the O'Donnell thing and then I didn't get how big that Vinnio thing was, and if I miss this one, I could be in big trouble." He started taking tiny steps backward, shuffling to the side to keep himself well inside the stationhouse. "Come on, Ken. Have a heart."

The sergeant glared at him, then relaxed. "Okay. I'll tell you what little we know."

"Thanks. You won't regret it, Ken. I promise you." He opened his notebook, pulled out a pen, and looked expectantly at the sergeant.

"You sound like a bad movie. Okay, okay." He raised his hands to ward off Mickey's obligatory defense. "Yesterday morning at about eleven o'clock Marian Davis, secretary of the Arbella Society, found Mr. George Frome dead in the attic. There were no signs of violence on his person and no weapons in the attic."

"What about in the rest of the building?" Mickey asked, eager to show how closely he was following the narration.

"It's a historical society. The place is filled with weapons. They got every kind of weapon you can imagine." He was not impressed with the question, and said in a whisper as he leaned into Mickey's face, "But none of them did it."

"Well what did do it, then?"

"Poison," said Dupoulis with dramatic satisfaction.

"Poison. Wow. Just like in those mystery novels." He made a hurried note. "What kind of poison?"

"We haven't yet received the medical examiner's report of all toxicological tests," Dupoulis said, watching Mickey struggle to get the last two words down. Dupoulis wondered if he'd notice the nature of the answer.

The young reporter added, speaking to himself, "The police have not yet determined cause of death. Wow. Great stuff, Ken, great stuff."

"Thanks, we do our best."

"What about Mrs. Davis's reaction? Anything there? You know, human interest stuff." He leaned forward; he was almost bent full over his notebook as he waited for a reply.

"She very sensibly called the police and waited for us to arrive before taking any further action."

"No words about the tragedy?"

"Not that you can print," he said maliciously.

"Thanks a lot."

"We do our best," Dupoulis said.

"So what was he doing in the attic? How come nobody heard him dying up there at eleven in the morning? Wasn't anybody else there?"

"First of all, we don't know what he was doing in the attic," Ken said. He didn't want to go into the business of the salad and the paintings, uncertain how much information Chief Silva was willing to release to the newspapers just yet. "But we think he was up there the night before. His body had already started to decompose."

"Ugh, gross," said Mickey as he went on taking notes.

"What a job you guys must have. I wouldn't do it for the world." Dupoulis held his tongue. "So you guys found him in the morning, well, Marian what's-her-name found him, and you saw that he'd been poisoned. Right?"

"No, Mickey. The medical examiner said he'd been poisoned and he'd let us have all the details in a little while. These things take time."

"Gee, do you think you could find out before my deadline tomorrow? I mean, it'd be really cool if I could get all that toxic stuff into my story. People really go for that. My editor would be really impressed too. And I can do with a little help."

"I'll see what I can do, but don't count on it." Dupoulis made no secret of his efforts now to edge Concini out of the stationhouse.

"Okay, okay, I'm going, but you should be nice to me. I always try to make you guys look good. I do," he wailed when he saw the look in the sergeant's eye. "Now, listen, Ken. You have to be nice to me. I'm a member of the public."

"I am being nice to you." He leaned forward and moved Concini back to the door, pushed open the screen door behind him, and urged him onto the sidewalk. "I'll tell the chief you were here." He smiled, and pulled the screen door shut.

■ ■ ■

There were few things Silva disliked more as a policeman than the random crime, the act of cunning and cruelty without motive, the person capable of destroying another human being either literally or figuratively without any more motivation than the tossing of a coin. It was a thought he kept pushing away to the back of his mind as he searched for a reason for the death of George Frome, a man apparently without enemies, secrets, or a past.

Silva turned into the paved driveway of Mrs. Rocklynd's home, his presence taken as a rebuke by a family that had stopped to admire the gardens along the road. The mother hustled the children into the car as the embarrassed father called to them to hurry; Silva waved but they sped on into town.

Despite the heat, all the windows facing the street in the Federal facade were closed, no cars sat in the driveway, and the small terrace in front was empty, no plant or chair or drying beach towel to suggest anyone was enjoying the summer at home. Mrs. Rocklynd belonged to the older element in town, old family, old money, old home. The place was patched, painted, polished, but hardly modernized. The chief rang the old bell and waited.

Catherine Rocklynd was testimony to the role of genes, rather than plastic surgeons, in keeping a woman youthful, but her rock-hard expression as she sat down across from Silva in her living room was testimony of another sort—to a determination and willfulness that had marked every year of her life. She was known to all as a generous but tough woman, who kept away from newcomers unless she wanted something from them; she had never wanted anything from Joe Silva.

"I know you have to go around asking questions because of the way you think George died, but I have other things to do this afternoon, so I don't want you taking up too much of my time," Mrs. Rocklynd began before the chief could get through the preliminaries. The living room was dark, from the draperies covering at least half of the long windows in the room, giving the large grouping of sofas and chairs a cool, cavelike feel. Everything had a tiny fraying at the edges, as if even the purest silk, the strongest linen had to give way eventually, no matter how hard Mrs. Rocklynd might try to prevent it. On the table between them were a vase of miniature roses, a candy dish, and an ashtray, the first two sitting on crocheted doilies. A few plants in the corners made Silva think of Victorian living rooms he had seen in old photographs at Arbella House.

"I'll try not to keep you too long," he said. "I understand that you hurt your hand Thursday night."

"I'm all right. Nothing for you to worry about," she said. "Nice of you to mention it just the same. It's George you want to ask about, isn't it? Well, get on with it." She lowered her head and waited.

"Actually, I was wondering about when you left and how you got home." Witnesses were their own mystery, as far as Silva was concerned. Some ducked every question, even one about the weather, if it was at all related to a violent crime, and others, like Mrs. Rocklynd, braced themselves for and expected tough, even threatening questions. It had to be a facet of personality.

"Edwin drove me. We left together. Registry took my license until I get my eyes checked again. Nonsense, but what can you do with bureaucracy." She looked with disgust in the direction of the garage beyond the house. To his answer about what time that might be, she snapped out, "We got here just after nine o'clock. No sense in waiting around at Arbella House. Most of those people can only handle one argument a night, and George sure gave us our quota on Thursday."

Silva wasn't used to interrogating this kind of woman, someone who looked like she should be a grandmother puttering around in her garden or playing with her grandchildren, and instead was ready to go head-to-head with a police chief. As much as he tried to open himself up to new ways of looking at people, he admitted that he found it difficult to look at elderly women without expecting to see his grandmother. She was a hard woman, but she didn't think it had to show, and so she left Joe and all her grandchildren with a loving but wary respect for any woman over seventy. Mrs. Rocklynd, on the other hand, just left him feeling wary.

"I have information that he was all set on buying your log house," Silva said, hoping to get her onto another tack. Despite his innate self-confidence, he didn't take easily to questioning a woman of Mrs. Rocklynd's class.

"What information? Who told you that?" She scowled at him.

"More than one source has chosen to help the police with our inquiries, as I hope you will too, Mrs. Rocklynd." Silva shifted in his seat so he could lean forward as he thought of the lawyer and Marian; he wouldn't want to have this woman for an enemy. Mrs. Rocklynd leaned back. "That log house seems to be quite important historically. When did you decide to sell it to Mr. Frome?"

Mrs. Rocklynd stretched her neck and tapped the arm of her chair, then smoothed out a fret of threads ready to break. She said, "I can't say I really know. He asked me several times and after a while it seemed like a good idea." She relaxed and cocked her head at him. Her smile said he was there on sufferance; she was being generous. Her attitude was having its effect on Joe. "I'm not as young as I used to be, though God knows I try not to think about it. I just can't keep up with everything anymore. The log house really is falling apart and George insisted he could restore it. I'd like to see that, I admit it. I really would. I guess I let him talk me into it." She turned to a window facing the backyard and the bank of trees blocking her view of the log house and part of the inlet beyond.

"Well, perhaps someone else will take an interest in it," Silva said.

"Oh no, I'll never sell it," she said vehemently, then laughed. "Once was enough. I wouldn't dare try it again." The outburst seemed to embarrass her. "My father always said it was bad luck to sell anything that belonged to the family, and he was right. Absolutely right. I'll just keep it and leave it all to Edwin. He'll know what to do with it. He's a good boy." She looked away, which was fortunate, for she missed Silva's expression.

Joe Silva had never been able to adjust to the Yankee habit of calling grown men boys. Any one of his brothers and cousins would have risen up with two fists clenched if he or anyone else (except one's father) referred to them as boys. And yet he knew Edwin Bennett and others like him probably didn't mind (or didn't say so if they did). It was one of the cultural revelations of Yankee English that forever astonished Joe in its insensitivity and unkindness. He suspected it was the way Yankees kept their own in line, planting in their minds the illusion that they couldn't break away, that they would always be the boys, the young ones, in the family, until it was obvious they were not boys but too late to do anything about it. It was one of the things that made Yankee life seem so thin, so frail, almost unable to fend off the passions and energies of a more robust world crowding up close to it.

"Can you tell me, Chief," she began diffidently, "what did you find? George, I mean. Oh damn," she said. "I'm saying this all wrong. I want to know what—" She nodded in the hopes of getting Silva to come to her rescue; she was used to her guests holding up their end of the bargain. "I want to know what you found when you found George? I mean, what, what was it like? I mean, he wasn't stabbed, was he?" She blurted out the last sentence, desperate to make herself understood. That really wasn't the problem, though. Silva understood what she wanted. He just hadn't decided what he would tell her.

"The medical examiner thought George Frome died of cardiac arrhythmia while he was eating dinner up in the attic. Then he came back and said that Frome was poisoned." Silva didn't have to tell her that the ME hadn't yet figured out where the poison came from, that so far both he and the ME were in the dark; knowing Frome had been poisoned was so little use that Silva thought it almost no use at all.

"This medical man doesn't sound very reliable, if you ask me," she said. "I mean, first they think it was his heart; then they think he was poisoned. I say, I certainly don't envy you your job, Chief." She smiled to commiserate with him.

"It wouldn't be so hard if I had any idea why someone would want to murder him, but so far no one seems to have anything against him, or at least if they do, they're not telling me about it." He smiled back. "Mr. Frome might have made enemies, at least on a low level, if he insulted people, say, by turning down their donations. What do you think?" It was evident from her expression that Mrs. Rocklynd didn't think much of Silva's idea.

"Some people do need to be redirected. We're not a charity for donors in quite that sense. People who need to feel good by making a donation would do better to stop by the Salvation Army. We are a museum."

"I thought perhaps it might have bothered you or some of the other members to know that Frome was inspecting donations before they were accepted."

"Really, Chief," she said, pursing her lips. "That's a procedure for nonmembers. I can't imagine how your informant failed to tell you that. Was there anything else?" She leaned forward with a quizzical smile.

■ ■ ■

Mrs. Alesander climbed the steep granite steps to Arbella House and banged the brass knocker against its plate; this wasn't her usual Saturday afternoon venue, or any afternoon venue for that matter, but she figured she knew enough people in town to find someone at Arbella House who would help her. When no one came at once, she

knocked again. Inside, through the sidelights, she could see
one or two people walking around. She pushed the bell.

Just as she did so, Marian Davis pulled open the front
door with an exasperated look on her face. For a few seconds
she stared at the elderly woman in front of her, then broke
into a smile of relief and welcome. "Elizabeth, I haven't seen
you in ages. Come on in."

Elizabeth Alesander climbed the last step to the front hall
and followed Marian into the library. The older woman
looked around her. "Actually, Marian, I'm not sure what I
want is here. But I thought you could help me, anyway."

Marian Davis was born and raised in Mellingham, just as
was Mrs. Alesander, and she was always glad of the chance
for a private gossip with another local expert. "Let's go into
the office. The crowd of thrill seekers has thinned out
today. Just a few tours, and the volunteers can handle them
all right." She motioned Mrs. Alesander into her office and
shut the door to the library. "Want some iced tea? Coke?
We're well stocked now." Mrs. Alesander declined and settled herself at the worktable while Marian went back to her
chair, protected from zealous volunteers, relentless
researchers, and curious tourists by her steel gray desk and
her steel gray typewriter.

"What do you know about the Portuguese?" Mrs.
Alesander asked.

"What? You mean like anthropologically? Or personally,
as in Silva?"

Mrs. Alesander chuckled. She had spent the better part
of the morning revolving ideas in her head, which now that
she was growing old was becoming harder and harder. The
only thing that got easier in her old age was keeping her
mind on one thing; the older she got the smaller her mind
became, leaving room for only one idea at a time. Her concentration this morning had positively impressed her with
her capacity for sustained thought. "I promised to help my

granddaughter put together a report about Mellingham in the past," she finally answered. "I thought she could focus on one ethnic community and get a little help from Joe."

"The only thing I know of for the anthropological part is a bunch of old photographs we have, you know, people who used to live here, the various celebrations different groups have had over the years, that sort of thing."

"Like festivals and parades? Portraits? People at work?"

"Yes, but I don't know what kind of help they'll be," Marian said. "They're not all identified."

"Where are they?"

"Where all our recent photographs are." Marian sighed. "In a box somewhere. They came in as a gift from a photographer just a few years ago; he had scads of stuff. We didn't do anything with them; we have too much else old stuff to worry about. So far we've only cataloged photographs up to 1894."

"I didn't know there were that many of them," Mrs. Alesander said.

"There aren't. I'll be right back." Marian disappeared up the back stairs as a tour group came down the front, its visit at an end. By the time the tourists had finished buying notecards and cookbooks, Marian was back with two large cartons, which she gingerly deposited on the floor beside the worktable. "These are photographs mostly from the 1940s and 1950s," she said, reading a note taped to the box. "I don't know where the more recent ones are, but as for Portuguese stuff the later ones probably don't matter. I think our Portuguese community, such as it was, migrated to the West Coast. More fish, I guess. Now," Marian said as she put her hands on her hips, "you have to tell me what he's told you about George's death."

"Nothing." Mrs. Alesander opened the carton on top. "Go back to work, Marian." The secretary stayed where she was, and Elizabeth was compelled to look up and acknowledge her. "I'd tell you if I had something. Okay?" Marian agreed, but back at her desk she kept her eye on her old friend as she piled pictures up on the worktable and started sorting through them.

"Good heavens," Mrs. Alesander said, "what on earth is that?" She passed the black-and-white picture to Marian, who studied it for a minute.

"That's a strawberry he's holding. That's what it is. That's the strawberry that won some prize at a fair one summer. It was his family that went to the West Coast. I forgot about him. He was Portuguese. He wanted to go somewhere else. He didn't fish. He grew strawberries. Delicious, as I recall. Course, I was only a kid then." Marian squinted at the picture. "Huge, isn't it?"

"I'll say. Hmmm." Mrs. Alesander went back to sorting photographs. "Why do you have pictures of these boats in Gloucester?"

"Some of them must be Mellingham boats that went to the Blessing of the Fleet," Marian replied. "Or maybe someone just wanted to give them to us. Lord knows, we seemed to take everything back then."

"Including family portraits at the Fourth of July carnival." Elizabeth studied a group of pictures spread out on the table before her. "Things must have been noisier back then. I don't remember any Ferris wheel for years."

"No bonfire either," Marian added.

"Good heavens," Elizabeth said. "That's Edwin. My word, he looks exactly the same." Marian got up and came around to look.

"He was a little old man even then. He must have been just a teenager when that was taken. What's the date?"

Elizabeth turned it over. "It's 1940 something. It's in pencil and fading fast." She mused over the photograph while Marian went back to her seat. "You know, here it is the 1990s, as my grandson constantly reminds me, and some of us are still living in the 1940s. Has Edwin ever said anything?"

"Him? You mean about his—?" Marian didn't have to finish the question for her friend. Elizabeth nodded. "No, never. At least not to me."

"I thought he might have, seeing as how he spends so much time over here. It's like his second home."

"Or third." Marian chuckled and Elizabeth repeated the comment, then chuckled too. "Are you finding anything of what you're looking for?" Marian asked.

"Not really. The tailor liked having his picture taken but he was Italian. Won't do me any good."

"Why don't you just buy a Portuguese history book? There must be something written about them in Massachusetts." After years of coping with the crises and disasters of a historical society, Marian knew what the easiest path was every time.

"That costs money. Besides my granddaughter wants something more local, more personal than that. Don't you remember anything about how the town used to be, back in the 1940s, 1950s?" she asked.

"Not very well. I would have been a teenager back then, if it was in the 1950s, and not all that interested in domestic life, I'm afraid." Marian shrugged. For the last several years she had come to regard herself as her own woman, true to her inner self, an identity crafted and nurtured over the years. Elizabeth's questions evoked a distant, earlier self who seemed strikingly similar to her present self.

"Here's something," Mrs. Alesander said. She carried the picture over to Marian. "Isn't that our man with the strawberries?" Marian squinted at the picture and finally agreed. "Do you mind if I borrow some of these? My granddaughter can use the pictures and then maybe interview Joe."

"You're rather fond of Joe, aren't you?" Marian said. She was rather fond of Joe herself.

"Well, he does live downstairs. Do you know that when that man moved in, he never changed the locks or told people they couldn't come in anytime they wanted? Now I thought he'd have locked the place up tight. Just from being a policeman. Be the natural thing for him to do, but he didn't. Think of that. So neighborly." Smiling to herself, she turned over photograph after photograph to the accompaniment of Marian's halting typing.

"Found some more?" Marian asked when her friend fell silent for several minutes. When Mrs. Alesander didn't answer, frowning at three photographs spread out before her, Marian went on with her typing. It had been some time since she'd had such pleasant company on a Saturday afternoon. She no longer minded the tourists traipsing through the house.

■ ■ ■

A heavy old seagull stood on the granite seawall as Silva pulled into a parking space behind the police station; he admired its pure white plumage rustling into great gray wings, and then he cringed. When in the last few months had he come to view the life around him in the same way as other Mellites, admiring a seagull, which was no more than a dirty scavenger with no mind for age or youth? Even worse, he was about to release things found in a crime scene for no other reason than the implicit approval of the Mellites involved in the investigation into the death of George Frome.

He felt a sudden backing-up in himself, pushing him again into familiar territory, remote, sometimes acid, but familiar. Fond as he was of Mellingham, and every other town he'd ever worked in, Silva was suspicious of the easy accommodation he saw in others, as though their personalities were never formed, always changing; he resisted those changes in himself, pushing against the enveloping character of place.

Silva parked the patrol car and walked across the village green to Arbella House, where the lines of tourists had declined precipitously as soon as word spread that the attic in question was off-limits to the touring public. Now the open front door beckoned only the chief of police, who wondered what the response might have been if it had been opened regularly during the last two days, instead of locked and barred most of the time, its usual state.

A middle-aged woman rose immediately from a Windsor chair when Silva's foot hit the first granite step, but her smile of greeting relaxed into one of casual recognition when she saw the chief's uniform. He made his way to the attic while the volunteer passed news of his whereabouts to Marian, in the office. It hadn't bothered him that he had decided to leave five oil paintings in the attic; after all, George had taken them up there or found them there after someone else had taken them up, and had kept them there at least long enough to study them, which raised a number of questions, not only about how they got there but also about how sensitive he was to the demands of art. Everyone else Silva had spoken to had made it clear that pictures did not belong in the attic, and Silva did not want to be known forever after in Mellingham as the chief of police who had destroyed the Arbella Society's finest paintings, which was just what they would turn out to be in coming years if he didn't let them be removed to safer storage.

Everything in the attic was still as he remembered it, and he justified his decision in part by rationalizing that there was nothing more to be gleaned from the area. The heat still pulsed against the wooden beams, and the main street once again seemed closer through the open skylight than it had on the first floor. The paintings still stood against the wall;

Silva lifted each one, taking it into the refracted light from above while he studied the front and back, looking for some sign of who had left it and why. Each painting was framed in the same way, with various stickers glued to a stretcher or the frame along with now fading chalk marks in white or yellow. Later when he was satisfied, he set them once again along the chimney and pulled out his notebook. When he was finished, he left, leaving the attic door open, and pulling into a bunch the yellow police tape.

"You're sure?" Marian asked rhetorically as she rose from her desk after he told her his decision. "I'll be right back." The stair runners muffled the sound of her steps as she ran up to the second floor. He looked around the office and into the library: Marian and the volunteer sitting in the front hall were the only people in the building as far as he could tell. A cardboard box stood on the worktable; inside were bunches of old photographs, some tied with string, others held loosely in old envelopes, some wrapped in paper around which an elastic band stretched, and still others loose in clusters among the bundles. He pulled out a few loose ones and turned them over one by one. By the time Marian got back, he had the box on the floor and was sitting down, so he could examine the pictures more easily.

"I just wanted to move the paintings," Marian said. She was breathing heavily from the exertion of running up and down stairs. "They're in the main storage room now. It's much cooler in there—no sun gets in with all the shades drawn; we turn on the fans a couple of times a day if it's really bad. It's not perfect but it's the best we can do. You look like you could do with some fan time yourself." She noticed Silva was hunched over the table, barely listening to her.

"I was just taking a look at these pictures. Are they all of Mellingham?"

"Most of them are. Someone gave them to us and they're

just waiting to be cataloged. I may have to push some volunteer to get to them; they seem to be so popular."

"How do you mean?" Silva replied, putting a photograph aside with a half-dozen others.

"First Mrs. Alesander, earlier this afternoon, and now you," Marian replied. She walked over to the table and picked up a color photograph and then a black-and-white one. "Remember when color first became popular and how excited we all were?" she said. "The older I get, the more I prefer black and white. It has so much texture. Color is just lots of—I don't know—color. There's no subtlety, no arrangement of shades and textures and contrasts the way there is with black and white. It's as though the artist gave up control. It's the same with movies. The old movies show a much stronger sensual visual imagination, to me, anyway." She went on pondering the images in her head until Silva proffered her another one.

"Is this who I think it is?" he asked.

Marian took the picture. A man and a woman stood in front of a church with a young boy in front of them, their long plain coats and hats suggesting a much earlier time.

"Good heavens, yes. I do think it is. Edwin Bennett. Yes." She turned the picture over.

"Do you remember him from school?" Silva asked, unsure how old Edwin was but guessing that he and Marian were of the same general age group.

"Vaguely," she said, still staring at the photograph. "He reminds me of someone in this picture, but I just can't get it." She shook the picture between her fingers and looked up at the ceiling. "It's so irritating not to be able to think of it."

"You were in school at the same time?" Silva asked again.

"Thanks a lot, Joe," she said, only half mockingly. "We were not in the same grade. He was five or six years ahead of me. But I remember him. We only had one classroom of students for each grade back then so it was easier to know everyone." Silva waited. "I used to think how lucky he was, always going up to Mrs. Rocklynd's. That was such a grand house, still is, I suppose, for a child—all those places to hide in." She laughed. "But now—"

"But now?"

She turned her eye on him; Silva wondered if he was being evaluated as a man or a police officer. "Well, I suppose it's all right, since you'd know anyway if you'd grown up here."

Joe had the feeling of emerging from a long dark tunnel, a decade of blurry life, like a river that runs underground but isn't named and known until it rises to the surface. "This sounds interesting. You're going to have to tell me now," he said, trying to sound easier than he felt.

"Well, the older Edwin got, the closer he grew to his aunt and the less his parents seemed to like it. I can't say when it happened, but by the time he was grown, maybe after Korea, he seemed closer to Mrs. Rocklynd than his own parents. I remember seeing them once all together and Mrs. Bennett looking at Mrs. Rocklynd. She was very angry, almost contemptuous. At least, that's what I thought it looked like, but it didn't last for more than a second. It may have been my imagination. But I never forgot it. It was so unusual for anyone to challenge Mrs. Rocklynd."

"I thought that's all anyone did around here—argue," he said with a smile.

She laughed. "We do, but even Mellites have their limits. No, this was different. Catherine Rocklynd may not be the richest old gal in town but she is a Hamden, and, well, her status is important to her. She wouldn't let herself get into a position that would undermine it. I suppose you'd have to be a relative, like Mrs. Bennett, to even think of challenging her personally." She put the photograph back on the table.

"Maybe she was jealous, Mrs. Bennett, of Mrs.

Rocklynd," Silva suggested. "The Bennetts didn't exactly live on the same level."

"Could be." She gazed out the window at the silver slivers of heat. "Mrs. Bennett certainly had cause to be angry. It must be an awful thing to lose your child that way, to watch it being taken over by someone else." Marian shuddered and went back to her desk, leaving Silva to wonder what story in her own life put such feeling into the telling of Edwin's.

7

Sunday Morning

This was the Sunday Joe was going to go down the coast and visit his family, to jostle among his brothers and sisters and their kids, eat *chauriço*, and let their home-generated happiness steal over him. Unlike the sergeant, Chief Silva was not eager for every job that came along; he liked his time off. More especially, he preferred not having to confront his mother with the news that he wasn't on his way down. She did not accept a change in plans with disappointment, wheedling, or even a well-placed jab with sniffles. She wanted to know why—in detail. And then, with unassailable logic, she insisted on hearing why Joe had to stay in Mellingham if the man was already dead. He was beyond help. The Silva family would remember the dead man in their prayers before dinner—right after Joe arrived. And every time it almost worked. These phone calls were never easy for Joe or his mother.

Although he wasn't officially on duty, Sergeant Dupoulis was already waiting for Chief Silva when he came in at 6:48 in the morning, before the mist had burned off and the sun made people complain that it was too hot, just as they had complained in the winter that it was too cold. The sergeant met his chief with a cup of coffee in one hand and a sheaf of papers in the other. He was back at 7:55, after giving the chief ample time to look over his reports.

"Nothing in the apartment to help us?" Silva asked.

"Sorry, sir. You saw it yourself. There wasn't much in the place at all. The man didn't live like normal people," Dupoulis said. Silva waited; he longed to hear what Dupoulis considered normal life. "He had practically no furniture, just a sofa and a couple of chairs, a bed on a frame in the bedroom, a few books, and that's about it. In the refrigerator he had all sorts of lettuce and tomatoes and stuff like that. No meat, no eggs, no milk, no nothing. It was like the guy was starving himself." Dupoulis wrinkled his face in disgust at Frome's dietary habits.

"I heard he was a vegetarian," Silva commented. "Anyway, I agree, it was pretty spare living from the looks of it. There were two things in the refrigerator I didn't recognize. I sent them over to the lab to find out what they are." He swiveled back and forth in his chair. "I had a long talk with Edwin Bennett yesterday, about small towns and secrets. He made the comment that in a small town everyone knows all the secrets; that's one of the advantages of living in a small town. You can know everything and still have privacy. You've lived here all your life. You agree?"

Dupoulis had followed Silva's discourse with a puzzled, then pained look. "I don't know about secrets, exactly, but there are things we all know about each other that we don't talk about. I don't know. Maybe you could call them secrets, but I don't see how they're really secrets if we all know about them."

"Give me an example," Silva said. "What do you know about Walter Marsh that fits into this category?"

"The president of the Arbella Society?" Dupoulis mulled over the question. "Maybe that there was bad blood between him and his father. My dad used to say that Marsh was nothing like his old man, never got into a fight, never hit anyone, never drank. So I guess his old man was a tough drinker and his son didn't like him for it. I'm not sure that's a secret, it's just something no one brings up."

"That doesn't sound like much now, but maybe a few years ago, I don't know," Silva said, imagining the morals of a time long gone; only the shame lived on.

"Wait, he was a navy man. I think that had something to do with it," Dupoulis said, getting interested in the idea of reexamining what he knew. "Who else are you thinking about?"

"Mrs. Rocklynd?"

"Geez, these are all my father's generation or older. Let me think." He did. "My mother used to say that things might have been different if she'd liked her husband more, but I don't know what you can make out of that. You know she married late, when she was getting old? Maybe about forty?"

Silva grimaced, then admitted he hadn't known that. Others might chide him for being touchy about his age, but Sergeant Dupoulis was making himself a candidate for sensitivity training.

"She might be running out of money too," Dupoulis added. "There was a big fund-raiser for the church a while ago and she didn't give as much as people thought she would. There was a lot of talk. I remember my dad saying she couldn't be rich forever; sometime the money just ran out. My mom disagreed. It was great dinner conversation for about a month." He laughed to himself.

"What about the rest of the people in the investigation?"

Dupoulis glanced at his notes. "Annalee Windolow is a social climber, but she thinks no one notices. Her father was a janitor, or something up in Lowell." Silva nodded, recalling the woman who looked him up and down one Christmas Eve when he told her she couldn't park in a no parking zone even if she was going to donate her time at the church.

"Kelly Kuhn was part of a small partnership that went bankrupt ten or fifteen years ago; he got it all paid off,"

Dupoulis continued. "One of the creditors let it slip when I ran into him a few months ago. Let's see. Who's next?" He looked at the list. "Gwen McDuffy's family was rotten to her when she was a kid, but she ran off to get married and her parents moved out of state before anyone thought about charging them the way we do today." Silva swung around to face Dupoulis, but the sergeant was staring out the window, the better to concentrate. "Now that's something that really has changed," the sergeant said reflectively. "Her parents would have been up before a judge in record time today. But, you know, she turned out okay. She's good with those kids. Neighbors like her."

The sergeant's ramblings continued, introducing Silva to a side of Dupoulis he hadn't seen as clearly before; his casual references to Gwen's early years were another surprise, but it made sense: the abused child taught to fear the very authorities that might help her thus grows into a wary adult.

"And Edwin never did anything to get himself in a compromising situation so his secret doesn't matter." Dupoulis looked back at the chief, now that he had finished.

"Doesn't matter?"

"That he's gay. I mean today it doesn't matter at all, but it used to. And he never did anything that I ever heard of. He's the one who wants to keep it quiet. Maybe he's embarrassed." It was obvious that Dupoulis wasn't bothered by any of it; he reached for another file.

"If you're right, we're starting to come up with motives."

"Come on, Chief. No one cares about any of this. It's just the way people are. And some people in town have a lot worse to hide, believe you me."

"That's not particularly encouraging, Ken," Silva said, but he didn't feel the lightness he pretended. No chief of police wants to be told he's been missing some of the more serious crimes in his area.

"Well, I don't see any motives, sir."

"What about George Frome? Did he have any secrets?" Silva asked.

"Not that I know about. Maybe you should ask Edwin? Or maybe Marian?" Dupoulis suggested.

It was a good idea, Silva had to admit, but he doubted that anyone would pass along secrets in the middle of a murder investigation; it was far too risky. "Edwin told me that George saw everything that was donated to the society before anyone else did. It's possible he found something that gave him information that could be damaging. It's also possible he had me over there on Thursday afternoon just before the monthly meeting to frighten someone; I never got the feeling my visit with him was all out in the open even though he pretended it was. It's also possible that he did uncover some theft from inside and wasn't sure who to accuse."

"Is there any way we can track that? Someone over there who can go through what they have and see what's missing?" Dupoulis asked. It was such a reasonable question and yet it only pointed up the irrational state of the Society.

"Not likely. Edwin doesn't like to admit it, and neither does anyone else, but Frome was the only one who knew everything that was over there. Shocking, I agree," he said when Dupoulis looked more than skeptical. "I guess they've been collecting for years and they're just getting around to doing the rest of it. It's all volunteer work, so it's probably hard to keep up with everything that needs to be done. No. We have to look at the hints he left us." Silva started doodling on his notepad.

"I don't see that he's left us much," Dupoulis said, still thinking about the man's apartment.

"He has," Silva said, chuckling at his sergeant's look of disgust; he too was thinking about the apartment. "First, he thought someone was stealing from the Society. Second, he was finally getting a chance to own an old house that was a real prize. Third, he was willing to push out of the way the person or persons who had a more realistic expectation of receiving it."

"You're going too fast for me," Dupoulis complained.

"He had me over there to talk about security, which became the main topic of the board meeting that night. He didn't put it on the agenda, or tell anyone else about it, but he knew that if anyone saw me over there or heard I was there, they'd want to know why, and the best time to get an answer would be at the board meeting, just a few hours later. Okay. We know he had theft and security at Arbella House on his mind and after that meeting it was going to be on everyone else's mind too. Next, he told his lawyer that he was going to buy the log house on Mrs. Rocklynd's property."

Dupoulis whistled. "That is a big deal. It may be a dump but it's like the crown jewels."

"So for her to sell it means something. Maybe she needed the money. Or maybe he had another way of getting her to sell."

"She could be short of money, but she sure doesn't act like it. It's hard to tell with people like that. They drive around in beat-up old cars, complain about how expensive everything is and how poor they are. Then they go home and write a check for ten thousand dollars for a trip to Tibet. She doesn't drive a car anymore, but that doesn't mean anything. She doesn't spend any money on her place, except out front. I don't know. I can't figure those people out." He shook his head at generations of selective parsimony. Silva sympathized with him; his own views weren't very different.

"Nonetheless," Silva said. "We really don't know what her financial condition is."

"True. The log house is falling apart, so maybe she does need money." Dupoulis shook his head at the fall of the great ones of his town.

"There's more to this than money, though. We can be sure of that. Selling the house to Frome means that Mrs. Rocklynd was willing to cut out Edwin Bennett, her nephew, who, if what I'm told is correct, has expected to inherit everything, including the log house, when his aunt dies. And that log house would be a big part of his personal expectations, sort of a family legacy that has nothing to do with money. So if Mrs. Rocklynd was really going to sell the house to Frome, and it appears she was, then in this last week Frome has upset at least three people. The question is, who has he upset enough to kill him?"

■ ■ ■

Gwen felt like a child again whenever she confronted the steps to the Congregational church. Like all the other steps to important buildings in Mellingham, they were of granite, but that was their only similarity. Each block in front of the church seemed twice as steep as an ordinary step, made high and deep in Gwen's imagination to remind the pedestrian townspeople who climbed them how hard was the task of the soul in its climb to heaven, and how far were they as penitents from the greater lives of the preachers who met them within. Another voice, the one with the giggle, suggested that the earliest church fathers had been men of vanity, proud of their gigantic granite blocks.

The more devout perspective on the granite steps came not from a fiery minister remembered from her youth but from her mother, whose imaginings of hell were as dire and as fearful as any conjured up behind a pulpit and cast among the cowering congregants. Sitting in a pew near a side aisle, Gwen in her childhood was pulled between fear of religion, which her mother considered the appropriate emotion, and affection for the minister, who was a kindly man who believed children should hear nothing distressing in a church building. Gwen's mother was sorely disappointed in him and ceased attending services and sending her daughter to Sunday school. After a few months of this, Gwen retained enough longing for kindness to elect on her own to attend services. When her mother objected, Gwen explained to her that it would serve as an effective camouflage, although she didn't use that word, for the townspeople, who always talked if a family deviated from what was considered acceptable behavior. Gwen's mother thought that clever, her father was suspicious, and Gwen was safely out of the house at least one morning every weekend.

To the young girl and later the woman, the church was a place of low-keyed sanity. The evangelists she met in later years were the crazy cousins she knew her own family represented and she was kind to them, grateful to have the opportunity, at least once, not to be the one on the outside.

Church was also an education for her, a time for reflection and analyzing what she had learned. She sat in her aisle seat, looking over at the other congregants, in their pastel-colored outfits in the spring, and wondered how they kept themselves so well. Her mother never seemed to be able to get the spots out of her skirts, or the lint from her blouses and her knee socks, or keep the buttons on her sweaters. These tasks were too much work for her mother, and Gwen had early learned to mend her own socks and the rest of her wardrobe, such as it was. Unfortunately, she wasn't very good at it, and her mother had once looked on her mending job in horror and said, "Don't you dare let anyone think I had anything to do with that."

Her mother had her pride; Gwen understood that. She also understood that she was never to mention how her mother was dressed before she went to school or out to play (her mother never dressed before noon), or what she had for breakfast (two beers, half a dozen cigarettes, and a candy bar or cold spaghetti, whatever was easiest to reach in the refrigerator). She was particularly not to tell about how her parents fought, a memory both amorphous and protean, flowing from shape to shape in her own mind, changing of its own will. That was the best she could do to defend herself against the memory that pushed behind her eyes, blinding her to the rest of life. But she couldn't shut it all out. Her home was always filled with voices, loud ones, calling, yelling, screeching; fights made up her earliest memories, but then, when she was in first or second grade, they stopped being loud and took on a different form. The voices were intense, hissing, and sometimes, late at night, the saliva from his mouth sprayed her ear as she awoke with a gasp and a whimper and the discord changed shape yet again. After that she grew adept in other ways—finding other places to be, other families to visit. She picked her friends according to their suggestibility, and succeeded in being invited for more overnights than anyone else in her class. She went to every church function, volunteered for every program; she even thought about joining a second church, to give herself more activities, other places to go. But in the end she decided not to; she thought it might look suspicious, to her parents if no one else.

Coming back to Mellingham had meant remembering all that she wanted to forget but it had also meant the comfort of familiar places she hadn't known since she'd left. It had been the distinct parts of her old hometown that had drawn her back, seeking a place of refuge for herself and her children.

Jennie jumped from step to step, feet together, until she reached the walkway, then turned around with a hand on her hip to disparage her younger brother's slower descent. Over the last few days she had swung back and forth between her ages, swinging her hips in mimicry of television heroines and older girls, racing her brother across the sand to the waves, standing composed while Philip argued with his mother. Gwen offered Philip her hand but he pushed away from her to grab the black wrought-iron railing, leaving room for the other parishioners to pass beside him; he assiduously avoided looking at his sister as they made their way to the car, parked just in front of the police station. A patrolman stopped a row of cars coming out from the dirt parking lot by the harbor to let Gwen and the children cross; when she had settled the kids in the backseat, he let the traffic take care of itself and met her in front of the car.

"Chief Silva would like to stop by later today, Ms. McDuffy, if that's all right. Will you be home?" The policeman was polite but there was no mistaking the imperative beneath the courtesy. Gwen nodded; he held the car door for her.

"Did he ask you about the murder, Mom?" Philip asked as soon as they pulled away from the station and the patrolman directing traffic. "Did he? What'd he want?" Still too young to control his excitement, he poured out his questions, too eager to absorb an answer even if he could have stopped himself long enough to listen.

"Were you there, Mom?" Jennie asked, leaning forward and grabbing her mother's seat from the back.

"Now, settle down you two." She put their questions out of her mind as she negotiated a left-hand turn. "I wasn't there when Mr. Frome died. And I wasn't there when they found him."

"Mrs. Davis found him," Philip said knowingly.

"We know that," Jennie said with disdain. "Do you know who the murderer is?"

"Do you, Mom?" Philip asked, suddenly seeing his mother in a glamorous light he had hitherto reserved for television stars.

"Of course, I don't," Gwen said, feeling the conversation was getting away from her. Philip sank back in his seat.

"Well, what does he want?" Jennie asked. Gwen recognized the streak of persistence in her daughter and on bad days feared what it could lead to; on good days she had only dreams of greatness for her Jennie.

"He probably just wants to find out if I know something about Mr. Frome that might help," Gwen explained.

"Do you?" Jennie persisted.

Her daughter's question went round and round in her head. Do I know that he was an underhanded, cowardly false friend who wanted to hurt people just because he was so unhappy he couldn't leave people alone to savor the little joy they have in their lives? But this she couldn't say to Jennie, or anyone else; she could only give another form of the truth.

"I don't know anything that could help Chief Silva, but he has to talk to everyone who was there on Thursday, and that includes me." She drove into the driveway of the double decker and around to the back, parking in the two-car garage. The backyard fell away into an old canal that wandered down to the harbor, passing under Main Street by the police station. In the summer Gwen sat on the back porch and watched the birds in the evening; in the winter she watched the neighbors skate. When they had first moved in, she had feared Jennie and Philip would tumble down the gentle slope and fall in and drown; later she feared the walk to school; then she feared the bike ride up the hill to the beach. Her return to Mellingham seemed to be a drawing away of veils of fear, each one revealing another, each thinner and more porous than the one before until she knew the last one would dissolve into sunlight and a smile. Perhaps facing Chief Silva was the last one. If it was, then she would face it. But she very badly didn't want to botch it.

■ ■ ■

Mrs. William Hamden Rocklynd, Catherine to her friends, might have been amused to learn how Gwen McDuffy regarded the Congregational church on the village green if she could have been persuaded to listen at all, for it would not have occurred to her that someone might have held a thoroughly different view of her Sunday morning ritual.

Catherine Rocklynd took pride in a pew that she had occupied—except for a brief period—since she was old enough to be carried to church services by her parents; her mother had felt the same way. Only four rows from the pulpit, the pew had received Mrs. Rocklynd's grandmother's embroidered cushions, then her mother's more modern ones, and finally her own corded rubber cushion fitting the full length of a quarter pew. The pillow covering was gold, to match the embroidery on the altar cloth, and reupholstered every few years. This was her place and she could reach it with her eyes closed. No one else had ever dared to usurp it, not for three generations and more.

None of this seemed to help her this morning. She rested her hands on the pewter top of her walking stick, standing straight against her legs, raised her head to attend to the minister, and ignored the throbbing pain in her left leg. It was a new pain, not more than two or three days old, unanticipated and thus all the more irritating. Never one to give in to weakness, she had ignored the erratic reminder of her own frailty and gone on about her affairs, running meetings, researching her family history, entertaining guests (such as they were), and attending church. With only one exception, long ago, she had never missed services. It was her place to set an example, a concept that she knew held less and less sway over others as the years passed, but it was part of her identity now, part of her definition of who she was. She couldn't understand people who thought everyone occupied the same station in life and moved around as a matter of choice.

George Frome had understood what it meant to have a place in one's community that was worth preserving; he had had one—in a manner of speaking—of his own for many years. Mrs. Rocklynd did not like to think of herself as a snob; she simply saw no reason to know some people just because she lived in a democracy. Unlike those who rambled from town to town, squandering their puny savings in the expenses of moving and setting up a new home every other year, and then creating friendships that were eminently dissolvable, Catherine believed in people staying put, building up the life they were born to, twining their roots deep among the boulders in the rocky soil of New England. George had spent virtually his entire life here; there was that in his favor, but not much else.

She regretted his death. It made life in Mellingham messy and at Arbella House, complicated. The sudden interest of tourists, and some residents, it should be admitted, had reduced the regular visitors, the members who came in to work or help out. Mrs. Rocklynd was one of them. She had no interest in fending off morbid curiosity-seekers who would invariably switch their interest to her work if thwarted in their gossiping about George. The library was, for her these last few days, unhappily out of reach, a place she wanted to get to but couldn't. It was an unusual feeling for the elderly woman, who was used to getting her own way at all times just by saying what it was. It had always been that way, except maybe once.

The minister moved down from the pulpit at the end of the service to bless the congregation and enter into dialogue with the congregants. The change in the form of the end of the service some years ago had unsettled Catherine, taking a constant—ministers delivering a blessing at the back of the church—and turning it into something less predictable. Now she never knew what he was going to say, though she calmed herself by remembering that he never said anything important. At least not to her. He mentioned parishioners who were sick, returned from a trip, in difficulty. People who were visiting in town and new members were invited to introduce themselves. It was his way of making a community of people who might not see each other for the rest of the week. Then he paused and Catherine knew what was coming next.

"We have had a great tragedy among us this week," he said. "One of our own members has met an untimely death." Behind her came a soft breeze of murmurings of acknowledgment. This was the only part of her position that Catherine didn't like—firmly fixed at the front of everything, she couldn't see what was going on behind her. She could turn around to look, but that was forbidden on principle. A Hamden, which is what she still considered herself despite her marriage, never looked back. So she braced herself not to know who was concurring and who was not, who was gathering up wiggling children and toys in order to depart, and who was fixed on the minister's words.

"Some of you may want to talk about it," he went on saying in a soothing voice. Again, there were murmurs, but not from Catherine. It had long been her opinion that people did far too much talking about such things. After all, George Frome wasn't a great friend of anyone here at the church, unless there was someone from the Arbella Society she didn't know about sitting behind her. She doubted it.

"I'm having an open afternoon tomorrow for just this purpose. Violent death is a tragedy for us all." He smiled sympathetically at the congregation, ending with Catherine. It made her uneasy. She liked her religion impersonal.

■ ■ ■

The last cyclist wheeled out of the driveway and onto Main Street, heading out of Mellingham for what Annalee knew would be a daylong ride. Winston spent as many Sundays as he could riding around the North Shore and southern New Hampshire with his bike club and Annalee was just as glad. When they were first engaged Winnie wanted them to do everything together, along with their parents. At first Annalee had been horrified, and then amused to find that his mother felt the same way. Now attuned to the family style, Annalee explained that her family couldn't possibly join in on weekend excursions because of her father's job. Always on the go all day long, he was never in one place long enough to be reached by telephone. And it was even worse on the weekends. When Winnie's interest moved to Annalee's mother, she raised equally compelling objections, and in time he let the matter drop. A quiet marriage in Bermuda (not quite an elopement, but close enough) avoided an awkward encounter and thereafter Winnie periodically commiserated with his wife on her parents' constant unavailability. He still didn't know precisely what his wife's father did for a living but had given up asking. Annalee knew he would. He didn't care to make extraordinary efforts where outsiders were concerned.

Annalee was not ignorant of what others in Mellingham said about her, having once overheard a group of her friends jealously reviewing her unsuspected capture of the chairmanship of a fund-raising committee; Annalee resigned as soon as she heard how large a donation she was expected to make. The rest of it didn't matter to her, for she had in fact said nothing untrue about her family. Her father was always on the go; how Winnie and her in-laws interpreted that was up to them. The only thing that mattered to her was that she be treated as a Windolow deserved; jealous or not, her friends complied. She might be enjoying her position in Mellingham right now, lounging by a friend's pool or playing tennis before lunch at a private club, if it weren't for Chief Silva.

Doing one's duty had always been a pleasure for Annalee; she was the first to volunteer for certain committees and to offer advice, but spending an hour with the chief of police about a man already dead, even if he was murdered, was a bore, hardly an effort that would benefit anyone she knew. But Chief Silva wouldn't take no for an answer, and Annalee ultimately agreed to meet him on Sunday morning. When she saw him turn into the driveway and climb the hill to the house right after Winnie rode away in the opposite direction, she thought he must have been watching and waiting, not a pleasant thought. After she showed Silva to a sofa in the living room, he gave no word of gratitude for her willingness to see him at this unusual hour for business; she thought him rude and uncouth.

If Silva divined any of Annalee's attitude, he gave no sign. He knew what her father did for a living even if her husband didn't, and was disgusted with her for not being mature enough to take pride in having a father who still did something with his hands instead of sliding money from one box to another. Her promise to answer questions to the best of her ability was perfunctory.

"Friday morning? Let's see. Why was I down there at Arbella House Friday morning?" Annalee frowned at the question, but Silva forbore from helping her recall the day. "That's when George died. I remember. The Arbella House. Right. Well, he was going to give me a few lessons in how to recognize a good painting, so I wouldn't make any huge blunders now that I'm doing some buying of my own."

"Is this something new? Lessons from Mr. Frome and collecting?" Silva asked.

"Oh no. Certainly not." She had the thick black hair that made him think of his sisters and their friends, but it was deceptive. She was as unlike his relatives as the Antarctic

was from the Sahara. "George showed me a few things a little while ago, what was valuable and why. That sort of
thing. It wouldn't interest you." She was taking a dislike to
Chief Silva with his easy looks and obvious ignorance of the
proper moments to be impressed. He was disconcertingly
unresponsive to some of her comments; it was obvious he
didn't mean to get ahead with the right sort in Mellingham.

"Early American paintings?" Silva asked.

Annalee's eyebrows went up. "Possibly. Why do you
ask?"

"You seem to have acquired one already," he went on,
ignoring her question and nodding at the wall.

"Yes, I have. Kelly Kuhn usually buys for me or searches
for the kind of thing I'm looking for, and he came across
some Early American paintings that he really thinks are just
right for me. He has a good eye. I don't think Winnie, my
husband, cares all that much."

"It's a little different from what you have," Silva said,
knowing he was taking a risk in venturing an opinion about
home furnishings, where his ignorance was almost total.

"Well, a little," Annalee said, squirming in her seat. She
wasn't sure how much Silva knew about American art and
she didn't want to reveal her limited knowledge. "Actually,
Kelly's been directing me. I generally buy whatever he sug-
gests. He thinks a few colonial portraits might work out
very well. Winnie and I are going to completely redecorate.
The place is such a hodgepodge right now. Everything's
going and then we'll keep only what is right."

"This was Mr. Kuhn's idea?" Silva asked.

Annalee twisted in her seat, wanting to say yes, but not
daring to go quite that far. Even she had her principles.
"He's really encouraged me to go into Early American
paintings. They're such a complement to a house like this."
She waved her hand at the large room. "At first I wasn't sure
what I wanted to do but when I looked at modern stuff,

Kelly got positively rabid. So I looked at earlier stuff and he seemed happier and more interested. Well, anyway, he seemed to want me to go with the Early American stuff, and I can see his point. It does suit the house." She looked around at the denticulated molding, the fluted window casings, and the parquet flooring. Silva held his tongue.

"How long have you been working with Mr. Kuhn and Mr. Frome?" he asked.

"Kelly's been helping Winnie for years but it's only been in the last few months that I've gotten George Frome to help me. Usually I could just ask him something when I'm at Arbella House and he would tell me what this was or what that meant."

"Is that why you were there on Friday morning?" Annalee could wander the byways of her redecorating woes for hours if he let her, but by now he had a pretty good idea of what she knew, and he wanted a few more specifics.

"Well, yes. I was supposed to meet him about ten o'clock and he was going to show me something about still lifes, I think it was. He was really quite remarkable. He had a great memory for the entire collection, although I think people were just beginning to appreciate that. I don't know what they'll do without him now."

"We found five paintings in the attic when we found Mr. Frome," Silva said.

"No!" said Annalee in her best indignant voice. "What do you think he was doing?"

"That is what we're trying to figure out. Did he say anything to you about any special business at Arbella House?"

"Not to me. But then he wouldn't. I know what I like but I am just learning, after all." She rose when he did and followed him to the doorway into the hall. At the last minute Silva turned back to look at a group of pictures sitting on the floor against the wall. "Are these some of the pictures you're removing to make way for new ones?" He picked up the top canvas and held it up, leaning the bottom against his leg.

"I got that just yesterday from Kelly. It was very expensive, but worth it." She drew closer to him and reached out to take the painting from him. "If there's anything else, Chief?"

Silva reached down to pick up the next canvas, which had been hidden behind the one Annalee was now holding. "This is the same sort. Is that right?" he said, lifting it up. "This kind of work is interesting, but it's all new to me. I'm even more ignorant than you are, Mrs. Windolow."

She smiled uncertainly, then preened a bit. "Oh well, in that case, yes. This is probably 1760s, from what I was told. The artist isn't very well known but at least he's known." She went on to describe the general area of the artist's work as Silva examined the painting, then swung it back to its spot along the wall, running his fingers along the rough and smooth spots on the stretchers and frame. He almost swore as a splinter drove into the flesh of his index finger.

Annalee gave him her best hostess smile when she showed him through the front door, nodding and waving as though she were a product of the 1950s, instead of the 1990s. It was all part of her image of the socially prominent woman.

■ ■ ■

On Sunday mornings Edwin Bennett liked to indulge his curiosity about unimportant things. As a child on his way to Sunday school he was delayed by a study of how ants cross a driveway; as a teenager he once disassembled his mother's favorite reading lamp. Later he practiced balancing half a dozen plates on his arms as though he were a waiter; it had taken him six months to earn enough money doing odd jobs to replace the plates that had fallen, reeling and rolling into the walls. His mother was furious but he had at least learned something that had tantalized him for years. And he never forgot it. With his beaten-up straw hat on his head, frayed Top-Siders on his feet, and khaki shorts, he carried small flats of flowers and plastic pots on his arms as he made his way from his car to Aunt Catherine's front garden.

Instead of ringing the doorbell when he arrived just before noon, Edwin honked the horn, feeling a bit racy as he did so, and went directly to the plants in the trunk of his car. Confined to a relatively small yard, he appreciated the bolder effects his aunt could achieve with her several acres; it pained him that she never experimented with anything more dramatic than the simple but lush borders she had tended for years.

After his parents died and he found himself living alone, his friends urged him to buy a dog or a cat, or even a bird, something alive so that he wasn't alone with only furniture and clocks and television to remind him of the larger world beyond the front door. He understood their reasoning and their motives. Finally, he admitted the need to feel more of life coursing through his shrunken world; so he was moved to garden. He planted eggplant along the short walk to the house, chamomile in the upstairs window boxes, squash by the driveway, holding up the pale orange vegetables in his mother's old nylon stockings tied to a trellis. He planted vegetables and fruits everywhere, and his neighbors began to take an interest in the man next door. He ceased to be Mrs. Bennett's boy and became Mr. Edwin Bennett, the man who had such original ideas about vegetable gardening. The new interest in him was a revelation and he set up a work area in the cellar, growing so much from seed that he had to give plants away to strangers. During some summer months he supplied the Harbor Light restaurant with all its tomatoes. When he tried to get Aunt Catherine interested in new plants, new arrangements, new garden configurations, she was amused but no more than that, and told him he could help her keep up her traditional borders as often as he liked. In a sense it was high praise.

Edwin deposited a flat of blue pansies, which he had grown from seed and was determined to plant despite his aunt's disdain for the surprisingly hardy perennial that was still being sold as an annual; beside the pansies he set two monkshood, two larkspur, two lupine (all blue), and two foxglove (white). Some had come from his own garden, repotted for the trip across town in case he was distracted into a long conversation; some he had purchased on sale from the local greenhouse, since their best period was now past. Edwin didn't care; he planted and tended for the future, willing to wait a year or two for a plant to get established before it gave its best blooms. His aunt was far less patient, wanting blooms right away. Sometimes he thought her impatience increased with her age, an uncontrollable challenge to what time was telling her. He knew she resented not being able to move around in her garden as freely as she always had; though she still gardened every week, she could do less and less without feeling the consequences in her legs and shoulders for days afterward. The flowering plants were for her.

The pots were spread along the ground as Edwin walked back and forth along the blue border considering each open spot as a site for one of his plants. The heavy morning traffic to church and the beach was thinning out for the lunch hour; Mellingham was suspended in an expectant stillness. To his right and up on the rocky hill Edwin could see a woman he assumed to be Annalee Windolow sitting on a terrace with a newspaper propped up in her lap. Such a view wouldn't last long, he knew; since she and her husband bought the old stone home they had let the shrubbery and brambles grow up until the thickets threatened to block any view from a nearby home, which was their intent, of course.

After twenty minutes of strolling, standing, staring, waving to friends driving by, and strolling some more, he was ready to position the plants. Putting the foxglove aside, he set the lupine, larkspur, and monkshood along the stone wall, about three feet apart. Each was placed to fill in a dead spot. Edwin began digging, working over the soil with lime and fertilizer. Behind him grew a pile of twigs, rocks, weeds, dead roots, plastic cups, and dying plants. Edwin liked his garden neat.

He worked over the soil for almost an hour before he was ready. He planted each flower in turn, trying to replicate the mornings earlier in the month when the garden had been at its best, the textures and shapes of the leaves adding a quality of complexity that would have been obscured by a showier display of colors. When he was finished with the blue border, he planted the foxglove in the white border, then aerated both gardens thoroughly, losing himself in the rhythmic motion as he worked the hoe among the plants.

Satisfied that he had done all that needed to be done, he gathered up his tools and stored them in the trunk of his car. The lime and fertilizer went next, and finally a newspaper folded around all the weeds and trash collected from the garden. He slammed the trunk shut.

"Edwin, is that you?" Aunt Catherine came around the side of the house leaning on her cane after Edwin had pulled a shirt from the backseat and slammed the door. "Just get here, did you?"

"Lord, no. I've been here for hours, fixing up the front garden." He put on the shirt. "Well, maybe not hours." He grinned at her.

"I didn't hear you."

"I honked." He was still pleased with what seemed rakish behavior. Mrs. Rocklynd strained to see the front garden. "New larkspur, new lupine, new monkshood. And pansies." He turned to her with a mischievous smile. "And foxglove, of course. Over there." He waved at the white border. "All planted and cleaned up."

Mrs. Rocklynd was nonplussed that all this had gone on without her knowing, while she sat peaceably on the terrace reading the newspaper and waiting for lunch. "It's almost two o'clock. Aren't you going to stay to lunch?" she asked, looking skeptically at his outfit.

"Why not? As long as you don't mind." He brushed some dirt from his knees. "You're eating outside, aren't you? And I feel great, just great. Time to go casual. Time to let myself go." He patted the hat on his head and stepped up to take her arm. Mrs. Rocklynd gave one last look at the garden and turned back to the terrace.

"You didn't tell me you were going to do all that," she said. "I didn't need that much work done. It's not as though I'd lost half my plants."

"I didn't say you had." He felt so cheery that he didn't notice the petulant tone in her voice. "But I had a bunch of plants that I thought would look good there, just what your garden needed, so I brought them over."

"You didn't go pulling anything up, did you?" she asked, not at all sure if she liked her nephew in such an exuberant mood. He pulled out a chair for her at the table, then when she was seated, went in to wash up. "I don't like my garden being rearranged," she said when he had returned and sat down opposite her.

"I didn't rearrange anything, Aunt. I just filled in a few gaps." He adjusted the yellow-and-white striped umbrella so that a larger shadow fell over her. "Plants do die off after a while. How'd you like the pansies?"

"You know how I feel about them," she grumbled. "Here, try this." She pushed a bowl of salad at him; he served himself. "There wasn't anything dead out there that I could see."

"This is excellent, Aunt, excellent. No, not too much had

gone, just one or two. But it does look good if I do say so myself. It really does."

"Well, don't leave anything around. I suppose I'll have to go out and make sure it's all clean. Be sure you put everything into the mulch pile. I don't want a mess." She pulled the salad bowl back to her side of the table.

"Don't worry, Aunt. I've cleaned it all up, including all that trash people throw out. You'll never see any of it again." He shook the bottle of salad dressing like a maraca, humming to the rhythm in his head.

8

Sunday Afternoon

Gwen McDuffy was not a coward. She knew the difference between doing what satisfied public policy, convention, abstract regulations, and doing what she knew in her heart was right. Not so long ago she had stood on a sidewalk in front of a courthouse only a few feet from legal absolution, from a freedom no one would challenge or question or impugn, and walked away. No one could have faulted her if she had followed convention and anyone might fault her now for holding herself to a higher standard. She was not a coward, but she knew what it meant to live in fear.

"But I don't want to—" Philip clenched his fists and leaned forward, his eyes shut tight as he squeezed out his complaint.

"Where's my Walkman?" Jennie marched into the living room with a pout on her face.

"I don't know. Look under your bed," Gwen said to her daughter before turning to Philip. "You have to just for a while, while Chief Silva is here. Then we're going to the beach and we'll have an early supper there."

"If we can get it," Jennie mumbled.

Gwen huffed in exasperation, then turned Philip around and hustled them both out the back door. She had come painfully close to losing it. In the yard below, Philip threw himself into a lawn chair, seething at this disruption of his

Sunday plans. Gwen knew exactly how he felt and was a bit ashamed of it; if she couldn't fend off superficial anger she should hardly be surprised if it showed up in her children. A problem for another time, she told herself as she rushed back inside to straighten up the living room before Chief Silva arrived. She had promised the children lunch at the beach right after church, but the patrolman's request that Silva speak with her today had changed all that. Now she hoped they'd get away by midafternoon.

She gathered up a pile of books and other toys and bundled them off to Philip's bedroom. The children should be doing this, she thought, but knew it would take too long to supervise them. Philip had entered a slow-motion stage and there was no way of knowing how long he intended to remain there. It frustrated her but she held her tongue; it was going to be worse when they were both teenagers, which wasn't all that far off. The slamming of a car door out front announced Chief Silva; Gwen froze.

She had never cared very much about the value of her property, about owning the newest television set, the trendiest sneakers, the fanciest bicycle, which was just as well, since her family could not afford to give her such things. She had cared about something else, about what other people took for granted, a home in which everything was clean even if only once in a while. Her childhood had left her with so many memories of dirty sheets, unwashed dishes, crud-encrusted kitchen floors that she vowed that her children would never be dirty or ashamed of their home. Her daughter would never wear safety pins in her underwear while her mother tried on a new dress; her son would never get a black eye fighting boys who laughed at the stains on his shirt. She had kept her vow, every day sending Jennie and Philip into the world in crisp, clean clothes, and often feeding them and their friends lunch or a snack in a tiny spotless kitchen. Jennie and Philip took their mother's care for granted, sometimes whining that they weren't allowed to dress in casual, well-crafted rags, but Gwen never took anything for granted. Each day it was a new pleasure to see them looking so perfect; her feelings hadn't quite caught up with the reality of her life.

Chief Silva's impending visit was bringing back the old fear of being ashamed of her home, blinding her to the new world she lived in. She still worried that other people might be pointing to her, talking about her. If she could hear what they were saying about her, she would have been embarrassed, but pleasurably so. Gwen McDuffy was the mother first brought to mind when social service workers wanted to remind someone on the other side politically that not all poor people kept slovenly homes. More than a few civic-minded women had been brought up short when a regular rotation of their committee meeting deposited them at Gwen's modest apartment, where they discovered that her sparsely furnished home was better kept and showed more attention to small, insignificant details than their own homes. They would not have recognized the quality of desperation in Gwen's housekeeping.

Nor would Joe Silva, but he felt at home as soon as Gwen showed him in. The neglect and lack of care in George Frome's home had disgusted him and brought out his less generous qualities. He had never thought of himself as a fastidious man but he disliked homes in which no one seemed to care enough to keep the place clean. He was a man of unshakable sanity, as his sister-in-law once said, but from her it didn't sound entirely like a compliment. She had also told him he was a sexist to place so much importance on housekeeping; since then he thought she might be right, but that didn't change how he felt. He liked a clean home.

"Nice apartment," Silva said as he took a seat on the worn green sofa. The large living room was sparsely furnished, with daisies in a vase on a coffee table and an arrangement of toy soldiers on the mantelpiece. "I didn't get around to asking you a few questions I meant to ask on Friday evening. I hope you don't mind losing some of the sun today."

"No. It's just as well that I stay out of it. I burn. But the kids are anxious to get to the beach. I'm taking them later." She looked down at her twisting hands. "I guess I'm nervous."

"Everybody is at first. There's nothing to worry about. I just wanted to get Thursday afternoon clear in my mind. Marian has told me most of what I need to know." The words came out of his mouth on their own while his mind was wondering why she was so nervous, why the kids were relegated to the backyard, why he couldn't treat her like anyone else who happened to be at Arbella House that day.

"Thursday. That's my regular afternoon over at the Arbella House. I usually have a sandwich at home and then go right over. In the summer Mrs. Alesander is here if the kids aren't in one of the summer programs." She paused to take a deep breath. "She was here on Thursday. Anyway, I was there all afternoon. I worked until about four-thirty."

Silva made a show of writing. There was something wrong in all this—her nervousness, her low-key recital, her lack of curiosity about the murder. She was lying about something. "Mrs. Davis said you were there at the worktable all afternoon, never leaving the office."

"That's right." Gwen nodded and pushed a thick curl back from her face.

"She was out of the room for a while, wasn't she?"

Gwen's face relaxed as she tried to recall the meaningless events of a weekday afternoon. "I guess so. Just about the time you and George came in. I think she left to answer the front door because George didn't. He was in the library with you. She went out one door and you and George came in the other." She looked at him expectantly, ready for the next question.

"It sounds like you never get any privacy while you're working."

Gwen laughed, more relaxed. "I don't go there for privacy. I go there for sanity. The solitude and camaraderie are wonderful. There's always someone to talk to if you want to but you don't have to. You can just work." They smiled at each other and Gwen blushed, wishing she didn't feel so foolish. She sometimes thought her heart was trapped in late adolescence, making her feel silly when she wanted to be taken seriously. She tried to pretend it was nerves.

"And last Thursday was typical? You were never alone?" Silva tried to sound casual but Gwen looked at him intently.

"I see. Yes, except for the two or three seconds after Marian left and George came in, I was never alone in the room. That's what you wanted to know, isn't it?" She was growing suspicious now, seeing his earlier friendliness as a calculated role designed to reduce her defensiveness.

"I have to know everything that happened on Thursday so I'll probably ask questions that sound trivial."

"Of course." Gwen slid behind her office persona and Joe noticed.

"What about Mrs. Davis?" he asked. "How many times did she leave the office?"

"While you were there and earlier while the UPS man was there for a pickup. She had to answer the door. It was only a minute or so."

"Out into the hallway and—"

"No. Through the library." Her eyes were on the floor now as she tried to remember the details, and Silva was tempted to call back her attention. Whatever else she remembered didn't matter. Gwen had just put Marian too far away from the kitchen to take any action.

"No one else has mentioned the UPS man before," Silva said.

"He comes and goes so regularly that we probably don't

think of him as noticeable. Poor man." She briefly recovered her sense of humor and Joe felt an unprofessional tug.

"You didn't like him very much, did you?" Silva asked. "George Frome," he clarified when Gwen looked perplexed.

"No." She wanted to show the proper feeling—whatever it was—for him; he had, after all, been murdered, but her insides were a confused mess, anxiety trampling sorrow, anger suffocating curiosity. "I should have learned to prevaricate better but I can't seem to get it right these days. No, I didn't like him at the end."

"Any particular reason?" Silva watched her struggling over whether or not she would tell him.

"He insinuated things," she said.

"What kinds of things?"

"Oh, just things. Nothing major. Just things."

"Give me an example," Silva urged her.

"I'd rather not. It's all so petty. It was just George. Most of the time he was all right."

"I'll keep that in mind but I would like to know what kinds of things he said. It might help me when other people talk about him to understand what he was like. It's not gossip and I appreciate your reluctance to talk about him. You think he was what?"

"I suppose it depends on how you feel about things," she said enigmatically. "All right. An example. He liked to make fun of Edwin. Mr. Bennett?" Silva nodded. "You know he's gay. Well, it's like a public secret; no one ever mentions it, but George sometimes acted like a jerk. Sort of mimicking and giggling. It was embarrassing and stupid. And irritating."

This was a side of Frome Silva had not encountered before, and he wondered how many other people had seen it. "Did anyone ever confront him about his behavior? Tell him to stop?"

"Most of us just cut him off and went on talking about something else. If he hadn't done so much work at Arbella House he might have been asked not to show up so much. But except for that childishness, he was all right." Gwen leaned back and crossed her arms over her lap.

"Were you there when Annalee Windolow arrived?"

"No. I saw her coming and that's when I decided to leave. We all know Annalee. I'm being catty. God, this thing is bringing out the worst in me." She shook her head as though that would break a spell. "I knew when I saw her coming that she would have Marian tied up and that it must be almost closing time. Annalee has her habits."

"Who else was around then?"

"No one. George had gone off to get something to drink. I'm sorry I didn't offer you anything." The mention of George's last errand reminded her of her lapse, but Silva declined her offer.

"So you just went out the front?"

"No. The back, through the kitchen." A light breeze tickled the back of her neck, making her smile. This interview business was much easier than she'd expected. She almost felt sorry for Chief Silva, who seemed to think he had to get more serious as the interview progressed, which was just the opposite of how she felt.

■ ■ ■

The black cat lifted its paw and stood poised on the edge of the garden before it leaned into the thicket of flowers, alert, cautious, silent. Mrs. Rocklynd swung her stick into the palmed lobate leaves, scaring the cat into a leap sideways and flushing out a female cardinal. The bird now gone, the cat swung its head back and forth, eyed Mrs. Rocklynd, then stepped majestically across the lawn. Mrs. Rocklynd turned back to the border, admiring Edwin's additions. Late moves in a garden do not bother some plants, whereas others shrivel and die if they are taken from the place they have grown accustomed to.

Every few steps Mrs. Rocklynd lifted a cluster of leaves to check the soil beneath, sometimes prodding with her cane, sometimes smoothing over roughly dug soil. The pinched-off deadheads from the bell flowers and balloon flowers were gone instead of being left to mulch. Other than that, Edwin had left the garden exactly as she might have—the ground aerated and well turned, dead leaves cut off, and the larger balloon flowers staked. It was just as he had promised—as nearly like the arrangement of the spring as anyone could possibly make it.

Catherine Rocklynd moved on to the white garden, glad to see that Edwin hadn't planted any pansies here. His behavior this morning troubled her, not just his lighthearted insistence that the garden be repaired but that he do it right away instead of waiting to see if any of the ailing plants showed signs of recovery. It wasn't like him to be so single-minded in her garden. He usually showed her such respect, such deference when he proposed working on her property, but today he had breezed over and gone to work before she even knew he was here. She probably couldn't have stopped him if she'd wanted to.

It was a new feeling, this sense that someone might affect her life in a way not anticipated. Edwin had always been so respectful, so conscientious in soliciting her views and wishes and then in carrying them out. Even after forty years of working in her yard he had never presumed what she might like, never undertaken any change without first seeking her approval. The idea of independent action was foreign to Edwin; at least that's how it seemed to Mrs. Rocklynd.

The change manifested in her nephew was not a welcome one; it put him beyond her understanding because it put him beyond her control, and she wasn't used to that. Moreover, this new behavior was so unlike Edwin. She had never thought of him as docile—his ways of doing things had always seemed to be genuinely in accord with hers— but this morning he was different, separate, moving in a sphere she could not enter, though he seemed to have no sense of the change himself.

His unexpected behavior was so dismaying that she sat at the lunch table long after he'd left pondering the events of the last several days in an attempt to identify the catalyst. All she got was a headache and the urge to walk along the front borders and reassure herself they were all right. She could see the changes, of course. A committed gardener knows if a plant has been moved, trimmed, or somehow altered even if others can't, and Mrs. Rocklynd could see the changes wrought by Edwin. No one else might be able to but she certainly could, and the whole thing made her uneasy. Edwin acting without consulting her undermined the stability of her world.

The church clock struck in the distance, with uncanny timing, reminding her of a nearly healed wound. Twenty years ago no one at the church would have dreamed of starting a fund-raising drive without seeking her out first, but now—Well, now, all sorts of people were jumping onto committees, people who had no sense of history, of place, of respect. It rankled. She couldn't bear the thought of handing over a check to them, and so she hadn't. She turned away from the sound of the chimes and headed to the walk leading to the back of the house.

Between the branches, waving like fans in front of royalty promenading to a throne, she limped on toward the old log house. It had never before held such prominence in her life and she now realized she had been taking it for granted, assuming it would endure until she got around to repairing it, never falling into such serious disrepair as to be unworthy of the ensuing effort at restoration. That had been a mistake. It drew the attention of others. George Frome was only the most aggressive of them; he had even suggested that she didn't truly care about the log house. He was so persuasive that for a while his plans seemed sensible. But it couldn't last. The house, with its split rails and thick muddy plaster, was too much a part of her family history and the history of Mellingham. Such a house could not be sold, not really, no matter how much the buyer promised to do. Such a house could only have one owner, only the people who knew what it represented. She had been foolish to think she could actually sell it, even to George Frome, who had proved his value to the town.

But now that George was gone and Edwin was acting so peculiar, she began to wonder what would happen in the coming years. Her time was limited. Even though she might have another decade or more, eventually someone else would own the log house, and as it stood before her now, it hardly seemed to count for much. Here was a dwelling more closely linked with her roots than anything else she owned, and she had never looked at it closely, noticed the rotting nails in broken clapboards, the sagging lintel over the door. For a second she was repulsed by this pathetic, dilapidated pile, outraged at her ancestors for carting with them this shameful beginning century after century, until she alone was burdened with it.

She pushed at the wooden door, woven into the tall grass though still on its hinges; a sudden scratching and rustling in the dark house answered her, driving away her sacrilegious thoughts. The place must be full of animals, she realized; raccoons, woodchucks, and field mice would love it. The thought of the amount of damage these animals might be doing to the interior was the last nudge she needed and she turned back to the main house determined now, this summer, to begin the renovations she had thought about idly for years. If she had to live with this hovel, she would make it an enviable one.

George had mentioned an architect who specialized in such projects when he had first approached her; he was certainly right that the age and construction of the house called for special skills. That was one point that had made the prospect of the sale palatable, brief though it was—George appreciated the value of the property he was buying. His ideas were detailed too, a sign he had spent a good deal of time thinking about the log house; some of them had captured her own imagination. The restoration project took shape in her own mind now; sample budgets, a schedule of the work, and a finished, fully decorated interior damped down the dying embers of a dream of destruction. She passed through the french doors to the living room and made her way to the kitchen and a cold drink. It would be a pleasure to have a new project to occupy her time, one that would also take her mind off Edwin Bennett.

■ ■ ■

For more than fifty years a woman, beginning in girlhood, is expected to be conscious of her appearance; many women comply intentionally or not, and almost all those throw away the mantle of concern about their looks sometime in the long span of years that is middle age. The reasons vary but the results are similar—a relaxation in personality and a corresponding slackening of requirements in apparel. Marian Davis took a hard look at herself one Tuesday morning several years ago when menopause came upon her, and decided that her age had finally caught up with her body. The thick ankles and spindly legs that had thwarted her attempts at appearing attractively attired in anything but long pants now seemed designed specifically for her new age. She threw away half of her long baggy slacks, pulled out the skirts that made her look like an umbrella resting on two buckets, and stopped dying her hair. It was a relief. Gordon, her husband, hardly noticed.

"Letting your hair grow, dear?" he said one morning after Marian had made changes extravagant enough to draw worried comments from her friends.

The next thing he noticed, just before they were all worn out and ready to be thrown away, were her first pair of khaki shorts, which she insisted on wearing with one of his striped jerseys. After that she took to wearing old rubber boots in the garden while she weeded and watered. Gone were her neat blue sneakers and denim slacks, the button-down blouses in pastels. On her head was a wide-brimmed hat that reminded her husband of one his mother wore to church when he was a boy. This was how Chief Silva found her after lunch when he walked around to the backyard after failing to get any reply to his knocking at the front door.

"Gordon's out on his boat," she said when he was only a few feet away from her. Silva never questioned Marian's appearance, since he hadn't known her in her more frivolous days. As far as he was concerned, everyone in Mellingham had a bizarre outfit or two in the closet.

"I didn't come to see Gordon." Silva's quick reply brought a startled look to Marian's face.

"Really? Should I be flattered?" Marian asked with a grin on her face. Her left hand held a bundle of weeds and her right a small trowel.

"That depends on how you feel about having your brain picked. I have more questions about George Frome and Thursday." This seemed the wiser approach to a woman who had access to Frome's fatal dinner and was also one of the most observant people in Mellingham.

"Yes, of course," Marian replied, immediately subduing her lighter nature. "I think I'd quite gotten over the shock of it all. Gardening is such a restorative." She plunged her trowel into the earth and tossed the weeds into a basket, depositing her gloves on top. "There are questions I want to ask, too, but I won't. I may not like the answer." Marian turned away while she said this, ostensibly leading him to the picnic table and chairs

"You make too much of my questions," Silva said. "Mostly I'm just cross-checking times now. Gwen McDuffy said there was also a delivery man there on Thursday."

"Oh him. Oh sure. Does he matter?" she asked.

"Not directly, but tell me what you do remember."

"He came near the beginning of the afternoon. I think Gwen made sure he had the right package."

"And you?"

"The door again, I suppose." She thought for a moment. "Kelly Kuhn. Now I remember. He came to leave an article for his intern to read before her session the following day, something about paint pigments. Poor Kelly. I forgot to tell him she'd had to change the time so he came back on Friday, around noon as I recall, right after you left, and she wasn't there. Poor Kelly. He was so caught up in his own problems that I couldn't even get him to stand still long enough to tell him about George."

"What kind of work does he do with the intern?" Silva asked.

"He started out evaluating our paintings and drawings. We really don't know much about what we have, so we were glad when we got him signed on." She remembered her satisfaction of a few months ago. "He seemed a bit confused at the first board meeting; I think he wanted to be paid, but we never pay professionals on the board for what they do for the Society. We're practically broke all the time."

"But he stayed on," Silva said, wondering how the Society had arranged to pay Marian but no one else.

"Well, he did agree. Then George saddled him with this intern—she really is hopeless. Kelly has been very good-natured about it." For the most part Marian liked Kelly despite his frantic air and nervous mannerisms; he had been a good sport about taking on a student, and he was doing a great deal for the Society.

"Where does he work? On the third floor? When I prowled around up there it seemed awfully dark."

"Kelly doesn't work up there. He won't even go up there, at least he wouldn't after—" Her eyes darted back and forth. "He prefers to work in the dining room."

"What did you start to say, Marian? He wouldn't work up there after what?"

"I suppose I can tell you. The first day he went up there, well, you know he's not exactly tiny. But I didn't think he was that big. Anyway, his first day he knocked over some boxes and chairs in the storage room on the third floor. I don't think it was anything valuable, but it might have been. George heard it, and caught Kelly in a ridiculous position—falling over a chair with a pillow on his head—and after that he gave Kelly a hard time about it whenever he got the chance." She screwed up her face as she began to mimic Frome. "'How's your diet, Kelly? Down one chair, are we? No? One colonial musket, then?' George really did pick on him. It made Kelly downright paranoid. He absolutely refused to go into the storage room after that. Sometimes he wouldn't even work in the building if George was there. One of us had to bring the pictures down from storage. Or the intern brought them down."

"Is he really that sensitive?" Silva asked.

"He's very touchy, Chief. Very touchy. About his weight. He's not that big but he's very sensitive to any comments."

"He took George's jokes pretty hard," Silva said. "Maybe he's gotten over it by now." Marian shook her head from side to side.

"Not Kelly. He refuses to leave the first floor. It really is getting to be an inconvenience. Sometimes the student intern brings down things that aren't worth bothering with, and he gets all het up and tells her to take them back up and bring something worthwhile down, but she doesn't know. I've had to get—" She stopped as she realized where she had been heading.

"Go on."

"Sometimes scholars or curators from other museums write to see if we have something by a particular artist or whatever. Well, we don't know if we do or not. We tell them they can come by and look. Kelly, of course, was no help with them. He wouldn't go near the third-floor storage. So George stepped in."

"He showed other curators around? Tourists?"

"No, not tourists. But he did sort of have free rein up there. I suppose that's how he got into that consulting business." Her voice trailed off. To Silva's muted request for elaboration, she said, "He ran into Annalee Windolow upstairs somewhere a few weeks ago and she asked him to teach her something about painting so she could do her own buying."

"Buying?"

"Art, antiques. She usually buys from Kelly but I guess she wants to do some of the searching herself. George offered to give her a few lessons in art appreciation and art history, although I don't think he really knew just how ignorant she is."

"Twenty tips to successful collecting?"

"That's about it." Marian grudgingly respected Annalee's goals despite how she felt about her as a person. As a former teacher, Marian was in favor of anything that prompted anyone to learn more. She was not above using bribery to tempt a student to read; Annalee fell into the category of unformed character ripe for shaping.

"How much had she done with George?" Silva asked.

"Nothing. Friday morning was supposed to be her first session, from what she said." She looked at Silva and gasped. "You don't think—"

"I don't think what?" he asked.

"That Annalee, that she, you know," Marian said, trying to get Silva to jump to the same conclusion as she had.

"You're way ahead of me. I thought you told me Annalee left at five-thirty. You saw her arrive and you saw her leave."

Marian resisted his rational dismissal of Annalee as a suspect. "She could have come back," Marian said.

"So could a lot of other people," Silva pointed out. "That's not what I want to talk about right now. What I want from you is a step-by-step description of everything that happened on Thursday."

"Again?"

"Yes. Go through it all again, so I can be sure."

So she did, and he was.

■ ■ ■

"I'm going that way," the old woman said as she pointed to the grassy walk that ran along the hill rising behind the revetment. The beach was dotted with groups of kids wandering around with buckets and shovels, parents under umbrellas, and men and women swimming or playing volleyball or walking the shore. A few were succumbing to the pounding heat of the sun by baking themselves even more—a kind of environmental homeopathy carried to an extreme. The path above the beach seemed to promise a cooler experience with its benches set near arching shrubs and a few old shade trees, but it was only an illusion. The branches lifted by a breeze worked only to heave more heat toward the walkers and bathers below.

"All right," said Mrs. Alesander, turning away from her friend toward the tiny canteen. She got in line behind a little girl still wearing her flippers and a snorkel. The brown-shingled bathhouse opened at nine o'clock in the morning but the beach was often already crowded by then, the parking lot filled with residents' cars. Youngsters ran up from the beach for a drink of water from the bubbler, to claim an important shirt or toy left in the basket in the cloak room, to meet a friend. Mrs. Alesander came for the view and today she was in line, not for the ice cream she just bought, but for the chance to talk to Gwen McDuffy.

"That's for yourself?" the old woman said as the two stood on the edge of the wooden deck. The sidewalk continued past them, to a wooden walkway that deposited people onto the beach proper. For the sheer length of the beach, the entrance was remarkably narrow. The rest of the open expanse between revetments rising to cliffs was a tiny rotary bounded by large white boulders, partly to keep cars from parking in the circle before they swung past the beach and headed back down the road to town. From the deck in front of the bathhouse, beachgoers saw all—cars, sand, swimmers, and the great Atlantic stretching all the way to Portugal.

In answer to her older friend's question, Gwen McDuffy nodded and molded her mouth over the ice cream scoops. Beachgoers sauntered past them on both sides. Some people were starting to leave now, moving on to late afternoon plans; others were arriving with their picnic baskets for a cookout on the beach. The cries of young children forced into cold showers rose behind them from the arms of the bathhouse. The two wings of the bathhouse were joined at the center by a walk-through with large barnlike doors at either end. Mrs. Alesander moved to a bench at the base of the beach path.

"I missed you at the Arbella House yesterday," Mrs.

Alesander began. "I thought you might drop by on Saturdays sometimes."

"Not me. One day a week is enough." Gwen liked Mrs. Alesander because she never felt uncomfortable in her presence, never felt that she had returned to Mellingham unwanted and unremembered, or, perversely, too well remembered. Mrs. Alesander had an easy acceptance of everyone, which Gwen especially appreciated. "What were you doing over there? Were you donating something?"

"I might in a few months—I have an old bureau that might work well in the upstairs bedroom—but yesterday I was there looking at old pictures. To help my granddaughter with a report on people and life in old Mellingham. She picked the now-depleted Portuguese community."

Gwen turned to look at her with a bemused expression. "Did you find what you were looking for?"

"Yes indeed." She sucked her ice cream. "I found a few other things too." Mrs. Alesander delivered this last comment with a change in tone; Gwen glanced at her while she ate her own ice cream. "I found pictures from the 1950s and 1960s." The two women watched a pair of small children carrying an inflated mat behind their father, who was carrying towels, buckets, and a picnic basket.

This was the time for Gwen to jump in with a question, to be curious about what her older friend had found, but she didn't say anything, only licked up the drips of strawberry ice cream tracking down the sides of her sugar cone.

"Someone gave a whole slew of pictures, mostly of the carnivals in town and parades down at the park. Almost everyone is in there somewhere," Mrs. Alesander went on. Gwen still made no comment. "Saw lots of people I recognized. Friends of my parents. Schoolmates. And old friends long gone now. And some still here." She turned to look at Gwen, who went on staring at the beach. When she turned to Mrs. Alesander, her face was hard.

"What's your point, Mrs. Alesander?"

"There's something you haven't told anybody, isn't there?"

"Maybe."

"You're going to have to, you know. Eventually it'll all have to come out."

Gwen looked at her speculatively, her hardness softening into thoughtfulness. "Maybe. Maybe not." She turned away.

"It's not right, this. You're making a mistake," Mrs. Alesander said. She looked over her shoulder and back around to the right. Satisfied they were far enough away from anyone else for her to speak freely, she went on. "Your family had secrets too when you were a child, and it didn't do you any good."

Gwen sat up on the bench and uncrossed her legs, as though she were getting ready to spring up and flee.

"We all knew your family wasn't an easy one, but you never gave much sign of what it was. You were a hard child to get to know, even though you seemed to have a lot of friends. The older you got, the more you kept to yourself."

Gwen leaned forward, torn between standing up with indignant outrage and an urgent need to silence this invasive advice. She cast around in her mind for a way to halt the conversation.

"I think you should be open about whatever it is. This secret business—it's not good for you and it's not good for the kids." Mrs. Alesander returned her attentions to her ice cream cone.

"What exactly did you find in the Arbella House photographs that prompted this conversation?" she asked.

"A picture of that boy you married when he was just a kid. I think he won something at the races on the fourth of July."

"So?"

"It was a color photograph, not black and white like most of them." Mrs. Alesander turned to Gwen and put out her hand. "Whatever it is, it can't be so bad that you have to be so secretive about it. You're all but lying to us. Well, I guess you have lied. That can't go on."

Gwen finished her ice cream and wiped her fingers with a napkin. "Maybe you're assuming something that isn't true. After all, it was just a photograph. You're making too much out of this." She threw away her napkin. "I have to get back to the kids." She walked off after an awkward good-bye. Mrs. Alesander sat on. She hadn't meant to speak to Gwen this directly when she first recognized the photograph of the boy who grew up to become her husband, but then she hadn't expected to encounter Gwen at the beach.

Mrs. Alesander's friend waved to her from the beach path; the old woman scowled at the rocky rise and began her ascent. She didn't personally care one way or another what Gwen was relegating to the past, but she believed nevertheless that a truth concealed became an illness that would ultimately destroy the carrier, no matter how innocent she might be.

■ ■ ■

In every neighborhood there is at least one who sits on the edge by choice or not, and is the last to know the important news, which makes its way up the street, leaping past the home in question, until the information is so common that sprigs of this tree of knowledge brush the shadowy person on his daily rounds. Kelly Kuhn was one of these. Sallies into auction houses on Friday evening had brought a cluster of disjointed questions that Kelly fended off with only half his attention. Forays into galleries on Saturday afternoon brought even more queries, and their repetitive nature finally caught his attention. By Sunday afternoon he knew most of what people were saying about Chief Silva, the Arbella Society, its board members, and, of course, George Frome. He was ready for Chief Silva's visit.

Chief Silva wasn't ready for him, however. Kelly Kuhn fell into that group of Mellites who tend to their own affairs and regard Mellingham as just another town to live in, not as a stage on which to present the drama of their lives. Kelly in fact avoided anything like public drama; he was happiest when alone in a room to contemplate one of his (or someone else's) impressionist paintings. The more time he could spend in this way, the happier he was. And until he had received a call from the police station asking him to be available all Sunday afternoon, that was precisely how he expected to spend his day. The sudden deprivation of his contemplative hours had the effect of all change on Kelly; it made him jumpy, and since he was already an edgy, nervous fellow, he now gave the impression of a bundle of fireworks popping erratically. Silva didn't quite know what to make of him when he looked across the small coffee table in Kelly's living room. The rippling fingers on Kelly's thighs moved from allegretto to allegro to presto.

"I'm sure I wasn't there on Thursday afternoon. Was I? Was I there?" His voice was jerky and the last phrases came out in a rising staccato. "My intern canceled. She does that. Canceling all the time." His fingers gripped his thighs. "I went to the house. I do remember. Marian said the intern hadn't come, so I didn't stay." There was no modulation in his voice; it was devoid of the rhythm of feeling, of aliveness. He spoke almost like an automaton. Silva watched him closely but as strange as his behavior was, Kelly showed none of the signs of the user of illicit drugs. It was the first time Silva could recall having been wrong about the reason behind someone's abnormal behavior.

"And Thursday evening? During the board meeting?" Silva asked.

"Would you like some cookies? I forgot to offer you anything." He scuttled off to the kitchen, where he made a great deal of noise before emerging with a tray of two glasses of iced tea and a plate of cookies. The mild exertion produced streaks of sweat down his temples and cheeks. Tiny beads of perspiration glistened in three rings around his neck. Silva thought how uncomfortable the other man must be and yet he had no air conditioner on the first floor. "I didn't do anything during the board meeting," he said after he had taken a gulp of his cold drink and swallowed two cookies.

Silva had declined the refreshments. Kelly Kuhn gave a nervous laugh, chewed a third cookie, stared at Chief Silva. "You were sitting at the street end of the library during the board meeting, and you had a good view of George Frome while he was talking. I want to know who he looked at when he started talking about my visit on Thursday afternoon." Silva waited for Kelly to react. The antiques dealer grew still, blinked.

"Why would you want to know that?"

"To get the placement of everyone correct in my mind."

Kelly nodded, staring. Silva's reasoning made no sense to him but he was willing to acknowledge his limitations. "I think he was talking to Walter, the president. Then he had to look at one woman over, ah, over, ah, I guess on his right. My left, sort of." Kelly waved his elbows from side to side as he tried to be sure of his directions. "Well, maybe sort of across from me." The struggle to visualize exactly where people had been seated served as a sedative, and at the end he let his hands rest on his thighs, his fingers stilled.

"So you think he was watching the president first," Silva repeated. Kelly nodded. "Do you know of any particular reason why he might do so?" Kelly shook his head, waiting for Silva to go on; he felt like he was going to be told a wonderful story and he didn't want it to stop.

"He thought paintings and other things were disappearing," Kelly said when he realized something was expected of him.

"Did he give any specifics?"

"I don't think so," Kelly said, trying hard to think back. "He just said things, old pictures. Not my sort." The last phrase popped out and both men examined it.

"He said what was missing wasn't your sort," Silva said. "What did he mean by that?"

"He knew I was interested in nineteenth-century art mostly," Kelly answered. His fingers started to twitch.

"Does the Society own much?"

"Nineteenth-century art? Some. Not impressionist art, though." His fingers again rippled on this thighs. "A fair number of old pictures. Early American portraits. Landscapes. That sort of thing."

"Do you happen to have any around? In your own stock?" Silva wondered if he was using terms that might offend but Kelly didn't seem to notice. He nodded while his eyes grew vacant.

"This way." He led Silva into the attached shop and started moving around chairs and canvases until he had six lined up against a wall. For the next half hour Silva was treated to a brief but intelligent survey of painting in North America up to the Civil War, illustrated by canvases, art books, and postcards. Silva was impressed not only with the art he glimpsed but also by the depth of Kelly's understanding of history and art movements.

"I've seen something like this recently," Silva said, pointing to one of the earliest paintings.

"It's not rare." He stood looking down at the still life, his face sad; the painting didn't appeal to him.

"Annalee Windolow just bought one like this, didn't she?" Silva asked, turning to Kelly.

"I sold it to her, yesterday." Kelly's breath came in short gasps as he thought of the check.

"She has two then. Very similar, same size."

Kelly looked over at Silva, his mind unfocused. "She does? Yes, she does. She bought the other one in New York. Her—brother?—someone told her about it. She likes that period." He turned a skeptical gaze back on his paintings. Silva picked up one and turned it over.

"What are all these tags for?" He motioned to the two stickers on the lower stretcher. Kelly peered at them.

"Old museum identification numbers. Anytime a painting, or anything else, went to a museum, donated, on loan, whatever, it got a number, and all museums had their own numbering systems."

Silva put the painting down and turned to a bright watercolor on the wall. He lifted it off and turned it over. "This one doesn't have anything on the back." He looked over at Kelly for a response, but Kelly's eyes, fixed on the picture, were sparkling, his fingertips trembling, his tongue tracing the shape of his lower lip; he took the picture in his hands and seemed to want to speak but his face only vibrated, his mouth working, his eyes bulging.

"It has no numbers on the back," Silva repeated.

"No, no it doesn't. It was never in a museum," Kelly replied without taking his eyes off the picture. Gently, lovingly, he held the picture until Silva took it from him and rehung it, then stood directly in front of it. The animation died in Kelly, sinking so deep into him that Silva wondered if there was something in the painting he had missed.

"I don't quite understand about pictures that were in museums. Every picture that has been in a museum will have something different on the back," Silva said. "Is that right?"

"Only in theory." Kelly spoke now in a normal manner, slightly bored, a little tired, mechanically. "In the last century curators didn't have many choices. There might have been three kinds of tags to choose from and numbering was very simple. Sometimes just a year and the number of the donation received up to then. So 93-24 might be the year 1893 and the twenty-fourth donation received to date. Sometimes they had group and item, 145 for paintings and 277 for item number. They're all about the same in the smaller museums. We only got a uniform system, something everyone in the country uses, in the 1970s and 1980s. So now everything gets a new number and most of the museums in the country follow one system."

"This isn't one of the newly cataloged ones," Silva said, pointing to one of the stickers. "But it did come from a museum." Kelly nodded and named the museum.

"Museums sell off some of their items if they get enough new stuff so they feel they don't have to keep less valuable stuff, especially if they're small and short of space. I'll sell these pictures and in twenty years someone will donate them to a small museum and ten or fifteen years later the museum might put them back on the market. With a number from Chenhall's *Nomenclature* right alongside these old ones. That's the system we're all using now, Chenhall's."

"Suppose one of your clients wants to buy something only if they know where it comes from," Silva said, setting down the painting.

"Provenance," Kelly said, absently, pulling open a desk drawer. "This is what a museum will give for anything it sells. It's like a withdrawal stamp in a book from a library. It's part of the package the client expects."

"Package?" Silva took the official-looking document and read it.

"A good dealer passes on whatever he knows about an object. Where it came from, who made it, anything special about technique. For this kind of art, I always have papers. It's worth more with papers." He flipped through the sheets.

Silva found himself with the irreverent thought that this sounded very much like buying a dog; in neither transaction did the pleasure to be gained from the purchase seem to bear consideration.

"Does the Arbella Society ever sell any of its pictures?"

"I was told it has in the past but I don't think they have recently," Kelly said. He was still staring with little interest at the six canvases as though they had disappointed him.

"And if I came across a picture originally from the Arbella Society I would have no way of knowing," Silva said.

"Well, that depends." Kelly was interested in this problem. "If it had a new acquisition number painted on it—"

"Painted?"

"Yes, after I evaluate it, I sandpaper a little section—actually, my intern usually does it, but not always. Anyway I paint the new catalog number on it and put the number in the accession worksheet along with any other old numbers also on the picture—the frames or the stretchers. If you have the numbers I can tell you if it was ever ours."

"So if I gather other paintings at the Arbella Society, I can pick out all the ones that have been recataloged," Silva said. Kelly nodded. "And only the newly cataloged ones will have painted numbers."

Silva's repetition made Kelly curious. "That's right. The intern has looked through all the canvases upstairs and we're just about done."

"What's her role?"

"Not much," Kelly mumbled. "She brings down two or three pictures at a time, sometimes more, for me to work on. Takes measurements, writes up a basic description, sands down a corner for the new number. That's about all she can do. She doesn't know what gesso is. Or tempera. Or a monoprint." He grew more and more depressed as he listed the girl's failings. Silva was compelled to interrupt.

"How long have you been doing this?" Silva asked, handing him back the documents.

"Months. It feels like years. Years and years and years of painting tiny little numbers." His whole body sagged.

"Did you ever think about going into another line of work, Mr. Kuhn?" Silva asked after he had thanked Kelly for his time. It wasn't a question for the sake of conversation; it was advisory, and it caught Kelly's full attention.

9
Monday Morning

At five-thirty on Monday morning, Joe Silva sat on the deck behind his house with a mug of coffee in his hands, his feet resting on the railing, his mind going over once again all that he had put together about the murder of George Frome on Thursday evening. It wasn't much.

In the early hours of the day Joe felt the world lay open to him, just as the sea had to his father, and he could see the path to his goal as though the ocean had routes marked all the way to Georges Bank. In the early morning, the town seemed organic, a single living organism in which the many separate families played their roles, like cells in a body. The sunlight was not yet tarnished by the activity of the day, and held its purest power. Sounds had weight and filled their spaces more thickly; the day had not yet attenuated the sounds of boats leaving the harbor, the voices behind a door opening to take in the morning paper, a car driving down the street. But it was an illusion.

In a little more than two days he had learned a lot about a part of Mellingham that had entered his life as chief of police only peripherally since he arrived in 1985, discovered most of what he needed to know about how George Frome was murdered, uncovered at least one theft from the Arbella Society, and identified the murderer. But he had no evidence, at least nothing that would serve in a court, and what little he did have to support his views was circumstantial. Even worse, he had no motive. Finally, the medical examiner still wasn't certain how the aconitine was introduced. A message on Joe's answering machine reported only that the ME hoped to have the answer soon. So did Joe.

Not a single thought about the murder of George Frome would cohere. Joe's sense of what kind of person the murder victim was disintegrated when the chief went to his home, a place antithetical to the man when he was alive. George Frome had seemed on Thursday afternoon an ordinary fellow, the kind of retired man often produced by small towns practiced in the skill of smoothing character into preferred shapes. George was active, but not threateningly so; he contributed his skills and time, but never openly pushed others to do the kind of serious work that required a salary and a title. He got along with people, at least on the surface, which was all that anyone had a right to expect, and he made a pleasant appearance, in his starched shirts and neatly pressed khaki pants. But George Frome's apartment said something else about him, and Joe wasn't sure what that was.

As often as he reminded himself not to, Joe could not get past the prejudice of judging people by how they tended themselves. It wasn't a moral issue, but a personal one. Short of mental illness, he expected people to expend a certain amount of care (not too little and not too much) as a sign of respect and consideration for themselves and others. George certainly did in his personal appearance, but his home said this was a facade. Walking out of Frome's apartment hadn't ended the unease Silva had felt his entire time there; the underside of George Frome's personality lingered, clinging to him like lint and just as hard to brush off.

The experience of Frome's apartment left him seeing a life fragmented, things standing apart with a film of dust connecting one to another, but nothing deeper binding them to the life lived among them. Sometimes since Friday night, when he had let himself in expecting to see an apartment furnished with little imagination but with taste, an image of a dish or a clock or a book vibrated out of its place in his memory, its place in the apartment, and grew and stretched and then finally collapsed back into memory. George Frome's apartment was a place, not a home.

Joe sipped his coffee, wondering if it was really, this time, a matter of not wanting to face other, entangled questions. Thursday afternoon was on the surface no more than a thorough tour of Arbella House by a man who knew the entire building intimately, it being his only interest in life for several years. And yet Joe knew at the end of the tour that Frome had wanted something else from the chief of police, something he could get without naming or identifying it. The man's insistence that someone was stealing from the Society wasn't corroborated by anything Frome showed Silva, but he now knew that Frome was right about that; moreover, before too much more time passed, the chief expected to alert the Society to the theft and leave it to the president to decide how to recover the stolen article. What he didn't know how to interpret was Gwen McDuffy and George on Thursday afternoon.

Joe had long been suspicious of the ability of other people to make a suggestion that imposed a new order, a new interpretation, on an old conversation that had seemed normal, innocent, bland, meaningless. George Frome's death had turned his casual introduction between Joe and Gwen McDuffy into a moment fraught with meaning; Joe was disgusted with himself for feeling the entire incident, all thirty seconds of it, altered through and through. George's casual comment about Gwen holding all the secrets in Arbella House might easily have been his way of threatening Gwen with exposure; her nervousness on meeting the chief might have been the result of a genuine culpability. Joe took another sip of coffee.

Gwen McDuffy's determination to maintain her current position in Mellingham was probably the only thing she had in common with Mrs. Rocklynd, Joe mused as he thought about the older woman. Gwen might show up at the Arbella Society to donate a few hours of her time, for the pleasure of Marian's company, a change in her daily round, the solitude of the work, or any number of other reasons, but Mrs. Rocklynd attended the Arbella Society meetings and programs because they were an extension of herself. She would welcome newcomers like Gwen for their apparent confirmation of the importance of the Society, but few would receive from Mrs. Rocklynd an acknowledgment that they might belong. Her love of her family heritage and her place in the town of Mellingham were so intense as to invite caricature, but it would be a mistake not to take her seriously if for no other reason than that she wouldn't tolerate anything less.

It was Edwin Bennett who surprised the chief most. Intelligent, interesting, pleasant, Edwin had let his life be circumscribed by Mellingham and gave no sign of disappointment, resentment, underlying ill will. It made Joe wonder what more there was to Edwin Bennett.

■ ■ ■

At precisely 6:27, Gwen McDuffy was imagining Chief Joe Silva in a most unfriendly light, a man with weapons dedicated to a job that she now openly acknowledged, at least to herself, might lead to his detaining her, not for anything she had done, or so it seemed to her.

Mrs. Alesander's admonition on the preceding afternoon might seem to be—it certainly did to Gwen in odd moments—the catalyst for her current melancholy, a mood slipping through her to make way for distress. Like any woman who has defied the gloomy predictions of her family and childhood guardians to emerge as a responsible, decent adult, she secretly feared that a fate of dramatically negative proportions lay inside her waiting for the moment to shift its burden and pull her from her chosen path. She feared her own inherent, ungraspable weakness, which is how she defined acts of will done in moments of crisis that brought her regularly to an unknown shore. But now the knowing nod of Mrs. Alesander and the probing looks of Chief Silva were pushing her back to a shore she thought she had left behind and she could imagine no way to dock safely, softly, unobtrusively. Every possibility floating before her ultimately made her groan, swing around on the kitchen chair while her mind darted off to wonder about Philip and Jennie, asleep still in their bedrooms, or to fret about her job and its sudden, solely to her mind, precariousness.

The passing of time pressed on her, pushing her back into the kitchen when she had wandered away from the telephone, slicing off moments of her future while her indecision sliced off moments of her past. She had gotten up early this morning to have time to do what she could not bring herself to do; yet if she didn't make any effort now, she might not be able to later on.

Occasionally a car drove past the double-decker and Gwen listened to the noise of its engine and wheels on the macadam blend into the sound of a town waking up. Nearby she heard Philip turn in his bed, but he would sleep another half hour at least. She let these noises fill her so that her hand might automatically reach for the telephone, not needing the will she could not draw out of herself. She told herself again and again that the early hour didn't matter; she had no intention of waking up anyone at four or five o'clock in the morning. This was a call for information, information she didn't want but had to have.

The operator was patient with Gwen's request, going down all the listings, spelling the name in different ways—an effort Gwen thought considerate but unnecessary, since she wasn't likely to forget how to spell his name. The operator was sorry, after three full minutes of searching. Gwen tried another town; she remembered the names—every one that might be possible—and went through them one by one without needing to write them down or check them off. And yet not one of these now empty towns with empty apartments could overlay the first image in her mind of the very last place, the one she had ultimately fled, angry, fearful, determined, almost broke. The last scene was burned into her memory, an eidetic image that would never leave her, never allow itself to be forgotten or replaced or even blurred with other memories. Her hand shook when she dialed the area code for that place but the politeness of the operator could conjure up no number to match the name. Names, she knew, would soon dissolve into syllables, then sounds—disconnected, wispy, unmeaningful. It made her feel potent; it was a lie. She was glad and she was not glad.

For the last several years Gwen had maintained to herself that she was the one in control because she held the secret—of where she was, who she was—but less than fifteen minutes on the telephone had shown her that wasn't true; it was false. In the months that she had wondered, when she had allowed herself to wonder, how he might feel, she had never been brave enough to let herself know how he might feel. But she was the vulnerable one; she was the one who had to worry about a surprise knocking at the door late at night. But why, her rational mind interrupted, why late at night? Can't the danger come late in the afternoon, at lunchtime, or even early in the morning, say, at around seven o'clock? When had she fallen into the pattern of thinking of danger in conventional terms, those defined by novelists and moviemakers who liked the poetry of darkness to enhance their fascination with evil? When the danger became real in her life, it took the ordinary forms of daylight, a danger too real to be dispersed with the sun at dawn. It made the evil concrete and the good of her heart insubstantial.

Jennie stirred. She was a slow waker, lying in bed on weekend mornings gathering her thoughts, as though she had to fit them back into her head in a proper order, one only able to butt up against certain others; no sloppy thinking for her. It had always been so. Gwen envied Jennie her young life in which she had not known a thought she could not examine fully, slowly, bemusedly. The child had no secrets she could not look at. She was not like her mother.

Ready to confront the worst, Gwen punched in the numbers for one more call, again listened while the patient, polite telephone operator explored variant spellings, checked new listings, unlisted numbers, and commiserated with the patron.

Gwen was drawing close to despair. She didn't want to reach the one she was seeking in towns across the country, but her failure to locate someone she had long assumed to be in a particular place made her rage against herself. She had been too afraid to act when she could; instead she ran, and now she couldn't act, now she couldn't prove good intentions, a responsible will. Now she was the criminal.

In the early morning heat Jennie wandered into the kitchen, her eyes fixed in their waking stare to reclaim the world and fit it again to her thoughts. At such moments she seemed hollow, as though her eyes needed to gulp down the world to fill herself up. She stared at Gwen, then blinked and was a little girl again, leaning into her mother's arms and yawning. Jennie's body was damp with sweat. Gwen embraced her, letting the fear of the last hour dissolve in the gentle tingling of awe and love for the life that was Jennie.

■ ■ ■

For the average worker Monday morning signifies the beginning of a long week, the chance to start out right once again, the chance to escape from a disappointing personal life, or perhaps a reminder that life shrinks as years pass. Monday morning had been all these things to Marian Davis at one time but no more. Once she had given up teaching and begun looking around for a job she could enjoy, she vowed never again to face Mondays with dread. The Arbella Society was all that she wanted. To friends who thought she was losing her ambition, her drive, her determination to make something out of her life, as they put it, she replied that she was no longer demented. She meant it. Twenty years watching young boys and girls grow into adults had persuaded her that the personality of many successful men and women was a distorted, unbalanced congeries of features never to be brought into harmony, never to produce the by-product of happiness that so many search for so compulsively, obsessively, even destructively. Marian Davis was happy at the Arbella Society.

At 9:07 Marian unlocked the back door and was soon settled at her desk with a mug of tea, a chocolate-covered doughnut, and all the work, such as it was, she hadn't been able to finish on Friday or Saturday. She never would have believed that she could spend so much time at a desk and get so little done until it actually happened. It was understandable, of course, she told herself, and then halted in mid-thought. Was it? Understandable? Had she just now reduced the death of another human being, someone she had known for years and years, to a merely awkward, mildly disruptive event in her life? Was that the mind of Marian Davis? Surely not. Surely she, of all the people George Frome drew close to in his retirement, was more deeply affected by him than that.

Marian let her mind drift while her mug of tea sent smoke signals before her unseeing eyes. Troubled by her reactions, she thought about how important George had made himself to the Society, getting to know it better than anyone else, insinuating himself into every facet of business, going from attic to basement, looking into boxes and corners and bureau drawers others had long neglected, popping up with old tales and forgotten facts. His understanding of the various collections and how they were interrelated, despite others' comments of how eclectic, disjointed, they were, impressed even those who had been actively involved with the Society for decades. Yet it never seemed to satisfy him, never to be perceived as an accomplishment, a natural rounding out of his work that brought him pleasure.

Over the last several weeks Marian had wondered, not unlike Silva on his visit Thursday afternoon, what George Frome was really seeking as he peered into corners, brushed away cobwebs in long-dark rooms, and provoked the board members at the monthly meetings. He could startle her by an offhand comment while stuffing envelopes and then never mention the topic again. Listening to the elliptical references to his most recent discoveries had become unsettling rather than intriguing. She had been astounded when he went out of his way not long ago to offer art appreciation sessions to Annalee Windolow at the Society. When Marian had learned about it from a woman who had overheard the conversation, she had to struggle to believe. Her resistance was not to Annalee, whom Marian considered capable of asking anybody for anything, but to George as a generous imparter of hard-earned stature as the significant figure in the Society, well, after Mrs. Rocklynd, of course. Even the president couldn't hope to be regarded in quite the same way as George, and didn't try.

For a few minutes Marian had considered George in the role of a lothario, caught up by Annalee's youth, beauty, and position in Mellingham, due, of course, to her marriage to Winston Windolow. But then she had decided that George might be many things—arrogant, charming, secretive, disdainful—but he was never louche where women were concerned, at least not as far as Marian had heard. And then there was Annalee, the other half of the equation. Marian hardly thought she would allow herself to be pursued by the likes of George Frome. So where did that leave Marian? The truth, it seemed to her, had to be already in her head, if she could just find it. Hers was a mental universe doomed by entropy except that others were forever interjecting their own ideas into her ruminations.

Chief Silva was one of them, planting ideas with his questions but not saying precisely what those ideas might be. She struggled over her interviews with him, trying to infer what each phrase might mean, but nothing came. For three days now she'd been going around in circles, still convinced that no one at the Society in the afternoon or at the board meeting in the evening could possibly be accused of murdering George. It didn't help to remind her that someone had.

Marian finally noticed the mug of tea and took a sip; it was lukewarm. The clock said 10:03. Impossible. Oh well, maybe not, Marian thought sheepishly, pushing away memories of having daydreamed herself into being late for her classes—a clear sign that it was time to quit teaching. She made herself another mug of tea, answered the door to the day's volunteers, and promised herself that she would somehow get to the bottom of the investigation—even if it meant asking her husband for help. Someone must know what Chief Silva was driving at.

■ ■ ■

For one person in Mellingham, Monday morning dawned like the day of execution, a day when the rest of his life was shortened, compressed, reduced to the few hours he could see before him; these few were devoid of the shading and striations that make time interesting. As a child he had toyed with the idea of turning back the clock, of finding himself in a universe in which it was possible to alter time and recover crucial moments and relive them so they were just ordinary again. He'd had the same feeling about matter at the beginning of his first chemistry course, when he had longed to be able to reverse the process of molecular change, undoing the damage of spattered shellac, but for the most part change had only one direction; Edwin Bennett accepted that, slowly at first, until it was finally part of his way of seeing life around him. It was in fact the immutability of life that truly depressed him on Monday morning.

Edwin Bennett was a kind man, unaccustomed to thinking ill of others, always willing to let the casually cruel remark pass unnoticed (and often unheard), quick to excuse the failings of others and to welcome in friendship the alienated or offended. His compassion grew out of a childhood of loneliness, was honed as a technique for surviving in a world that seemed otherwise to shun him. He spent Monday morning thinking forgiving, compensatory thoughts of another; then he called the police.

Chief Silva was less inclined than Edwin to find mitigating circumstances around every antique, but he was eager to listen to the other man's rationalizations, believing that mixed in would be a few facts that would aid him.

"I really didn't want to come down," Edwin began as he looked around at the police station. "This is very hard for me. It's not something I want to do. She's a lovely woman. I wouldn't hurt her for anything." The distastefulness of what Edwin had to say could be measured by the profusion of his introductory apologies and protestations of regret. He sighed after an especially long-winded protest.

"You're looking at me as though you don't believe me," Edwin said at one point.

"Not at all. Just take your time, Mr. Bennett." Chief Silva had managed to seat Edwin comfortably in his tiny office while Edwin alternated between regret, surprise at finding himself in a police station, and reluctance to say what it was that had brought him down in the first place. "Have you come across something about the death of George Frome that you want to pass along?"

Edwin's eyes bulged. "Didn't I say that? I guess I am a bit rattled. It was such a surprise."

"What was a surprise?"

"The plant." Edwin's face had the wide-open look of dumbfounded innocence. "I found a plant with the root missing. Monkshood. It looked like it was dying. You know, they don't like too much sun; the heat's too much for them, and they get stunted-looking. They just don't flourish. I figured it had had too much. That wasn't such a good spot for it, on the border. Oh dear, I'm sorry. I'm rambling." He took a deep breath.

"Just start from the beginning. Where did you find this plant?" Silva asked.

"Yesterday afternoon I was replacing a few plants in my aunt's garden—lupines, pansies, well, those were my idea; I'm very fond of pansies. Anyway, I pulled up a monkshood because it was obviously dying and just tossed it aside. I knew at the moment that something wasn't right but I was so enjoying myself. It was such a lovely day, my plants looked great, I felt wonderful. Then when I hoed the garden and cleaned up all the weeds and trash I collected, I didn't stop to think about it. But when I got home and started to dump the stuff on my mulch pile—"

"Yes?" Silva said. He knew it could be worse. Some witnesses came into the station after a long struggle, barely convinced they were doing the right thing, and then changed their minds, walking out with their information still a secret. At least Bennett was talking, even if he was making no sense.

"Well, I thought I could save the plant. I hate to waste anything and I'm pretty good at bringing back sick plants." He smiled, his feelings for his gardening obvious. "Those fruit trees out back I started from seeds when I was a boy." He blinked with modesty, then blanched at his own insensitive wanderings. "Sorry," he mumbled. "Where was I? I thought I'd try to save the monkshood so I separated it from the weeds but all I got was the stalk and a few surface roots. I looked everywhere but I couldn't find the tuber."

Chief Silva looked blank, not at all sure where Edwin had wandered from the path he thought he was on. "The tuber," he repeated, trying to sound as though he knew what he was talking about. He knew about roots and taproots, but not tubers. Why hadn't he gone to work on his uncle's farm during his summers in high school when he'd had the chance?

Edwin looked back at him expectantly. "Right. The tuber. It wasn't there."

"What exactly is a tuber?" Silva asked.

Edwin sagged in his chair. "It's part of a root. Some plants have long thin roots, some have clusters of fibers, some have what look like potatoes or carrots along the roots. That thick part is the tuber. Am I making any sense?" he asked.

"Enough. Go on," Silva said.

"Well, I couldn't find the tuber. So I examined the plant. The head of the tuber had been cut off. It was gone. It didn't fall off—they don't do that—and I hadn't picked it off by accident. It was cut. Once I stopped to look, it was obvious. I could see the cut."

"Why is this important?" Silva asked, able to guess the answer.

"The root is toxic, very poisonous," Edwin said.

"How poisonous?" Silva asked.

"Highly poisonous," Edwin whispered.

"What's the poison?" Silva asked. "Do you know?"

"It's aconitine," Edwin replied. He and Silva looked at each other across a widening chasm. It seemed to Edwin that the man he had thought of as a friend was changing before him, the muscles around his mouth coding for interrogation rather than conversation, the sinews beneath the navy blue cotton shirt stretching the weave in readiness. He was beginning to regret he had come, afraid of this new form of Chief Silva. "It must have been an accident, a horrible mistake," he insisted as Silva receded behind his official persona. "I'm sure she couldn't have meant to do such a thing."

"That may well be," Silva agreed. "That would be—"

Edwin stalled in his protestations, now aware that he could still back away from some of his confession. Silva watched him questioning whether or not to answer.

"Mrs. Rocklynd?" Silva suggested.

"Oh no," Edwin said, genuinely shocked. "Annalee Windolow. She lives just down the road, up on the hill on the other side. You can see her place from Aunt Catherine's garden. Haven't you noticed?"

"So you think Mrs. Windolow stopped by on Thursday or maybe earlier in the week, pulled up a plant and cut off a poisonous root, which she then cut up and added to George Frome's salad at the Arbella House." Silva waited while Edwin tried to digest this scenario.

"You make it sound ridiculous," he conceded. "And impossible."

"Not impossible. Improbable maybe, but definitely not impossible." He paused to study Edwin while he reconsidered the unsuspected direction his narrator had taken. "It's a possibility for more than just Mrs. Windolow, too."

"What do you mean?"

"The garden is accessible to a lot of people. You go in and out of the driveway all the time. Mrs. Rocklynd likes to garden as much as she can, if not every day then every two or three days. The garden is right along the road, where anyone can stop, steal a flower or two, and drive away without being noticed." Silva delivered his possibilities in a soft, even voice but to no avail. Edwin was still shocked. He had struggled through the early morning to come to grips with his suspicions of Annalee Windolow; he counted himself brave in his efforts. But Chief Silva seemed to be entertaining the same suspicions about him, his aunt, and everyone else on the board of the Arbella Society, an emotional leap that terrified Edwin.

"Is the root the only part of the plant that's poisonous?" Silva asked.

"No," Edwin began, glad to have the topic changed, at least from a list of suspects. "All of it is poisonous. The flowers, leaves, stem, roots. All of it. Especially now." When Silva looked doubtful, Edwin explained. "The plant flowers in July and the poison is strongest just before it flowers. Not everybody knows that," Edwin said. "I mean, it's a very popular plant and most people who garden today have no idea how poisonous a lot of their plants are."

"But you do," Silva said in a more challenging tone.

"Well, yes, I do, but—"

"Did you get along with Mr. Frome?"

"With George?" Edwin grew perplexed. The conversation with Silva was nothing like what he had imagined it would be. "Of course. We worked together all the time, on committees and whatnot."

"All the time. Hmm. He never gave you any trouble? Never tried to"—Silva paused as though looking for the right word—"embarrass you? Make you uncomfortable? Make fun of you?"

Edwin's face turned blotchy. "Why would he do that?"

"To intimidate you, push you aside, to make room for himself?" Silva suggested.

Edwin tried to dismiss the chief's accusations. "I was no threat to him. There's plenty of room for everyone. And besides, we are adults, you know. Frome might have been pushy sometimes, but he wasn't so different from anyone else. He made a comment or two, nothing worth bothering about."

"About being gay?"

■ ■ ■

There were times when Silva hated his job, especially when he had to probe for vulnerabilities and gauge their relevance to a crime. He tolerated much of what he had to do because a man was dead, murdered, and no one has the right to do that. Edwin Bennett's initial reaction had been shock, then resentment. Neither man spoke; the one waited and the other thrust his way through the thoughts and feelings bombarding him.

"You're trying to provoke me," Edwin said, making it sound almost comradely. "You're not the first. But I don't provoke easily."

Silva swung sideways in his chair, consulted a sheet of paper on his desk, then faced the other man. "You made yourself something of a challenge to George. Is that it?"

Edwin struggled to remain calm, to appear helpful, pushing down anger and outrage. He came with the offer of information, but his suggestion of what it might mean had pulled him into a mire that sucked him deeper the harder he tried to extricate himself from it. "You're making this very melodramatic, Chief. Perhaps you're just a bit out of date."

"Perhaps I am," Silva agreed. "But I'm not wrong about George, am I." It was not a question.

"No. But you're not right about what it means, either."

He took a few short breaths, still stifling his anger. "I don't belong to your generation or your sergeant's. I grew up being taught, indirectly, of course, that what I was was not something anyone ever mentioned. I understood almost right away that it meant becoming two people, hiding my true self and letting people think the exterior public self was who I was. I lived in the shadow of my life. You can't imagine what that means." His words challenged Silva with the strength gained from decades of self-discipline. "You can't imagine. But back then, we—people like me— had no choice. The price of tolerance, of a place to live even, was silence if not outright denial." His voice softened. "I envy the younger men today but that doesn't mean I can be like them. I'm sixty-five years old. The way I am in every sense is fixed." He gazed at Silva, his eyes recording the shifting of various ideas in his head. "Yes, I'm gay. I don't know how much of a secret it is, and I'm not sure I care anymore."

Silva recalled Sergeant Dupoulis's cataloging of the secrets of Mellingham and silently agreed with Edwin. "Did George Frome ever threaten you with exposure?" Edwin's reaction gave Silva his answer.

"Frome could be extremely puerile sometimes. Specifically, yes, he did, once or twice."

"What did he have to say about it?" Silva asked. "This may not seem important, but it is."

Edwin didn't answer right away. "George implied once that he might tell Aunt Catherine." The memory was obviously distasteful to Edwin; he screwed up his mouth. "I believe he said, 'What would your aunt—it is your aunt, isn't it?—have to say about that?'" Neither man heard any of the sounds of the station beyond the chief's office door or of the street outside.

"And that scared you. Understandable; it could have ruined your relationship with your aunt."

"No, it couldn't," he said, pleased to add to Silva's surprise. "I told him she already knew."

"That was quite a risk, wasn't it? He might have—"

"It was true." Edwin interrupted. "I told her years ago." His voice rose angrily, broke, then softened as his heart opened again to a brief but formative chapter in his early life, one he had never shared with anyone else. "When I was a teenager. I'd figured it out when I was pretty young; you do, you know. But it wasn't until I was a teenager that I understood what it meant for my life. That it was the way I am. That I'd always be the way I am." He grew thoughtful, calm, meditative, and Silva let him wander.

"I told my parents, after a great deal of soul searching and doubt and personal revulsion. I just told them one night over dinner. No preparation, no warning, nothing to prepare them for the truth. I was a bit impulsive back then."

Silva shook his head; he could imagine the scene—the shock, denial, anger; later would come the pleadings and perhaps even rejection, for a while, but only for a while, for Edwin had lived in apparent contentment with his parents until their death. "That must have been difficult," Silva said, wanting to be kind.

"It was, oh it was, but not the way you mean," he said. "They looked at me like blanks, no expression, nothing. But I saw them look at each other, you know the way people do when they have the same reaction to a third person and they check in with each other to see if the other one got it. And then they said they loved me anyway, that it didn't really matter. But they withdrew. If I live to be a hundred I will never forget the way they looked. My mother went inside herself into a place I didn't know was there, and my father did too. They were just gone, sitting in front of me, but gone. More gone than when they were dead. I think it's the closest a human being could ever come to being invisible. They were completely gone from me." Throughout his narration, Edwin kept his eyes locked on the ground between them, his feet pulled in under the chair, his hands clasped in front of him as he leaned forward, his elbows resting on the arms of the chair. In the silence that followed a group of teenage boys ambled past the open window, their easy rough banter carrying into Silva's office.

"You said your aunt knew. Did your parents tell her?"

"No, I did." Edwin leaned back, crossed his legs, and met Silva's eye. "My parents pretended nothing was changed, but things were different in little ways. One day Aunt Catherine asked me if I'd had a falling out with my parents. I told her I'd had to give them some bad news. She asked me what it was so I decided to get it all over with." He laughed. "I must have been feeling a bit melodramatic there, sort of imagined myself cutting my last tie to Mellingham and my family before leaving home and doing God knows what. Thrown out into the world. A sinner." He chuckled at the adolescent memory.

"And?"

Edwin dropped his hands to his lap, his head hanging forward. "Her eyes flashed with a pain I had never known could be so deep, so intense. It was a shock to her. It hurt her more than I feared it would, much more than I thought it would hurt my mother and father. But she covered it up almost instantly. I remember exactly what she said to me. 'Well, Edwin, aren't you the gentleman to think to tell me just in case I might mind. But, of course, you know I don't.' It must have cost her a lot to say that. She didn't hesitate for a second, not a second. She insisted I stay to supper and we talked about my plans. There was no pretense. She never suggested anything that might mean I had to lie. It was a great relief. We've been best friends ever since." He paused. "I wanted to go to college. My father wanted me to go into the army before—"

Silva nodded. The story didn't surprise him now that he

watched Edwin tell it. "How old were you when you told her?"

"Just seventeen. Her husband had died in the war a few months earlier, her parents were quite old by then. I began to feel I was the son she's never had." He smiled at Silva. "We are so melodramatic and self-important at that age."

"She's remained something of a benefactor in your life," Silva said.

"She has indeed. She put me through college, even offered to pull a few strings and get me out of the service when I was drafted. But I wanted to go, after I got used to the idea—sort of a chance to prove myself. And my father was pleased in his way. He wasn't so cold after that. Sometimes in the evening I'd catch him looking at this." He touched the scar at his temple. "Things were better after Korea, at least for me."

Joe Silva could well imagine what it might mean to reduce a father's ire by joining the military. One of his sisters had dated a man opposed to the Vietnam War with a passion that allowed of no meals eaten in peace; she dated him for almost a year, giving her father one of the most painful periods in his life. It was a relief to everyone when, the many paper-sharp issues still unresolved, she simply broke up with him. Silva never understood how some families could live with tension as a constant in their lives; it was to him unbearable. Getting through Edwin's initial hostility and suspicion hadn't been all that pleasant either.

"So you never made a point of concealing or revealing," Silva said. "Which means George Frome wasn't really tuned in to life in Mellingham, was he?"

"We didn't move in the same circles, if that's what you mean. I guess people around here have figured it out." He glanced at the chief. "I went into Boston once in a while when I was younger, back in the sixties, but my friends moved on and I got caught up in my life here. It's different today. This new generation is changing things. They'll never know what it means to look into the future as a teenager and wonder if you will ever have someone of your own to be close to, or just the freedom to be that is our birthright as human beings. Wow, I do get maudlin, don't I?" He laughed but his eyes didn't.

Silva nodded. It wasn't his place to say that a man didn't have to be gay to feel as Edwin did.

10

Monday Afternoon— and Later

For the last several hours Chief Silva had let Edwin Bennett's story rattle around in his head while he tended to the other emergencies of life in Mellingham—a resident who threatened to file suit to reclaim what she regarded as her beach, since it lay at the end of her lawn, and wanted the police to remove the hundred or so trespassers at once; a tourist whose car was towed only five minutes past the time limit on the sign; a lobsterman who found his underwater locker broken into and suspected his catch had been stolen. He and Silva both knew the police could do nothing for him, but he had to tell someone his paycheck was gone.

When Edwin Bennett left Silva's office for the second time, he left a dried-out dirty brown root about eight inches long, tapering like a carrot. With the aid of a large pair of tweezers, Silva gingerly lifted the evidence and packed it off to the medical examiner's office, using the few hours' delay before he could get any response as a reason to slip the case out of mind and let his unconscious work on it. He knew what he thought about it but still needed to let his ideas settle. Consciously, he could reconsider the perspectives Edwin had offered; they certainly had merit.

Any time of the day or night a passerby could stop in a

car or linger on a walk past Mrs. Rocklynd's front garden, and merely reach down and pull out the monkshood long enough to cut off its tuber. Done quickly and efficiently, the cutting would be over before anyone noticed. Not even Mrs. Rocklynd need know anyone had been in her garden.

Even I wouldn't have known, Silva mused, if Edwin Bennett hadn't been such a keen gardener, eager for a place to plant long after local gardeners had set out their plantings for the season. Now was the time to enjoy the work of the spring. But Edwin had waded in among the blooms, adding more and removing the failures. Silva liked to think he would have found the evidence anyway, but he was honest enough with himself to know he might not have. Edwin's appearance with the root was more a relief than the chief dared reveal to the other man. There was nothing worse than having a murder without weapon, motive, or suspect, unless it was a murder with all those but not enough evidence to convict. And Silva knew he was coming dangerously close to that.

Nevertheless, Edwin was right about one thing— Annalee Windolow was a guilty party in all this, and she did have reason to fear George Frome. Bringing her to book, however, was not going to be easy. Perhaps Frome knew that. The idea struck Silva as far too possible, and he momentarily set aside the duty roster—summer was always a difficult time with the influx of summer residents and tourists.

Since his unpleasant visit to Frome's apartment Friday evening, which now seemed like weeks in the past, he had given relatively little thought to the victim, and that could well be a mistake. Interrupted briefly by the telephone, Silva felt a longing for the days of his thirties when he had a left-brained precision in his investigations, each piece of material evidence leading inexorably to an end—and a person—already clearly marked out by circumstances. The certitude of those early investigations was reinforcing, and probably thoroughly undeserved, Silva reminded himself. After listening to a carefully couched argument, Silva advised the telephone caller to consult the Fish and Wildlife Warden and transferred the call to another officer; this was a person who needed to be told officially that an egret picking its way across a private lawn—for whatever reason—did not constitute found property. Silva hinted there might even be a law against interfering with egrets and certain other shore birds. The caller snorted and waited on the line, unimpressed.

It occurred to Silva that Frome might have known the answer to that question, as he had known so many other answers to security questions last Thursday afternoon, making Silva wonder why Frome had pressed him to undertake the inspection. Frome had in fact known almost everything Silva had come prepared to tell him, which was part—but only part—of the reason Silva had wondered about Frome's real agenda. The man made no secret to anyone of Silva's visit and its purpose, though he apparently had not meant to bring it up for formal discussion at the board meeting the same evening. This led Silva to suspect a hidden agenda and he now believed he knew what it was. Still, that didn't mean Frome was right. As smart as the man was, Silva was convinced that George Frome had drawn erroneous conclusions about a board member and then set about conveying that conclusion through Silva's visit. But Silva couldn't prove it.

The case was like the man—an emptiness below the dust. Silva still had trouble imagining a life ending, even in violence, that did not evoke a choir of mourning relatives full of stories of the deceased's foibles and successes, greatest moments or sweetest secrets, all told between plates of food and embraces. No one had emerged from George Frome's life to mourn, to remember, to love the ongoing life that is memory and family. No one even revealed an implacable hatred, an old grudge; no one was made empty by his death.

It was this that troubled Silva most—though he had seen it before—even more than the slim material he had gathered in his investigations. It was a tragedy for a man or woman to go through life without coming to the end loving and beloved. Joe took Frome's life as a personal warning, for he had gone on thinking of himself as part of a large family that kept getting larger and larger every year, but in that he had been deceiving himself. His brothers' and sisters' families were getting larger, but he was not of them; he was an appendage, a remnant of their earlier family. Having taken his natal family in his heart into adulthood, he didn't see his siblings moving away into their own orbits. They loved him no less but they could not do what he had to do for himself. When Joe thought about his own apartment now, it was obvious to him that he expected to share his life with other people, though of late he hadn't. Frome's apartment warned of a hostile greeting to anyone who strayed inside. His home was designed to repel others; he was a man who wanted to be alone, whereas Joe felt he was alone partly by choice and partly by accident.

This distinction between himself and the dead man soothed him. To find himself in the same strange world as George Frome would have demoralized Joe, a measure of his too great sympathy with a lonely man dying alone rather than any inherent alienation from society. But it was nevertheless cautionary. Now, in his late forties, Joe was disinclined to begin the life he should have started in his twenties. Confronting George Frome's death was giving him the unexpected opportunity to grieve for a life that might have been—his own.

■ ■ ■

Some leaders receive the news of an offending employee, from petty theft to murder, as a moral obligation they would rather be spared; others regard the news with relief, as one more problem solved. Walter Marsh, the president of the Arbella Society, fell into the latter category, at once alert and eager upon receiving Chief Silva's call at his office in Mellingham. When the chief arrived just before three o'clock, a bystander would not have marked Joe Silva as a bearer of bad, or even awkward, news, but rather as a valued client. Silva perceived this, too, and momentarily worried he had not made himself clear over the telephone.

The president was loose and lanky, much like his attitude to life and the Arbella Society, easily twisting himself into expressions of delight, pleasure, curiosity, and goodwill. He thought Joe Silva a rather decent sort and was pleased to have him stop by.

"This is what every one means by protocol, I suppose," he said energetically after the chief declined anything to drink. By midmorning the heat had settled into the small town like a conquering enemy, provoking slowdowns and stoppages by the weary and sweaty victims. The president adjusted the fan to include the chief in its orbit. "I mean, here you're coming to let me know what you've found out before arresting anyone." He sat down again, stretching his neck upward in enthusiastic anticipation, reminding Silva of a hysterical chicken.

"I think you misunderstood me. I'm not about to arrest anyone. What I want to talk to you about first, before I go any further, is my suspicions about another matter," Silva explained.

The president was vastly disappointed, and deflated in his chair. After he took in Silva's words, he brightened up a bit. "Oh well, that's something. Go ahead."

"It's about my visit to the Arbella Society last Thursday," Silva said. The president winced.

"It was the topic of some discussion at the board meeting that night." The president tried to conceal his disappointment at another meeting gone awry.

"Mr. Frome never made it clear to me exactly what he was looking for. He made a lot of general comments and a few dark allusions to things going missing," Silva said. The president grimaced; Silva continued. "It bothered me, especially since I couldn't see any signs of illegal entry and he gave me no examples of things that were missing."

The president pursed his lips and said, "True, true. Absolutely true. The other board members pointed that out right away."

"That made me wonder why he had wanted me there," Silva said. "That seemed to be the key. He worked very hard to persuade me to go over there. Suppose it wasn't a security investigation he wanted but the presence of a police officer. My visit there was sure to be talked about, so that got me thinking about other possibilities."

"What?"

"I think he wanted to warn or maybe frighten someone," Silva explained.

"George Frome?" The president gaped. "That's downright devious. Why, the old—" He stopped as the idea sank in. "Warn them about what?"

"About stealing from the Arbella House," Silva suggested.

"You think someone's stealing from us?"

"Frome thought someone was."

"Who? Half the board members own most of the good stuff and the other half don't seem to care all that much." His own words caught his attention, making him sit upright in his seat; his arm shot out. "I don't mean they don't care. They do. They do. But they're not interested enough to steal. Not the board members."

"Mr. Frome may have disagreed with you." Silva waited for the other man's surprise to abate. "I agreed with him that the Arbella House is porous but I don't think anyone has broken in recently. That's what he wanted me to think but it didn't work. That was just a cover. He wanted the board members to sit up and notice what he was doing, especially one in particular."

"Who?" The president was agog now, listening intently though he had no idea where Silva was going.

"Kelly Kuhn," Silva said.

The president's mouth dropped open, then he sputtered his protest. "I don't believe it. I don't believe it for a moment."

"Neither do I," Silva said.

"But, but, you just said—"

"George Frome singled out Kelly Kuhn, but I think he was wrong," Silva said.

"I'm lost. Is someone stealing from the Arbella Society? Kelly? Is it Kelly?" The president pulled out a handkerchief and dabbed at his forehead, then pulled the fan close.

"I don't think Kelly Kuhn's stealing from the Society, but someone else may be. According to Marian Davis, Mr. Kuhn has been up to the third floor only once. That time George came across him knocking some things over, commented on his size or awkwardness or whatever, and generally made Kelly feel self-conscious. At least according to Marian Davis."

"Oh well, if Marian said so, she would know," the president said.

"After that he stayed on the ground floor and the intern brought down paintings for him to work on." The president nodded in agreement.

"Well, that solves it then. It can't have been the intern. George was just unduly suspicious," the president said.

"Not quite," Silva said. "Someone else was removing paintings from the Society, paintings probably uncataloged by Kelly and so untraceable. This is part of what

George caught on to but he thought Kelly was doing it."

"I'm confused," said the president.

Silva felt the sweat dripping down his chest and hoped he didn't have to explain the same point many more times. "George Frome was the only person who knew the entire house, all the floors and everything on them," Silva said, beginning again from another angle. "He made a point when he first joined the board, according to Marian Davis—"

"She would know," the president chimed in.

"He made a point of getting a look at everything that was there, and he had a good memory. He could remember what he'd seen and he could reconstruct what was missing, with enough time."

The president narrowed his eyes and looked hard at Chief Silva, his doubts displaced by intense curiosity. "It was amazing what he knew sometimes. He kept count of the teacups. Who ever heard of a man doing that? It was amazing, simply amazing."

"Yes, I'll bet it was," the chief said. "That's what I think he was doing up in the attic that night."

"The attic? I'm lost," the president said. "For the life of me I can't figure out why anyone would want to look at old oil paintings up in that stifling, smelly place." The man's distaste was obvious. Gone was the eager leader, the hardy manager; beneath it all was the incipient Philistine.

"It must have seemed easier to pull out a group of paintings and store them separately while he tried to figure out if one of the group was missing," Silva explained. "I'll have to ask Kelly, but those must represent a grouping of Early American paintings; George took them from the third-floor storage and moved them upstairs."

"But why?"

"To give himself time to remember the whole group, particularly the one or ones that were missing," Silva said.

"So someone was stealing paintings?"

"I think so. I found a sketch in Frome's notebook in his apartment. It was done after Monday; his notes for the day are dated. The drawing doesn't look like much but it kept coming back to me and I finally realized it was a bare outline of another picture I'd seen recently."

The president stared, then swallowed and said only one word. "Where?"

"In Annalee Windolow's living room," Silva answered.

"No! Well, I'll be—" What he would be he didn't say, just stared in amazement at Chief Silva. "How do you think she got it?"

"By taking it. She knew her way around the building, and when the house is full of people downstairs no one is going to notice someone going up to the third floor. After that, all she had to do was wait for Marian to go to the door. If she picked a day, morning or afternoon, when no volunteers were working in the office, she could slip out with whatever she wanted and no one would ever notice."

"I don't believe it. I mean I do, but, well, it's so bold," the president said, with admiration.

"Frome was right. The house does leak, but it's not the board members' fault."

"Well, that's a relief." The president expanded as he sat back in his chair.

"I've told you what I've surmised from the evidence in Frome's apartment and his behavior Thursday. I've seen a painting at Mrs. Windolow's house that may be from the Society. It has on it, in the back, the same kinds of stickers that are on the backs of the paintings Frome had in the attic," Silva explained.

"Oh, that's important," the president agreed. "Yes, definitely." He nodded vigorously, imagining his duty as president of the Arbella Society in this time of crisis.

"It may not count for much," Silva said. "Kelly Kuhn

pointed out that such stickers were fairly common. What is more important is the newly sanded corner as though someone was getting it cleaned up for something. Kelly told me he sanded a spot, then painted on the new number. This one may have been next in line to be recataloged. His intern may have done the preliminary work; Kelly didn't recognize it when he saw it at Mrs. Windolow's."

"Maybe we should ask him again," the president said.

"Kelly or someone else has to identify the painting as formerly in storage at the Arbella House and the property of the Society, and then request Mrs. Windolow to produce a bill of sale or turn the painting over to the Society."

"Oh yes, very good." The president's plan of attack grew more elaborate. "Do you think she'll do it? Give it back? Can Kelly identify it?"

"I don't know. He's not very interested in that period but he might be persuaded to look at the painting. Mrs. Windolow may fight you."

"Yes, yes, I'll speak to Kelly at once."

"I must remind you, sir, that all this is circumstantial so far. This is just a thread I had to follow out in order to eliminate it from the murder investigation. No one has pressed any charges or made any accusations outright. I'm telling you all this so that you can take care of it yourselves, or call in an attorney, as you see fit," Silva explained. "This is not officially a police matter. It won't be one unless you choose to make it so."

"Oh, I understand," he said. "I wonder if Kelly will do it, though. I think Mrs. Windolow is a client of his."

"If I were you, I'd present what you have to him. In clear, concise terms. Don't hold back. The jolt won't do him any harm," Silva said. And it might do him some good, he added to himself.

"Yes. I'll be unaccommodating in this," the president said. "Firm. To think George was right, after everything that was said at the last meeting." A bemused gaze came over the president's face, mystifying Silva, who could not have known that at that moment the president was having a vision of a different sort of board meeting, a different sort of discussion arising out of a different sort of agenda, a vision of a dream becoming a reality.

■ ■ ■

On the drive over to the police station, and all through the wait in Chief Silva's office, Gwen McDuffy assured herself that she would look back on this moment with an indulgent smile if not laughter, but she didn't really believe it. She was here because she had no alternative. That was all. She wasn't going to aggrandize her behavior by indirect references to sacrifice, responsibility, or anything else. She was here because she couldn't run and didn't know what else to do. Ironically, now that she was finally here, Chief Silva was not.

It was tempting to view this turn of events, at five-thirty on Monday afternoon, as a sign from heaven, an opportunity to retract one decision and try on another, or at least revert back to the one she had been living with, but she could do no more than toy with the idea while she waited for Silva. For some time she had felt trapped and now, like a man sitting on a ledge, she just wanted to get it over with, whatever "it" might be. The struggles of the last few years had left her more ashamed than afraid, and still vulnerable. That was about to come to an end but it didn't make her any happier. By the time Chief Silva arrived, Gwen had retraced the steps of her reasoning, jumping from fear to fear, like stone slabs on a garden pathway, until she once again had arrived at her resolve, therefore greeting the chief, not with the tentative, falsely brave facade of her arrival, but with the tense, brittle veneer of courage about to collapse.

"It's about my children," she blurted out at once.

"They're not mine." It was done and she took a deep breath, still gripping her hands in front of her but easing back in her chair. Silva nudged the office door closed with his foot.

"Where are the parents?" he asked.

"I don't know." She looked at him with the eyes of a guilty child.

"You've tried to reach them?" His question was put calmly but it belied the surprise he felt. For the last several days he had imagined excuses for her sometimes remote behavior during the investigation and he didn't like seeing how wrong he was.

She nodded in reply to his question, then said, "I've called every place I can think of; they're gone."

"Who are they?" It was hard for him to separate the members of the small family from each other in his mind; they looked so much alike, behaved so naturally in public. In fact, the more he thought about it, the more far-fetched Gwen McDuffy's confession seemed. She had none of the traits of a kidnapper, nor did the children behave as though they were kidnapped. She lived in a town where her family was known, living in the same place for years, not just a few days; the children went to school, participated in youth activities, spent long stretches of time away from her, with other adults or other children, or alone. People were welcome in her home. Gwen was never nervous or anxious in the manner of a kidnapping parent. "You know their names? The parents' names?"

"Oh yes. I know them." She sighed and studied him speculatively. "It doesn't make much sense but it happened. Probably happens a lot now."

"What happens?" Silva asked. "When did you first meet them, the children and their parents?"

"When?" She tried to smile. "In another lifetime. They lived down the street from us." She took a deep breath and crossed her legs. "I left Mellingham when I was eighteen and got a job and then I got married, to someone from around here. He wanted to go out West so we started to work our way across. It was going to be fun," she said ruefully. "This was back in the early seventies. Well, we got about halfway there, after I don't know how many years, and just stopped. It was this crummy town out in the Midwest, and we just ran out of money, ran out of energy, I don't know. We just realized one day that we weren't going anywhere."

Gwen's breath started to get rough. "Jimmie got really bored and miserable; he spent more and more time at the bars downtown. I went with him in the beginning, but they were so dirty and smelly. I got tired of being in a dark place on Saturday afternoon. Besides, I kept hoping we were going to move on."

She laughed, perhaps at herself, perhaps at the situation of her youth. "Whenever I pushed him about it, he told me to quit nagging him. We had awful fights about it." Silva nodded sympathetically.

"Anyway, there was a family down the street from us. The woman, Polly, used to come by in the evenings after work and complain about her husband. We'd have a beer and sit out back on the porch. We lived on the first floor. I thought she had the same problem I had only longer and maybe that was why she found it easier to drink her way into a good mood. Then Mark, her husband, came by one night and blew up at her and I realized she was pregnant and I didn't even know. Jennie was just a baby. It drove Mark crazy when Polly drank and she did it sometimes just to get him going. It was awful. I started to worry about the baby, with all that drinking. When Philip came along, he was fine." Gwen looked up at him for the first time in long minutes. "I felt so guilty that I might have contributed to some horrible problem in the baby by sitting out drinking with Polly. You can't know how relieved I was that he was okay. Boy, was I dumb!" She shook her head. "It got to be how I always felt about them. I felt guilty for things I couldn't possibly be responsible for."

"He's a fine-looking boy. Seems bright, too," Silva said.

"He is," Gwen said with a broad smile. "But that's not the problem, is it?"

"I don't know. You haven't told me, yet. What happened then?"

"The rest of what I didn't know was that Polly had been working to stay clean until Philip was born and then she was gone again. I thought the alcohol was bad enough, but she was into much heavier stuff. Sometimes she said she was too sick to go to work but as soon as Mark left in the morning, she was gone, too, but not to work. Finally she quit her job. Sometimes she'd be gone all day. She wouldn't come home at night. When I hadn't seen her once for a few days, I went over to their place and found the two kids in a crib with their diapers soiled and no one around. The door was locked—I had a key—but Polly wasn't there. She came back later, happy, hyper, ready to conquer the world. That's when I knew. It finally dawned on me how bad things had gotten. I don't know what she was on, but she was on it all right."

"What about your husband all this time?" Silva asked.

"What about him is right." She shrugged. "He couldn't hold a job. He started to get nasty. And then after he finally—" She glanced up at Silva. "He hit me, so I smashed the laundry board over him." She looked away. "I had no idea I could be so angry. He was gone after that. He left, just took off. So did Polly a little later."

"Together?" Silva asked.

"Jimmie and Polly?" Gwen laughed heartily. "Not likely. Jimmie thought Polly was total scum and Polly thought Jimmie was a rat." Her laugh subsided into a tremulous sigh. "It was a nightmare. Anyway, that's how it happened.

The children, I mean. Polly just had to have her stuff and off she went. One day she was there and after a few more we all realized she wasn't coming back, at least not for a long time."

There was nothing original in Gwen's story of two families falling apart but Silva could never listen to anyone repeat the cliché of familial destruction without feeling a penetrating sympathy. "So you and Mark—"

"No." Gwen shook her head with a half smile on her face. "No. Definitely not. I went on working and taking care of the kids and Mark went on complaining about Polly. Then one day he started being real nice to me, taking me shopping, asking me how I felt, taking me to the movies. In the end he asked me to move in with him and I did. I got a divorce from Jimmie, but, well, I don't know. Mark was overwhelmed with the kids. He started coming home later and later after work, which meant I was getting to work later and later. I worked nights then. You can guess the rest. By the time Jennie was three, Mark was a yelling, swinging drunk, just the way he'd been when he married Polly. He couldn't stay straight any more than she could."

"And he left too."

Gwen nodded. "I almost went crazy. Those were the worst years of my life back there but they turned into the best."

"So you moved back here after Mark disappeared," Silva said, but Gwen didn't reply immediately.

"Not exactly. We were always broke. I couldn't count on the older women in the neighborhood any more—they were kind of disgusted with us, at least they were fed up with Jimmie, and Mark and Polly and I just sort of got tossed in there too. My job wasn't going anywhere either so I quit and went on welfare. I'm not proud of this but I didn't have any choice. I talked them into giving me a one-time supplement for clothing and housing, and with that and my first month's check, I packed up the kids and left." She swallowed hard and then glared defiantly at him. "I left all the bills unpaid and just took off. I figured no one really knew who I was. I'd kept Jimmie's name after the divorce and never told anyone my maiden name."

"What about Jennie and Philip? Did you think about putting them in foster care?"

"I'm the only mother they've ever known. They trust me. I'm their mother. I wouldn't do that to them. I couldn't." She leaned forward, grasping the arms of her chair, the tears welling up in her eyes.

"And yet you're telling me all this. Why now?" Silva asked.

"I haven't any choice." She leaned back, dropped her head into her hands. "Back then I didn't think about the future. I just had to make things better, get away from a rotten life, a rotten place, a rotten past. I just wanted to put it all behind me. And I did. At least I thought I did."

"George Frome," Silva said in a moment of inspiration. Gwen gazed at him in admiration.

"How did you guess?"

"How did he?"

"That's what I wondered. And then when it came to me I had to laugh." And she did again, softly, kindly, as though she and Chief Silva were talking about nothing more serious than the innocent follies of their youth. Silva was enchanted by the change in her.

"We were in the drugstore and Jennie was picking through the fingernail polish and trying to find matching lipsticks. I told her if she picked the one she had in her hand, she'd look just like me. It was my shade. She said in great disgust," Gwen said, stopping to chuckle, "'But I don't want to look like you.' So she put the package back. But then Philip piped up with, 'You can't look like her, she's not your real mother.'"

Silva whistled softly. "So they know?"

"They must," Gwen said with some of the surprise she had felt at the time. "I didn't think they'd remember but they must have. I was stunned when he said that. You know, I heard them once talking about their dad, about Mark, but when I asked them about it, they just wanted to know if he was a McDuffy too. I told them he wasn't."

"Someone overheard you in the drugstore," Silva said.

"I saw George at the checkout so it must have been him because a few days later he said something to me at the Arbella Society about how fortunate some women were to have their adopted children turn out to look like them. It was a leading question but I pretended I had work to do and he went off to do something else."

"When was this?" Silva asked.

"That time was over a week ago," Gwen said.

"And the second time?"

She tilted her head back and said, "Thursday. This past Thursday. I ran into him in the drugstore right after I got off work." Her breathing grew short and quick and she looked warily at him. "He started talking about some children whose parents kidnapped them from their grandparents who were their guardians." Silva listened to the details of the encounter, but his thoughts were given over to Mrs. Alesander's worried visit to him a few days ago and her description of Gwen on that Thursday.

"So you thought he was hinting that someone might take Jennie and Philip," Silva said when she was finished. She nodded. Silva rubbed his chin with his right hand; he needed a shave, a shower, probably a haircut too. He was tired, tired of the ordinary, everyday misery people inflicted on each other, tired of feeling like he was caught in a half world of failing lives, tired of not having his own dreams anymore. "Why are you telling me all this now? You could have let it go."

"Because I don't want it hanging over my head. I want it

SUSAN OLEKSIW

to be over with. It frightened me too much to have George suddenly know. I want to get out from under this constant threat of discovery. I say to myself everyday, 'I'm not dishonest, I'm not sneaky, I did what I had to do to survive. They're good kids. I did the right thing.' But then I look at what I did. I took money from the state. I left the bills unpaid; they weren't much, but I left them. I ran off. It's not who I think I am. I want it to be over with."

Gwen looked out the tall narrow window facing the harbor, where working boats and pleasure craft tugged at their anchors side by side. Joe knew what she was seeing; he too turned to that scene time and again. The view often brought to mind, his at least, a sense that men and women, no matter how different they might seem on the surface, like bobbing lobster boats and day sailors, were tethered by the same human passions lying far below.

"I don't want to take any chances now," she said in a whisper. "I've raised them. They're like my own. It would destroy me if anything happened to them. I want it legal." Silva nodded; it was what he'd expected.

"There's no guarantee, you understand," he said. She nodded. He continued, "If you're sure about this, then you should call the Department of Social Services for this area and double-check the procedure, but I think it's pretty simple. You'll have to go over to Probate and Family Court, and file a petition for emergency guardianship. The court has what they call an attorney for the day who'll help you fill out the forms. And then later you can go back for permanent guardianship." It was a process he had guided other desperate men and women through often in his earlier years, and the information came out readily.

"You make it sound so simple," she said.

"It is. It's in the state's interest to keep the children in a stable home. There's no reason for them to object," Silva said. "I'll put in a word as a character witness, if you like."

Gwen was not prepared for this generosity, and Silva was not prepared for her gratitude. Each glanced out at the harbor beyond.

■ ■ ■

Catherine Rocklynd was expecting Chief Silva on the back terrace, sitting in the mild and glowing twilight, looking straight out toward the harbor glistening through the trees. She didn't rise to greet him, barely turned her head in fact as he came around the side of the house, keeping to the flagstone path. He hadn't bothered to knock at the front door, since he'd seen the housekeeper driving into Mellingham as he left the station. Mrs. Rocklynd had asked him to come late when he called her earlier in the evening.

"There's iced tea there," she said as he approached her; she waved her hand in the direction of a small table. Silva declined and pulled a chair closer to her, putting her at an angle to him. She continued to stare into the distance; he placed a paper bag on the ground beside him.

"Edwin Bennett came to see me this morning," Silva said. "He found a plant in your garden missing a root, a poisonous one. It's the same poison that killed George Frome. The plant showed signs of the root having been cut off with a knife."

"Really?" she replied. "What else did he say?" She was tired from the heat and sounded it, but there was an undercurrent of resolve and strength in her voice still.

"He suggested Annalee Windolow, or someone else, might have cut the root out."

She laughed. "He can be fanciful."

Silva waited in vain for Mrs. Rocklynd to look at him and could not speculate on what was going through her mind. Her disparagement of what she presumed to be something in Edwin's report to the chief put the conversation on another level, and Silva wanted them to be talking about the same thing at the same time.

"He brought me information," Silva countered. She turned to him then, but only for a moment.

"How can you possibly need a plant and an irresponsible suspicion about one of my neighbors? Is your murder investigation in such desperate straits?" The words hit the air like pebbles falling on a pile of rocks.

"I don't have to take them as a package deal; I can separate the two," he said. The coming of night depressed their voices; they spoke softly though there was no one else around. "It's the root that interests me."

A male cardinal touched down on the edge of the lawn, near a cluster of strawberry plants, and jabbed at the last remaining berries before flying off.

"People who don't know anything about the natural world are always so surprised to learn that the male of the species is so much prettier, so much more colorful, than the female. They expect nature, in animals and birds at least, to reflect the human world. Why, I can't imagine. We seem to do everything topsy-turvy, turning life inside out." She followed the cardinal's flight into the tree branches above.

"He said the root came from your garden," Silva said, as he edged his way closer to the real topic.

"He's a very keen gardener. It started after his parents died. Well, maybe it didn't start then, but it certainly blossomed, you might say." She brushed away a few wisps of white hair from her forehead. It was still hot.

"He said he dug it up yesterday, around noon, after he'd noticed that the plant wasn't doing very well," Silva went on.

"Monkshood are temperamental. They don't like heat. I shouldn't have had the branches of the oak thinned out quite so much," she replied. "It lets in too much light now."

"He thought it might be something else," Silva said.

"Such as?" A trace of belligerence crept into her voice but she checked herself.

"Such as damage to the main root, the tuber."

Mrs. Rocklynd surveyed the back garden, the wildflowers growing beyond their allotted space, the dead blooms on iris stalks that leaned down to the ground. It needed work and her knees were no longer up to it, nor the rest of her.

"I have more squirrels than you can count, and a few rabbits too, along with the usual complement of raccoons and woodchucks and lord knows what else." She sighed deeply. "I'm surprised I have any plants left."

"It's not likely they'd dig up a tuber from monkshood and leave a clean cut behind," Silva said.

Like the second hand on a clock, Mrs. Rocklynd's head turned in tiny spurts toward the chief. "A clean cut?"

"That's right. No other part of the plant was damaged; the tuber was severed with a single cut," Silva said.

"I probably shouldn't have such poisonous plants so near to the road; anyone can stop and take whatever they want and I'd be none the wiser," she said, turning away.

"That's what your nephew thinks too, but it doesn't go anywhere," Silva said.

"What does that mean? Doesn't go anywhere? If you're going to ask me questions, please don't use slang. I don't like it," she replied with spirit.

"I apologize," Silva said, unmoved. "Anyone might have stopped to take a plant or a root, but that by itself isn't enough." The chief waited for the obligatory response but Mrs. Rocklynd was silent. She had reached for her walking stick, an antique ivory cane with silver tip and handle and designs engraved on the creamy smooth body. The stick waved in her hand like a palm tree taking the brunt of a monsoon wind.

"Whoever took the root also had to get it into the refrigerator at the Arbella House," he said.

"Really, you are imaginative," she said.

"The monkshood tuber contains the poison aconitine, which is especially toxic just before flowering. In your front garden, that would be right about now." He looked out where Mrs. Rocklynd was staring. The gardens that had always seemed so sweet and domestic now were ominous, shielding dangers ready to kill or cripple as decisively as wild animals or car accidents. The summer evening took on a different cast and Silva found himself thinking of the fear and respect accorded to medicine men in tribal cultures. Knowledge of the plant world meant power, and that power was dangerous. Had there ever been an Eden?

"I know what's in my plants," she said. "What's that got to do with George Frome's death?"

"George Frome died from what he ate in the attic Thursday night. His salad contained aconitine, which someone added to it sometime on Thursday," Silva said.

"That's a lot of time. Anyone could have done it," she said. "You're pretty sloppy for a police officer, if you'll forgive my saying so. I can hardly be responsible for what might happen if someone takes a plant from my garden." The confidence in her voice had an unmistakable edge to it, the edge of class, the edge that cut Joe Silva when he presumed too much, challenged too much, risked too much. But he was Joe Silva, the son of an adult immigrant, not bred to believe in an unwritten code though he could read it as well as anyone.

"It only seems like a lot of time," he said, ignoring her jibe. "And only two people could have done it." The silence scooped in the sounds of a small motorboat entering the inner harbor, filling the straining space between them.

"Two?" she said in a flat voice.

"Marian Davis was alone at five-thirty while George Frome was out, but I can't find any reason for her to want to harm him." Again Silva paused. "That left me thinking about the only other person who had the opportunity to put the root into his salad."

"Aren't you forgetting something?"

"I don't think so."

"Why would George eat a poisonous root in his supper?" Her disdain for Silva was palpable.

"A very good question," he agreed as he reached down for the paper bag. He placed on the small table between them two nearly identical roots, long, tan-brown, with dirt still clinging to them, both shaped like a medium-sized carrot. Mrs. Rocklynd stared at the dirty pair; she ground her teeth, working her jaw as her hand gripped and ungripped the handle of the cane.

"So?"

"One is the tuber from a monkshood plant and the other is a horseradish. Remarkable how similar they are; almost identical," Silva said. Mrs. Rocklynd glared at him. "We found a horseradish in Mr. Frome's refrigerator and slivers of horseradish in the Arbella House attic, along with the rest of his salad. We also found slivers of the monkshood tuber, sliced in precisely the same way." The discovery of how simple it had been to introduce the poison had sent the medical examiner's office into a flurry of discussions about gardens, their neighbors, florists, and flower shows. There hadn't been so much excitement since a man walked into the office ten years ago, stripped off his clothes, and insisted he be allowed to help with his own autopsy.

"How many people know that this tuber and this vegetable are nearly identical? A lot of people may know what George Frome ate regularly—he was a man of rigid habits—but only one knew how to take advantage of it."

"That is a ridiculous assertion." She turned to face him. "The idea of coming here and accusing me! No one for a minute would believe this. No one." The blood rose to her forehead. "This is outrageous."

Silva waited impassively. "Only one person was able to get to the kitchen alone and tamper with George Frome's dinner. Ironically, probably no one would have noticed or even remembered if you hadn't made a single mistake."

Catherine Rocklynd was torn between curiosity and revulsion, curiosity to know what mistake Silva meant to dangle in front of her and revulsion at the very idea of being questioned in this manner by a police officer. But she couldn't ask; she could only hunger for Silva to keep talking.

"When you went out to get the dip, you dropped the shredded tuber on top of the salad, just like a little more horseradish. You used your handkerchief to pick up anything you dropped because the poison is absorbed through the skin. Then you took the dip back to the meeting and settled back for a good discussion."

"This is nonsense, but if you're enjoying yourself, I suppose I can't stop you."

"Then you had something to eat and another board member pointed to a crumb, perhaps, on your lip and automatically you reached for a napkin, found you had none, and just reached for your handkerchief. You got hold of it in your purse on the floor. I don't know exactly what happened then—if it was juice from the tuber or a tiny piece—but you suddenly felt the first signs of aconitine poisoning. A tingling, then a burning sensation, maybe even numbing?"

Mrs. Rocklynd looked away.

"There wasn't enough to do more than startle you, which it did. You pulled your hand away. Everyone thought you'd scraped your hand on the chair, gotten a splinter or cut yourself," Silva said. "Your shock, even temporary, scared your friends. Marian Davis and your nephew thought you were in trouble. You must have looked pretty bad there for a while."

"This is preposterous." She spit out the words.

"Everyone after that was aware you'd been out of the room for a while," he said. "You were the only one. You alone had the chance to introduce poison into Frome's meal." His even voice drifted across the darkening shadows but Mrs. Rocklynd heard only the charge. She rose.

"How dare you! How dare you! The nerve!" One hand grasped her cane with thick bony fingers still strong and hard, the other held to the chair. She leaned away from Silva in elegant outrage. He gave her a stern appraising look in return and waited for her to return to her seat. She was an old woman and he was a man and the chief of police.

"Do you realize who I am? Why would I do such a thing?" She curled her lip and her white hair flew out in twisted spokes as she tossed her head.

"Why did you agree to sell him the log house?" She blenched at Silva's question and again he knew he was right.

"You assume too much," she began. "He was very interested in historical architecture, that's all."

"He was expecting to gain ownership; you had agreed to sell," he said.

"You still don't give me any reason," she said. "I hardly need the money."

"No. If you'd needed the money, you could have sold it to Edwin easily, or anyone you trusted to do with it as you wanted. You sold it to George Frome because you didn't have any choice."

This time her eyes were fastened on his face, her breathing growing heavy. Her shoulders tensed and she drew back as though she feared being struck.

"That's, that's—" She struggled to refute him with emotion.

"I suspect it has something to do with Edwin," he said. The pain flickering across her face confirmed his guess. "He's starting to look a lot like you."

She lifted her chin, perhaps to keep it from quivering, perhaps to block his accusation, and slowly shook her head from side to side.

"George would have noticed something like that," Silva said. "He could have figured it out for himself just by looking at the two of you, or he might have caught on when he came across some old photographs. He saw everything that came in and not long ago someone donated a large collection of old pictures. Something there might have given him the idea. He had several in his apartment that we can probably have identified, if we need to; I suspect they'll turn out to be pictures of you and Edwin at various stages in your lives. It doesn't matter now. He knew." Throughout, Silva kept his voice level, even, low, slipping the truth through the interstices in the wall of her passion, outrage, denial.

"And you?" she asked. It was a question Silva had been hoping to avoid, for it revealed the weakness of his case against her but not the level of truth he had reached.

"Your nephew told me about his early years, including the time he came to you to tell you about his being gay."

She was horrified. "Edwin? He doesn't—"

"He doesn't know. If he ever thought about it, he's repressed it. He loves you deeply but as a nephew." Silva could go no farther; he had brought her to the edge—of truth, of crisis, of defeat, of what he wasn't sure himself—and she stood on the precipice, swayed and buffeted by her past, her future, her feelings, or more that was still hidden from him. He calculated roughly that Edwin Bennett had been born in 1929 or 1930, during the Depression, in another time, almost another culture, when Mrs. Rocklynd was still the young, beautiful Catherine Hamden, a girl whose world was untouched by the unpleasant, inconvenient realities of desperate searches for work, for food, for safety.

"You must have been very young," he said.

"He was raised by my cousin. He had a very good

upbringing. I saw to it," she said. "It cost me what might have been one of the best years of my life. Right after my debut. But I never begrudged him that. I had to fight my parents to make sure he didn't drift out of my life. They wanted him given to strangers, but he was my son, family. I couldn't let it happen." She shuddered as she gave up the truth. Even now the implications of that year in her life for who she was, Catherine Hamden Rocklynd, were more than she could lay out before him. "I did everything I could for him. You have no idea the sacrifices entailed. Today women, girls even, lug around all sorts of children without any sense of responsibility for them. I saw to it he was raised properly. My cousin knew from the start how I felt about it." She jutted out her chin. "She knew what it means to have a heritage to pass on; she was born in the Hamden line. If she'd married better, well, too late now," she grumbled.

"George pressed you for the log house with hints about what he knew," Silva said.

"You could tell he wasn't— The very idea of thinking he could just buy something like that." She turned a hard face to him. "There's nothing you can do about it. You have no evidence, just the ravings of a weary old woman."

He nodded. She was right, as far as she'd gone.

"What're you going to do?" She pushed the cane out and straightened her arm as she lay back in her chair.

"I'll send a car for you in the morning and you can come down to the station for questioning," he said matter-of-factly. She paled and gazed simple-mindedly at him.

"You can't. Don't you realize who I am?"

■ ■ ■

Just after nine o'clock Edwin Bennett looked up from his back porch, out across the shallow backyard, and wondered why he felt so tingly all of a sudden. He looked around him for a reason, as though scanning the darkening, cooling space might reveal something, but it was nothing outside himself and he knew it. He felt guilty, unsettled, anxious. Courageously he had walked into Chief Silva's office; fearlessly, as he now remembered it, he had related his experience of the day before, at his aunt's house. It was the right thing to do, he kept repeating to himself, just as he had for most of the afternoon. And yet, and yet.

For some inexplicable reason, Edwin felt uneasy, with that nagging, undermining sense that in his effort to take all he knew and had found to the police, he had forgotten something. Playing around the edges of his worry was a darker one, that he had tipped someone he knew into danger, nudged a friend or acquaintance into Chief Silva's suspecting view. He felt disloyal. The quiet of the evening and solitude of the back porch, now that his neighbors and their children had withdrawn into their homes for the night, invited forth the secrets from their caves, like bats out into the night sky, and he squirmed at some of his thoughts. He had never, in all of his sixty-five years, been disloyal to anyone, friend or family, and today, unthinkingly, and uniquely, he had failed to warn his aunt of an action that concerned her, for surely she would not relish finding police officers trampling through her flower beds, looking for clues to connect the tuber with her garden, since they certainly couldn't take his word for it, could they? They might even want to reconstruct—that seemed to be the right term—Annalee Windolow's theft of the root.

Another, darker thought occurred to him. He had accused Annalee Windolow and, really, he had no proof that she was actually guilty. One moment he was digging and planting, and the next he was looking up and seeing the Windolow house and its terrace and marveling at how close it really was. Good God! He'd accused a woman of murder for no stronger reason than her proximity to a garden.

Whatever might have caught his eye in the yards and homes beyond his screened-in porch was blocked from his view by his shame confused with guilt and regret. What had he done? Long familiarity with the darker feelings of life had taught him to draw back and recover his perspective and he tried that now but he felt like he was finding only slick wet spots on a marble floor that sent his feet shooting out from under him. He would have to stop Chief Silva before the man took his accusation seriously. After all, anyone could have taken the root.

The thought of Chief Silva alone was calming, reassuring, suggesting not a robot programmed by others' suspicions but the professional able to sift through the odd bits of information that the board members as a whole must have been feeding him the last several days. With this perspective, Edwin felt much better, confident that the chief would seek more certain evidence before he pursued Edwin's erroneous (but passionate) accusation. He shifted aside his sense of guilt for one of foolishness; that was much easier to bear. He propped up his feet again.

In another few minutes the disarray in his soul was back, and this time no amount of rationalizing could rectify it. His aunt would not be pleased that he had gone directly to Chief Silva rather than to her; it was, after all, her property, and she was, therefore, intimately concerned. For no other reason than corroboration, Chief Silva might simply take his questions about plants to her, confronting her with the horrible news of how her openheartedness had been violated and the accusation against one who lived nearby. He dropped his feet to the floor and tossed his book into another chair as he strode into the kitchen.

The lights at the entrance to Aunt Catherine's driveway were off, as was the light at the front door, but lights shone in the downstairs hall and upstairs, through the small-paned windows, leaving a pattern of shattered glass on the stone walkway leading to the front door. He let himself in with a key after ringing the doorbell; pushing the heavy wooden door shut, he called to his aunt. The downstairs rooms were dark so he climbed to the second floor and followed the hall to his aunt's upstairs sitting room; it was dark.

He became uncertain and embarrassed as he started to picture his behavior from his aunt's point of view. On the flimsiest of motives, he had scuttled across town well after nine o'clock at night to confess an inconclusive, minor conversation with Chief Silva earlier in the day, a confession that could have waited until morning. He wished he hadn't come but he didn't feel he could leave without seeing his aunt. If she saw him going away down the drive, she might wonder who it was, not recognizing his license plate at such a distance and thinking it a stranger. What a fool he was, to give into a phantom feeling of fear and worry and regret and guilt.

He looked around him. If the upstairs lights were on, she must be still awake, he reasoned. Ready to explain himself and laugh along with her at his less than dignified behavior, he continued on to her bedroom, rapped lightly on the door, and pushed it open. The room was empty. He opened the door wide and walked into the center of the room. There wasn't even a sign that Aunt Catherine was planning on retiring soon, although she regularly went to bed at ten o'clock.

Curious, he walked back into the hall, looking up and down. The house was still, the heat absorbing the tails of sounds waving in from the road, deadening his footfalls, the chiming of clocks, the hum of a refrigerator, the clicking-on of a time-controlled lamp. He walked back to the main hall at the top of the stairs, and looked down to the end. A bulge of golden light lay at the bottom of the farthest door. In seconds he pushed the door open to the best guest room where his aunt kept a bedroom suite her parents had purchased in

England on their honeymoon in the last century, her favorite crystal lamps, an Aubusson from her grandmother. It was the scene of many transitions in his gradual elevation from callow schoolboy to connoisseur and heir; it was a favorite room for them both.

"Aunt Catherine," he said happily, affectionately, when he saw her stretched out in the chaise longue. He moved across to her and slowed to stillness with his last step. She only lay there, not responding, not turning to him to chide him for such a late visit, an unseemly entry, the dirt on his sneakers, in his fingernails. He was so dirty and grubby from gardening and she was so lovely in her favorite green silk suit reserved for splendid luncheons in Boston in fall or winter, not summer, not weather like this. Confused, uncertain, he went closer and called her name again. He laid a gentle hand on hers, wrapping his fingers into her palm. He gasped, squeezed her hand, drew back, turned to the side table.

The light shimmered down the crystal wineglass, darting through the amber liquid like guppies in a pond set in motion by Edwin's step. Beside the glass stood a bottle of liqueur her father had purchased at her birth, a bottle Aunt Catherine had talked about but never shown him. Beside that sat a small plastic bottle of capsules, the prescription refilled only two days ago. It was a few more seconds before he could comprehend the nature of her silence.

11

Thursday

In the early hours Joe Silva raised the sash window over the kitchen sink and the heat rushed past him, into the cool interior, brushing his cheek like a kitten's tail; by midmorning it was still, sinking heavier on the shoulders of the men and women gathered in the far corner of the cemetery. Children who normally played among the headstones lurked in bushes in the rocky hill beyond, studying their counterparts in dark shorts and navy jackets. The grief of the mourners was quiet, and the departure to the cars punctuated by exclamations and questions, the same ones repeated hour after hour since Catherine Rocklynd had first been found by her nephew.

"I told her some time ago," Marian Davis said as she moved closer to Chief Silva. "I told her she should have someone there. That's exactly the kind of thing we're all afraid of." She shook her head, then stopped to wave to another mourner getting into a car.

Since being called to Mrs. Rocklynd's home by Edwin Bennett, along with the ambulance, Chief Silva had had no doubts about the nature of the death and he waited for the forensic reports to make that clear, but so far they hadn't. Silva had been left with a report of what might have been a careless accidental death by a frail old woman.

"She should have had someone there," Marian repeated

as she eased herself into the backseat of a car, clapping a hand on her head to keep her hat from being knocked off. "It never should have happened."

To every comment that Mrs. Rocklynd had gotten careless under the stress and confusion of the investigation into George Frome's death, Silva nodded but thought privately she had taken great, meticulous care. The lack of a note had predictably biased the medical examiner and would predictably bias everyone else who thought about her death. The deepest the discussion penetrated was to the irony of dying from the excesses of wealth, from mixing a rare liqueur with expensive pills, as only Mrs. Rocklynd might do.

"You will come back to the house, won't you, Chief?" Edwin popped up on the other side of a black limousine, his pained eyes imploring Joe, who nodded and crossed the street to his own car. At first he had avoided attending funerals of crime victims, sympathizing with the families and their needs to withdraw and grieve. In later years he watched over mourners, friends and relatives, for signs that one of them might be of interest to the police. More than once he saw what he came for only to be frustrated days later by an inability to turn up enough evidence to take action. For Joe, funerals were for mourning the criminals who got away.

This wasn't Joe Silva's first Protestant funeral, but he was not easy in the muted, subdued gathering in Edwin Bennett's home. Quiet, their voices modulated and faces composed, the mourners ate tea sandwiches, sipped coffee or wine, and spoke decorously of the departed and local politics. No one cried openly, no one told jokes or stories beginning with "Remember when—" and no one laughed. This way of mourning was a mystery to Joe.

"The two biggest benefactors of the Arbella Society," Mrs. Alesander said to Joe by a table laden with plates of sandwiches, cookies, and other sweets. "Both gone in a week. Exactly a week. Whatever shall we do?" She shook her head and plucked another sandwich from the pile.

Edwin appeared behind her, a platter of food trembling in his hands. "It's hard to imagine the Society without Aunt—" He swallowed hard. "Don't you worry. We'll be fine. We have a good group on the board. We'll bounce back," he said with false bravado.

"Edwin, you're a dear. Thinking of us at a time like this," she said, taking his arm. "You're going to lean on us now. We've leaned on you long enough." She patted his arm and went off. For some time Joe watched Edwin be the perfect host, soothing his guests' grief as much as his own while the chief wandered among them, doing his duty and mulling over how he was going to close the Frome case. He was alone in the kitchen considering the possibilities over a plate of sandwiches when Edwin found him.

"Here you are, Chief. I'm awfully glad I found you." He motioned Joe to follow him to the back porch. On a board resting on two sawhorses were rows of flats of pansies. "I start them from seed several times a year so I'll always have fresh ones. They get so leggy in the hot weather. But I seem to have outdone myself. I was going to drop some off at your place before—I thought you might like them. I hear they're popular where you come from."

Silva glanced over at him but he was gazing at the multi-colored blooms. The chief thought about the city south of Boston and the island the family called home; it didn't matter which one Edwin meant. Pansies were a favorite at least with some Portuguese.

"These are good," Edwin said, pulling out two flats. "There's something you're not telling me, isn't there?" He pulled out two more.

That question always reminded Joe of the trick questions unscrupulous recruiters and salesmen used; he felt trapped. He didn't want to lie, but he definitely didn't want to tell

Edwin the bald truth in the middle of the back porch less than two hours after burying his aunt. Joe fingered the velvet blue flowers. "I can only tell you what the medical examiner tells me," he said.

"She wasn't careless. Not ever." He turned to look boldly at the chief.

"She didn't seem to be," Joe agreed.

"It was an accident, wasn't it?" he asked. "Or wasn't it?"

"They're lovely plants. You could go into business," Joe said.

"I'm not asking for anything secret, Chief, just the truth. She was my family. I have to know." He shook his head. "She was so proud, so sure of herself, of her place in the world. She would never lower herself in the eyes of her friends by doing something so cowardly. It doesn't make sense."

"It doesn't now, but it will," Joe said. "If you come by the office tomorrow, I'll tell you everything I know. Before you do that, though, go through her papers as carefully as you can. I have a feeling you'll find most of what you want to know in there, in the house, somewhere in her papers."

Edwin nodded, skeptical but grateful. "Thanks."

It was what he had to do, Silva supposed. But between now and then, he would pray that Edwin found what he wanted at his aunt's house.

■ ■ ■

"I took your advice."

The voice was soft, so soft that at another time Joe might not have even heard it over the traffic passing by, and not known anyone was behind him on the sidewalk until he had backed into her. In her navy cotton dress, Gwen stood demurely fingering a navy veil; she looked tired, jumpy, afraid to smile.

"It wasn't nearly as bad as I thought it would be. The judge was very nice but he told me I might have had a close call. It was a good thing I came forward." The sweat glistened on her throat and collarbone inside her white collar.

"I'm glad." He couldn't think of anything else to say. Another couple walked by them on the sidewalk, heading for Edwin's house, and Joe and Gwen fell silent until they passed. "It's better for all of you." She nodded.

"I told the kids. They were relieved. Can you imagine? Relieved. I guess they've been talking about it, about what might happen if I got sick or run over. They even thought I might get tired of them. Can you believe it?" Her expression said she couldn't. "So it was good. I'm glad I went." She looked vaguely at the ground while she spoke, then raised her head. "Thanks. I'm not out of the woods yet but I'm getting there."

"The kids will be okay." He forgot about the case he had to leave unsolved, the man whose life he might have to unravel; he liked thinking about children whose lives were getting better.

"Yeah, they're tough little guys." She smiled. "The lawyer said I should make an effort to pay back any debts I left behind so that will help my case when I go for permanent guardianship." The smile that had stretched sagged, and the sadness brought age. Her chestnut hair fell toward her green eyes.

"That sounds positive," Joe said, surprised at the change. "What's the problem?"

"I'm worried about what happens when they're older, when they can understand the choices I made." She leaned against his car, lost in her thoughts, talking absently of her love for Jennie and Philip. Joe let his eyes dwell on this woman, not so many years younger than himself, who had risked so much of her own life for children not her own, at least not in the strict biological or legal sense. In the house behind them, friends were mourning a woman who could not or would not acknowledge, even privately, her own son, a man who had grown to love her above all others even so. It seemed that no matter how much society tried to move past specific prejudices, failings, or perverse rules, the result stayed the same—children without their parents, to be raised by strangers who only want to love them.

He started to speak but it caught in his throat. Perhaps it was better. She didn't need comforting phrases from him, not someone who had kept her head and her health and her heart in an environment designed to destroy them all. Not every woman would have defied the law, avoided the easy path, to love the children of another. He could barely hear her, so intent was he on the emotions passing across her face as she sifted through the doubts and fears that had ruled her past few weeks. It amazed him that any woman could be so quietly strong and sure.

"I've done some things they're really going to be angry about," Gwen went on, oblivious to the change that had come over Joe's face.

"I can't believe it," he said. "You're letting fear tell you what to think."

She laughed. "That's exactly what drove me. When I looked at them I saw myself when I was a child. I knew exactly what could happen to them. That fear was a real shot of adrenalin. I even scare myself sometimes."

"Whatever it is you think you've done, they'll forgive you," he said.

"You think so? I wonder." She smiled. "I went through all our photographs, burning almost all the ones of their mother and all the ones in which they looked like her instead of like their dad or me. I kept some so they'd have a record of her, but I hid those. I put the best ones of us into a scrapbook, like we were just a normal family." She blushed. "I tell myself I was just—just, will you listen to me? Trying to justify myself. What I was doing was destroying clues to who Jennie and Philip really are. That's what I tell myself when I'm trying to be totally honest. But even that I think is a cover-up. In some strange way I think what I was really trying to do was make them mine." Her limbs grew loose with the ease of honesty. "I couldn't bear the thought of them belonging to someone else, even in a picture."

"That's not much of a crime," he said, surprised at the tenderness of her conscience.

"You know what else?" she said, beginning to see the humor in her behavior, "I even cut off all the tags on our sheets and towels and our clothes that I bought out there so no one could ever tell where we'd lived. Now that's paranoia." She started to laugh again. "But they're going to make me answer someday for those pictures. They'll make me pay, just you wait."

■ ■ ■

"Those must be Edwin's," Gwen said after she and Joe had moved on to other topics, no longer conscious of the guests still trickling into the funeral party. The sun was still high, vibrating through the haze that came and went at midday, giving only the illusion of relief from the striking sun. She nodded to the pansies still sitting on the hood of his car.

"I promised him I'd take some and see that some of these flats made it to your house." He pulled out two with the tightest cluster of blooms.

"Wasn't that nice of him?" She smiled. "It's just like him. At a time like this he's still thinking of others. He was so welcoming when I first moved back here. I must thank him." She looked toward the house, where guests were milling about in the backyard and sitting on the front steps. Through the front door she and Joe could see people crowded into the hallway and onto the stairs. "Maybe I better wait. I had no idea it'd be so crowded."

"Neither did Edwin." He turned to her. "You're only a few houses down the street, aren't you?" Joe asked, picking up two flats. She fell into step beside him. "Edwin has some idea they're especially popular where I come from."

"They're not?"

"Not that much more than any other garden flower," he said. "They're one of my mother's favorites but my aunt doesn't like them."

"What're they called in Portuguese?"

"Amor perfeito."

"What's that in English?"

"Perfect love," he said, putting a flat into her outstretched hand.